DOUBLE
THE BULARI SAGA
EDGED

JESSIE KWAK

ALSO BY JESSIE KWAK

The Durga System Series

The Bulari Saga

Double Edged

Crossfire

Pressure Point

Heat Death

Durga System Novellas

Starfall

Negative Return

Deviant Flux

Standalone Novels

From Earth and Bone: A Ramos Sisters Thriller

Nonfiction

From Chaos to Creativity: Building a Productivity System for Artists and Writers

For Robert,

I couldn't have done this without you.

BULARI

N

University of
Bulari

Carama Town

Blackheart
Territory

Dry Creek

Downtown

Tamarind District

Jet Park

Casinos

Geordi Jimenez
Terminal

To Julieta's

PROLOGUE

ORIOL

Busting up a casino has never been at the top of Oriol Sina's bucket list, but here he is, standing in the middle of the *Dorothy Queen* dressed for trouble in a suit he'd much rather be admiring on another man.

From the outside, the *Dorothy Queen* looks like a golden top orbiting New Sarjun, glittering levels faceted like a cut stone surrounding a tapering spindle. On the inside, it's one hundred and fifty levels of gaudily themed hotels, over-priced restaurants, dubious recreation spaces, and raucous gambling. You don't get on the *Dorothy Queen* without a work permit, a vendor license, or a bank account large enough to turn the Demosga family's eyes vivid green with greed. And the first two won't get you on the casino floor unless you're young and look good in a dress.

Oriol is neither, and his bank account is definitely lack-ing. What he does have is a contract with a woman who's got far more secrets than he prefers in an employer.

Pays well, though.

Oriol drums his fingers against the sensitive pressure

plates of his thigh, stretches calves both real and manufactured, scans the casino floor. He'll be glad to leave. He can see the fun if there's a paycheck in it, but damned if he'd spend actual cash on the pleasure of visiting the *Dorothy Queen* again.

Jobs he usually takes these days, they're the low-intrigue, high-pay type that help him afford the ever-increasing bills for his aging mech prosthetics. Which means he spends most of his days knocking back whiskey with working folk and fighting the occasional scrapper, not fending off insistent waitstaff and pretending rich people have a sense of humor. But Oriol's a professional. He can manage any gig so long as there's a definite end date with a return ticket to New Sarjun attached, and in two days' time he'll be home and working his tan back up.

He loses another ten New Sarjunian marks of his employer's money at Devilier before he finally gets the message from the woman who's code-named Frog:

"Target's here. By the alien, I'm going in."

Her voice is routed through the scrambler they're all using, flat and distorted in Oriol's earpiece. The words crawl across the bottom of his vision as well. He's running an ops lens, which he hates. The disorienting overlay flashing in his peripheral reminds him too much of the darker work he did in Alliance special ops, those days when anyone back in the home office could jack in and take whatever they want from him: vital stats, sensory inputs, fears, dreams. He's been batting away low-level flashbacks tonight, flashbacks reminding him why he should stick to his rule of taking only tech-free jobs, jobs that rely on instinct and training alone.

But right now he's got a voice in his ear and a glowing

lattice of lines across his vision, and at least the flat voice in his ear isn't the nameless ops tech who was his most constant companion in the Alliance — for the morning wake-up call, for the evening check-in, in the bathroom, in those rare times he had a spare moment to visit someone else's bed.

There's no feeling in the world like the inability to unplug from your masters. And none quite like the joy he felt waking up in the hospital with no leg and realizing he was too damaged to go back in, that he would be decommissioned with enough salary and savings to buy out his own indenture and do whatever the hell he'd always wanted to.

Turns out, what he wants to do is crime for money. It pays well, you get to see the universe, and you meet the most fascinating array of people. Like Frog and Rabbit, his co-heisters. Like their boss, the woman in the white suit. Like that man over there by the "alien."

The alien Frog was referring to is an oversized blinking sign advertising a drinks bar. It's a cartoonish imagining of what aliens would look like if they existed: gangly and green-skinned, with an array of lumpy appendages and tentacles sprouting from its head. Stereotypical, of course — the Demosga family has no imagination Oriol's heard of, except for famously in the secret-level chambers where they take cheats and thieves. No, this creature's something out of a horror vid with the copyrights filed off.

Or not. Who's going to sue someone like Aiax Demosga for copyright infringement?

The target's hovering at a low-roller's table like he's deciding whether or not to throw out some coin. He's tall, with a paunch born of beer and worry and thinning, nutrient-poor hair. He's got the wide-eyed look of a first-timer to the *Dorothy Queen* and the cheap suit of someone who's been told to dress his best even though it's still levels below what the rest of these rich asses throw out as too threadbare for work clothes. Even if Oriol didn't know why the man was here, it would be clear he doesn't belong in this crowd.

Oriol blinks three times to mark him, and a floating star appears above the lanky man's head. It tracks him without delay even as he decides against the low-baller's table, gawks at the alien, and weaves through the crowd to the cashier. Oriol can see the star out of the corner of his eye as he scans the room for Aiax Demosga's security guards, each marked with a red exclamation point like he's in a goddamn video game.

Never again with a job that requires an ops lens.

Frog's neon-blue exclamation point, superimposed above her sleek bun of silver hair, passes by the target's star; even watching for the drop, Oriol doesn't see her pause.

"Package is away," she says. "I confirm he's got the ring."

"Copy package away," says mission control. "Starting clock now."

A clock appears in the corner of Oriol's vision, counting up. The three-minute mark is the time when the drug Frog slipped into the target's drink should take effect.

It's go time for Oriol.

Oriol places another losing bet on Devilier, sighs with unfeigned remorse — he would've welcomed a few more marks in his pocket — then tosses his last few chips to the dealer and twines his way through the glittering crowd, following the star.

"I see him," Oriol murmurs. "Rabbit take the Gold entrance; Frog take Platinum."

They call him Tiger. The code names were assigned by the bosses; Oriol doesn't ask if it's not going to get in the way of his work. He sees his teammates begin to move through the crowd. They're already coded into the tracker overlay, Frog in the blue and Rabbit — a man — marked by an exclamation point in sizzling green.

The graphics may be cheesy, but damn, this ops lens is the good tech. Almost Alliance military grade. Oriol's dying to know who's backing the lady in the white suit, but he doesn't make it a habit to ask where his employers get their funds. He didn't when he took the Alliance's offer of food and family as a kid, and he isn't going to start now.

The target's star bobs towards the cashier, then abruptly changes direction, making a straight shot towards the bathrooms.

The clock reads 03:07.

Oriol feels his body get loose and ready for action; it's a feeling better than any drug.

"On it," he murmurs.

The lady in the white suit had found Oriol on his shore leave on Maribi Station, just off the back of a security job that had been disappointingly uneventful. No space pirate battles, no lasers, no explosions — and no hazard pay. His former crewmates had been off drinking away their earnings; he'd gone for tune-ups to his prosthetic leg. He and it both were getting on in life, requiring a little more maintenance and a little less partying than in years past.

The job came across his comm while the fake leg doctor had him plugged into a diagnostics harness: WANTED, SECURITY FOR A SHORT TRIP TO THE DOROTHY QUEEN. EXCELLENT PAY.

His thumb — hovering a moment over reply — hit Send

on the message without a second thought when the diagnosis came in. The biomechanical interface at his hip joint would need to be completely replaced in the next six months.

With that on the horizon, Oriol could use a little extra cash before he headed home. And the *Dorothy Queen* would carry him back to New Sarjun.

He'd met his new boss: an olive-skinned woman in a simple white suit with three stars pinned to the lapel and smooth black hair bound tight in a bun. The man and woman flanking her wore gray suits, no stars. She'd introduced herself as Sister Kalia; she'd not introduced them at all.

They needed a simple job done — a criminal job, she was careful to warn him, with the plainspoken concern of someone who'd never hired a mercenary before and didn't want to offend him.

They wouldn't be robbing the casino itself, she said — probably for the best, given that the stakes for robbing a Demosga casino, including in the *Dorothy Queen*, the *Lucky's Double*, or the *Little Brother*, were a visit to Aiax Demosga's private family jail.

No, his job would merely be to intercept a critical item before the carrier had a chance to complete its sale.

"So you're with the OIC?" Oriol asked, and got a cool look. "NMLF? The Coda?" Three strikes, but he wasn't surprised. Sister Kalia and her friends didn't look like they were working with one of the many anti-Alliance resistance groups; they looked well-fed and even more well-funded.

His next guess was going to be that they were corporate spies, until a chime sounded softly through the room and Sister Kalia informed him they'd finish the conversation later; now was time for prayer. He was welcome to join them if he liked, she said, with one perfectly plucked eyebrow raised in question.

He'd declined.

"Your soul burns pure," she said as he turned away. "It wouldn't hurt you to spend some time refueling the flame before it begins to sputter."

He stopped with one hand above the palm lock, turned back to look at her, intrigued despite himself. "What do you mean?"

"Your true human soul. We'll need all the bright ones when it comes time to pass the test."

"I'm good at tests," Oriol answered, but the intensity of her smile had churned his gut like poison.

Oriol props the target as comfortably as possible in the bathroom supply closet, then slips the ring off a pudgy finger and into a lead-lined zippered pocket in his suit vest. He riffles through the man's pockets for anything that seems valuable.

"Sorry," he mutters, but this will play so much better if it looks like a basic robbery. After all, who would steal such a chintzy ring?

There's not much, just the man's scant winnings and a black plastic ID badge; turns out the target's some breed of bioengineer working for an Arquellian agricorp. Agricultural tech can be worth its weight in gold on arid New Sarjun, out in Durga's Belt, and even on fertile-yet-crowded Indira. And the Demosga family still makes a good portion of its fortune from food production, so it makes sense that he'd be trying to make a deal here.

Not the sexiest intel Oriol's ever stolen, but it's probably worth good money to the right buyer.

"I've got it," he murmurs as he shuts the door to the supply closet. Hopefully the target'll wake up with only a headache, plus lighter a few New Sarjunian marks. "Heading back to base."

"Copy."

His job had been to take care of the target somewhere private and let Sister Kalia's tech team handle the surveillance monitors, but he's having trouble walking calm. Any moment now one of Demosga's thugs is going to land a meaty hand on his shoulder and the whole game will be over. But he coaches his posture into relaxation, tosses out smiles and congratulations and winks as he crosses the casino floor, then leans casually against the gold-plated wall of the elevator while it whisks him to level ninety-seven.

Level ninety-seven is one of the full-floor suites, no worries about your neighbors down the hall wondering why so many people are coming and going from a single room. In another time, Oriol would've taken the time to appreciate the room's luxe amenities. But this job hasn't given them much time to explore — and they're not about to linger now that they've got the goods.

He can smell the blood and ozone the instant the elevator's doors slide open.

A pistol whines, warming to the palm of its owner.

"Out of the elevator," commands a voice.

It — and the plasma pistol — belong to a pale-skinned man Oriol's never seen before. He's not simply a new addition to the crew, Oriol notes. Sister Kalia's two gray suits are both dead, and she's bound in a chair beside the bed, gagged. Her white suit jacket blooms deep red.

Another armed stranger is sitting at Sister Kalia's ops

desk, monitoring the feeds from his, Rabbit's, and Frog's ops lenses.

Fucking ops lenses.

"Rabbit, Frog, come on home," the woman says into her headset, her voice echoing flatly in Oriol's ear. The same scrambler that was meant to keep Sister Kalia's team's identity obscured hid the fact that they were being fed direction from an unfamiliar voice.

A third stranger, another man, is sitting on the bed beside Sister Kalia. Tanned complexion, shaved head, eyes blue as ice. An old scar bisects his cheek, twisting his lips down as he smiles.

"You thought you could beat the Dawn to this, Kalia?" says the blue-eyed man. He watches her as though expecting her to speak. Sister Kalia's eyes go wide, then her eyelids flutter back down. The red stain on her suit is spreading. She's not long for this plane if she doesn't get medical care in a minute or two.

"I'll take the ring, please," the man says.

Oriol's mind is racing. They didn't kill him right off the bat; they may not be planning on it — or maybe they just don't want to risk firing a plasma pistol on this ship. Looks like the gray suits were both done with knives.

Oriol holds up his hands, but the man with the pistol's not going to get close enough to him to pat him down.

The man gestures with his gun. "Get it. Slow."

"I got no part in this, man," Oriol says. Sister Kalia's eyelids flicker open at that. "I give somebody the ring, I get a payday. That's what I'm here for."

But Oriol can see in the gunman's eyes that he's not doing deals with mercenaries. Whatever Sister Kalia and this new band of thugs both want, it's not just about greed. There's something deep-seated and calculating in the terrible gaze the gunman turns on Oriol.

Oriol is split seconds from reacting when the elevator door opens once more with a stream of profanity. The man with the plasma pistol spins and shoots, burning a hole in Rabbit's chest.

Oriol may be paid like a merc, but he still fights like an Alliance special ops soldier. He pivots and kicks, the blow from his prosthetic foot snapping the shooter's wrist and sending the gun flying. A second kick breaks the man's sternum, and he collapses, blood in his mouth and gasping for breath.

The desk operator flings herself at him. Oriol snatches his karambit from its sheath at his groin, blocks her left arm with his right as she tries to get a clear shot, twists to hook the curved blade into the meat above her elbow and bring her screaming to her knees, releases to slash the abdomen. A prosthetic knee to her chin and the woman's head snaps back. She slumps to the ground.

"Drop the knife."

Behind him, Frog has scooped up the pistol, and she's got it aimed squarely at his head. He doesn't even have to turn to know: her feed is still running to the ops desk and he can see the back of his head just beyond the sights.

He's got another view, too. Rabbit lying in the elevator, the doors trying repeatedly to shut on his body, his dead eyes rolled up to see Frog with her military-styled silver bun, her mercenary's muscles, her double-crosser's right arm straight and sure.

"You can have the ring," he says. "I really don't care."

"Drop the knife," she says again.

He loosens his grip on the karambit, letting it dangle by its ring around his index finger.

The man with the ice-blue eyes is watching him. Sister Kalia is watching him, eyes open and aware, with the peaceful calm of a woman who's accepted the warm silk of death winding around her body. She meets his gaze and hers sharpens suddenly, ferocious. Her chin dips — decision made — and Sister Kalia lets out a low, guttural keen, her body racked and shivering.

In the feeds, Oriol sees the exact moment Frog's attention wavers to Sister Kalia. The moment the sights of the pistol sway off-center.

He pivots to the left and steps into her outstretched arm, bringing the karambit in his right hand under and up, slashing the curved hook back down again past ear and neck and shoulder and clean in a spray of her blood. She's already tripping forward, and he uses the rest of her momentum to fling her at the blue-eyed man standing by Sister Kalia's body.

Oriol leaps over Rabbit's body and pushes him out of the elevator; the doors finally sigh closed. He slams his hand on the panel; he doesn't care where it opens so long as it's not on level ninety-seven with Frog, the blue-eyed man, and far too many bodies.

He pinches the lens out of his eye between two fingers, crushes it to a sizzle of smoke.

He's got no clue what's on this ring, but one thing's for sure. It'd better not be tips for growing soybeans.

For such a svelte casino, its escape pods are shit. Oriol must've blacked out in the rocky reentry, because he wakes with a start, gasping for breath and choking on what air he finds. Hot, arid atmosphere sears his sinuses with the sharp bite of pollution, the odor of hundreds of millions of humans crammed together in a volatile brew.

Oriol laughs with relief, breathes deep once more.

He hopes wherever Sister Kalia's religion has taken her is peaceful. But him? He'll take New Sarjun, thank you very much.

No feeling in the universe is quite like coming home to the city of Bulari.

1

JAANTZEN

The air is fresher out towards the hills, yet Julieta Yang's estate is as far from Bulari's city limits as Willem Jaantzen ever cares to go.

The streets widen here, historically to allow massive crawlers out to the southwestern mines and heavy-laden magtrucks back into the city, though now they're breezy boulevards, paved to keep down the dust and lined with public art in lieu of trees. A few low scrubs thrust spiked branches into the heat of the day, a few silver-needle fern cacti fan their spines in a pale blur outside his window.

They're not late, but Starla Dusai's pushing the spinner, a glossy black Dulciana JX, into top speeds to take advantage of the open road. His goddaughter's gleeful velocity isn't doing a thing to calm his already-taut nerves.

Julieta's message specified no crew, no weapons. As though he would ever come armed to meet his old friend. Julieta Yang — thief, smuggler, blackmailer extraordinaire — might have her share of enemies, but she has nothing to fear from him. And so her request nags at him, like a distant alarm he can hear only when he turns his head the right way.

Starla's going to tear right past the turn onto the private country road that leads to Julieta's estate. Jaantzen lifts a hand to point it out, but she's already slowing, maneuvering the spinner into a fast, smooth turn that shifts Jaantzen's weight against the door. She's smiling.

"We have plenty of time," he says, and if her lens transcribes that, she doesn't respond. He takes a deep breath; it doesn't soothe him.

Julieta's estate is surrounded by stone walls topped with elegant metal spikes and edged with a particularly vicious variety of sword palm she bred herself. The result is a low-tech throwback look he knows is augmented by cutting-edge defenses. He helped install those defenses himself, but he's under no illusions that he knows all Julieta's secrets.

The Dulciana is scanned at the gate — pale blue light washing over them in a flash. He expected that, but the following flicker of green isn't a standard part of the biometric entry package his security company, Admant, installed here years ago. He glances at Starla, who's craning her neck to find the source. She spots it before him, jerks her chin at a low-profile box affixed to the top of the gate. "Scans for gentech mods," she signs as the heavy wrought-iron gate slides out of view. "I read about those, first time seeing."

"Those scanners. Do we carry them?"

Starla shakes her head and types something into the gauntlet on her left arm. A note to herself, probably. Admant Security will be carrying gentech scanners by this time next week, but Jaantzen isn't interested in that right now.

Why would Julieta be scanning for gentech mods? And who had she gotten the equipment from?

ACCEPT INCOMING MESSAGE? blinks across the windshield.

Starla presses the Accept button on the spinner's dashboard, and an overlay map pops up on the windshield, a pulsing green dot marking one of the outbuildings in the complex. Julieta's greenhouse. Starla waves the map away and drops the spinner back into gear.

Julieta's transformed her little pocket of the suburbs into an oasis, practically a bioreserve; this is as lush as it gets on this desert planet.

Jaantzen hates it. The dusty gray and silver-blue foliage could be hiding anything, and the constant shiver of wind through dry leaves is an unsettling undercurrent of static that drowns out his thoughts. Not to mention the *klik-klik-krrriiit* of whatever insects call Julieta's wonderland home.

Give him the sharp angles and predictable lines of downtown Bulari any day.

Starla slides the spinner into a dock in front of the greenhouse. They're not alone here: a pair of well-muscled guards, a man and a woman, armed to the teeth, stand on either side of the greenhouse door. Private security team? Or new employees? If she's hiring out her security, Jaantzen wishes she would consult him. She doesn't have to hire his company, but he has people he could recommend.

Plus, he'd like to know who's walking around with muscles and guns this close to one of his oldest friends.

The two guards straighten as he approaches the door, shoulders back to assert their claim to the territory, but their gazes aren't on him. Jaantzen glances back. Starla's a pace behind him, measuring up the pair like she'd like to put those muscles to the test.

She's lanky and tough, and taller than the guards due to a youth spent in low-G. Black combat fatigues and bleached hair, razored in the back and spiked in the front. The contact lens over her right eye goes mirror-finish for a second, then glimmers as she scrolls through information. Probably scanning the pair for stats.

She catches Jaantzen's glance and arcs a sharp eyebrow: What?

Youth. It's a powerful drug.

"We're here to see Ms. Yang," he says to the pair of stony faces.

But before he gets an answer: "Mr. Jaantzen," says a familiar voice from behind them. "I'm very glad you're here." He turns to find Aster, Julieta's youngest daughter. Thick black hair cut short now, sweeping down and forward in a sharp wedge to brush her shoulders. In her smart business suit she looks so much like her mother did when Jaantzen first met her thirty years ago that he almost does a double take.

The security guards step aside and Aster palms them through the door. Jaantzen feels the crackle of a forcefield against his skin as he passes through, and his comm beeps to alert him that he's entering a dead zone. It won't work here without joining an encrypted private network — which of course he won't do. The last thing he needs is Julieta's people combing through his communications.

She's always been careful, but this is verging on paranoia. Jaantzen sits with the feeling, puzzling through it. The message about not bringing crew or weapons. The extra security check at the gate. The muscle at the door, the comm dead zone.

"My mother is with her plants," Aster says. The door shuts behind them with a gentle click; the air in the greenhouse's antechamber is a pleasantly cool relief from New Sarjun's constant dry heat. Aster turns to Starla. "Would you like some coffee while we wait?"

Starla nods with a too-bright smile; she's never liked Aster, but a decade since growing out of her angsty teenage years, she's gotten decent at feigning politeness, if she doesn't have to do it often. And she does love coffee.

"Be nice," Jaantzen signs. Starla winks.

Aster leads Starla to the sitting room in a clatter of clicking dress heels and scuffing combat boots. Jaantzen pushes open the greenhouse door. The humidity hits him full force when he steps inside; his skin drinks it up. Julieta calls it her secret for looking so young, a need for humidity imprinted in her genes. She was born on New Sarjun, but her family comes from New Manila, a country on the lush planet of Indira. She likes to say she remembers the ocean, ancestral memories layered like watercolors onto willing brain cells.

If her external bioreserve of desert plants is unnerving, Jaantzen finds Julieta's greenhouse downright claustrophobic. Pink-streaked palm fronds brush his shoulder, droplets soaking into the fabric of his suit jacket. He steps gingerly over a trailing vine resplendent with buttery blossoms; the petals flinch shut at the closeness of his dress shoe. "Julieta?" he calls.

"Back here," comes her voice, though "back here" could be anywhere in this humid maze.

He finds her picking dead leaves off a vine, little wispy husks clenched in her equally papery fist. The plant itself is lush and happy, deep green and vivid purple leaves trailing in a magnificent cascade. Her tables are filled with orchids: spidery white clusters, fuchsia starbursts, fat and showy yellow kings. He knows better than to touch.

One in particular catches his eye with its series of thumb-sized blackish-purple blooms spiraling around a central spike. A blood-red stamen quivers in each tiny throat.

"You've added to your collection," he says, and Julieta turns. He's not prepared for how old she looks. He's suddenly aware that he's towering over her, and he settles gingerly on a nearby stool.

"I have." Julieta says, and he notes that the strength in her voice when they've spoken lately hasn't been a product of voice correction — it's got every ounce of power and authority he's used to. "It's a type of *Aerides*, a new breed I'm developing."

"It's very . . ." *Beautiful* isn't the word; *unsettling* might be a better one. Each bloom grimaces and yawns like a greedy predator. "Interesting," he finishes.

But Julieta waves a hand. "You don't have to start feigning interest in my plants now, Willem," she says. "I've known you far too long for that. And I'm — "

"Too old for small talk," he finishes for her. "I know."

But she doesn't jump to the point, not like she usually does. Since he's known her, since back when her hair was glossy black and her gait was sure, she's never been one for polite conversation, for bloated filler words. Her hands haven't stilled, but her fingers are combing aimlessly through the vine as though she's stalling. Or as though she hasn't yet figured out how to say what she needs to.

Jaantzen is struck by an unsettling realization: Julieta Yang is at a loss for words.

"What is it?" Jaantzen asks.

The crisp, involuntary whisper of paper-dead leaves in a tightening fist. Julieta plucks a healthy leaf from the vine and adds it to her refuse pile without noticing. "Thala's dead."

The room's suddenly too hot. Or too cold. Whichever it is, Jaantzen's hyperaware of the blood surging in his cheeks, though Julieta may not see it beneath his dark skin. Her hands are completely still now; she's watching for his reaction.

But Jaantzen isn't sure what that reaction *is*, let alone what she hopes it will be. That hollowness in the pit of his stomach could be relief, or a shell that will fill with rage. And underlying it all, a deep, quiet clench of old grief never healed.

Thala Coeur — Blackheart — is dead.

"How?" he asks.

"Bullet to the back of the head."

A twinge of satisfaction, now.

"Who?"

There's a faint, familiar click overhead, and around them misters whisper to life, covering Julieta's plants with velvety dew. She releases her handful of dead leaves to a wastebasket on the floor, brushes fragments from her palm. She's stalling again, and Jaantzen frowns at her. Surely not Julieta. She must be the only person in the city who didn't have a personal feud with Thala Coeur.

"You didn't — " he starts.

"I wanted to ask if it was you," she says.

Jaantzen laughs, surprised, and Julieta's gaze cuts him sharp. Her thin lips quirk into a frown. "People are saying it was you."

"What people? Street thugs? Other crews? The police? Justice Leone?"

"My people are hearing it on the street," Julieta says, and Jaantzen relaxes a fraction.

"Don't I wish I could take credit," he says. "But I made a promise."

"Promises are broken every day," she says mildly.

"Not mine."

"Even after Tae? The children?"

It's unnecessary to say, and it still hurts, just like she must have known it would, even after all this time.

Time is such a fluid thing, isn't it? Reach back fifteen years to try to remember the name of a favorite restaurant, or the details of a particular job pulled, and all you'll grasp is smoke that dissipates more and more every time your fingers pass through it. But behind that smoke some fires still burn with furious heat. Moments like the last time he held his wife and children, like the concussion of the bomb that destroyed his spinner, with them inside, while he waved goodbye from the curb, the concussion still echoing through his chest like a drum. Fifteen years or fifty, those are the memories that will never fade.

But Jaantzen no longer gets trapped by them, not like he once did. And that's what Julieta's testing for, that involuntary petrification, that rage response he no longer allows to blind him. Jaantzen realizes suddenly the sharp pain in his jaw is his teeth ground tight. He forces himself to relax.

"That was a long time ago." Jaantzen says. "Coeur's been off-planet for almost a decade."

Over fifteen years ago, when Coeur had cheated her way to the position of mayor of Bulari and Jaantzen was just beginning his most recent reincarnation as the type of man who made deals with signatures instead of bullets, it was well-known that there was bad blood between them. It was a selling point, in fact, to Julieta's influential friends when she convinced them to enlist his help in getting Coeur exiled from New Sarjun for good — once it became clear her transition to politics was becoming a disaster for the rest of the city.

Turns out you can only double-cross so many people before your enemies finally band together against you.

Julieta's still watching him. "*Was* it you?" she asks again.

"No, Julieta. It wasn't me."

"That's too bad."

Jaantzen shrugs. He'd thought he made his peace years ago, but now he can't shake the nagging voice saying that it *should* have been him. To hell with the promises he made to Coeur's sister in exchange for Starla's life, to hell with what his wife would have wanted, to hell with being a good role model for his goddaughter, and to hell with the empire he's built.

Life on the streets may be far behind him, but there's still a scared, scrappy boy inside who'd rather fight with his fists than his mind.

Jaantzen locks that thought back into the darkness it came from.

"That's too bad," Julieta repeats. "Because if it *was* you, you'd have an easier time with the dust storm her death is going to stir up."

Coeur had been in exile for over a decade, but that hadn't kept her from running her operations on New Sarjun through her lieutenants and continuing some of her business partnerships with other families. The death of any family head without a proper plan in place holds the potential for chaos, but Coeur's crew is already divided. Peace in the Bulari underworld is a delicate balance, and someone's put a bullet in one of its major linchpins.

"Naali can't hold them," Jaantzen says. Level-headed Naali Hinoja is the natural successor, but she doesn't have the iron grip and silver-tongued charm her boss had. "Half the Blackheart crew only follow her because Coeur's told them to."

"So they'll follow Levi?" Julieta makes a little sound of scorn. Levi Acheta, Hinoja's lieutenant, is the sort of old-school thug Coeur had been in her youth, eschewing alliances in favor of turf wars, preferring easy drug money to long-term business investments.

"I'll talk to Naali," Jaantzen says. "She'll see reason."

"I was hoping you'd say that. This could be a good move for you. If I can help . . ."

"I should have killed Coeur back then," Jaantzen says. "You shouldn't have stopped me."

"But then you and Starla would both be dead" is what Julieta normally answers. This time she only takes a sharp breath and picks up a pair of pruning shears, turning to regard a fat-leafed jadau. Her hands are steady as she slices off a finger-sized branch at its base.

"I had another reason for asking you here," she says, voice brusque. "A job."

"Yes?"

"I had a bad delivery get through my people. I need the shipment eliminated."

Jaantzen relaxes a bit at that. Despite the rented security guards at her door, she'll still turn to him for her muscle work.

"Not recalled?"

"Eliminated," Julieta repeats.

"Eliminated." It's an odd request, even coming from an old friend. Jaantzen waits.

Julieta shoots him a look of irritation, then concedes. "Thala asked me to ship things for her from time to time since being exiled on Indira." She busies herself with pruning the jadau. "You know this, of course."

He doesn't bother answering. He's suspected, but it still stings to know for certain that Julieta has been working with his fiercest rival. Suddenly he sees the security guards, the gentech scan, the communication dead zone in new light. Thala Coeur has been murdered, and Julieta must be wondering why. Wondering if it has anything to do with this shipment, their most recent job together.

It's unlikely, of course — Coeur's the target of grudges going back decades. But it doesn't hurt to be cautious in case someone goes looking for anyone who has ties to Coeur.

"This shipment is hers," Julieta says. "I want it gone."

"Still in Bulari?" Jaantzen asks. "Or has it gone on?"

"I diverted it as soon as I heard the news. It's still here."

"Send Starla what you know. I'll ask her to take care of it personally."

Julieta nods sharply, then tucks the jadau branch into a scrap of cloth and hands it to him; the cut end weeps sap thick as blood. "Let this heal, then root it. I'll have a pot and some soil sent up to your office. It could use some greenery."

His office has plenty of greenery — most of which are gifts from Julieta — but Jaantzen just nods. Wraps the cloth around the branch and tucks it into his suit pocket where it lies light and knobby as a severed thumb.

She's turned back to her pruning. He should go, it's none of his business, but he can't let go of this overprotective feeling when he looks at his aging friend. He wonders when Starla will begin to feel the same for him.

"Your security guards," he says. "You're happy with them?"

She doesn't look back. "I trust them. Aster set them up."

"Glad to hear it. Remember you can always ask me."

"Thank you, Willem." But he knows she won't; she does like to keep her secrets. "You're attending Justice Leone's dinner party tomorrow night? I can't imagine what the talk of the town will be."

"I'll be there."

"Good. It will reassure people."

He waits a moment to see if there's more, but she simply shears another branch with a *snick*. "I'll see you then."

"Good day, Julieta." He gives a slight bow to her back and pushes his way out of the greenhouse into the blessedly cool air of the rest of the complex. Starla stands, overeager, when she sees him.

"Thank you for the coffee," she remembers to sign to Aster, who slips into her mother's greenhouse as they leave.

Back out in the oppressively dry heat of midday Bulari, Starla catches his elbow. "What was that?"

Jaantzen sighs. "Trouble," he signs.

"Another job for Julieta's guard dog?" she signs, flippant, but her frown deepens as his expression darkens. "What's wrong?"

Jaantzen just holds up a finger — One minute — and reaches for his comm.

I JUST HEARD, he types. His finger hovers over Send. A death in the family deserves a call, not a curt message; if he'd learned of the death of any other business partner's family member, he would meet in person. But he isn't ready for the emotional navigation it will take to meet Coeur's half-sister Ximena. Isn't ready to see her trying to hide her own emotions.

For a second he almost types, I'm sorry, but he catches himself in time. *MY CONDOLENCES TO YOUR FAMILY,* he types instead.

He's not sorry.

He takes a deep breath. It wasn't difficult to type; maybe it won't be too difficult to sign.

"Coeur is dead."

He gets a flash of recognition and a tiny frown from Starla. "And we have a new job," he signs, before she can respond. "Julieta will send you information."

She watches him a moment, fingers flexing on the spinner's controls as though she's trying not to sign something. Finally she just nods, palms the gearshift, and the Dulciana's engine purrs to life.

Jaantzen takes a deep breath as the landscape blurs outside the window. He wants to pound his fist into the dash, wants to tell Starla to take them back home, that the day's second order of business can wait.

But, no. He's off to make one of the biggest business partnerships of his career, and dead or alive, Thala Coeur isn't going to get in the way.

2

MANU

Manu Juric's hand is on the door to the bar when he feels his comm going off in his pocket. It's an urgent alert, of course, flashing an insistent red.

He's never had a job title, though he thinks of himself as Willem Jaantzen's Executive Problem Solver. Whether it's a maintenance issue with Admant Security, an unruly patron at the Jungle, or a shipping problem for Rosco Kudra Enterprises — as in this particular message — his domain is urgent problems.

The thing with urgency, though, is that there's a spectrum. Maybe it just needs to move to today's to-do list, or maybe he needs to drop everything and solve a literally life-and-death issue. Maybe he needs to cancel his current appointment, or maybe he can just swing by and deal with it after.

It would be nice if the urgent tag let him know this, rather than flashing at the top of every damn message that shows up on his comm.

He's explained this.

It doesn't stick.

Manu parks his shoulder against the bar's doorframe and thumbs through the message, light sparking off his metallic purple manicure.

Cedra from RKE tends to be the biggest offender in the message urgency department. It's rare that the fully legal restaurant-supply importer has an emergency that requires Manu's skill sets — and Cedra isn't from Manu's world; she doesn't have a full sense of what those skill sets even are. He's been through life-and-death more times than he wants to remember. To her, life-and-death is a metaphor to be employed when a shipment of barware shows up in the wrong colorway.

He envies her that.

He scans her typically bubbly opening to get to the "urgent" bit:

OUR DOWNTRIPPING CONTRACTOR FOUND SOMETHING ODD IN THE ME3 SHIPMENT. HE WOULDN'T SAY WHAT OVER THE COMM, HE WANTED ME TO SEE IT IN PERSON. CAN YOU CHECK IT OUT? I CAN SEND MAELIN INSTEAD IF YOU DON'T HAVE THE TIME.

Manu mulls it over. He *is* already at the terminal, and he has a couple of hours to spare in his schedule. And the fact that the contractor wouldn't say what it was over the comm is intriguing. Could make for a good story later, maybe.

The Executive Problem Solver doesn't always get to solve sexy problems.

I'M ON IT THX, he writes back. Four words, Cedra. Sometimes all you need is four words.

He slips his comm back into his pocket and pushes open the door to Le Comptoir Darna. The bartender looks up from his cutting board, then slides a pair of coasters into their usual place at the far end of the bar.

Geordi Jimenez Space Terminal is two stories above-ground and three stories deep, layered like a pit with the trash settling to the bottom. Manu's favorite drinking establishments and cheap meal spots are on the lowest level, Level C, though he always appreciates the chance to use Jaantzen's expense account to impress potential clients by meeting them in a Control-level restaurant with the expensive plates and great launch views.

Le Comptoir Darna is two levels below ground, on Level B. It's Louis Oni's favorite, and close to his prosthetics repair shop. Low ceiling, like all the places on Level B, but it's been built out nice to look like a retro pub from Indira's early days, with that reclaimed, unfinished look like it'd been built from salvaged parts of the original *Ark Matsya*. It's all for show, but it's well-done: buffed-out rivets, molded plastic seating, a bartop filled with replica colonist stickers under thick scratched glass.

Manu slips onto his favorite stool; under the glass a sticker with a girl in a flowered skirt and crop top encourages him to visit some place called Mauritius. Above the bar, a newscaster is waxing poetic about the latest round of peace talks between the Alliance and one of the many resistance groups on Indira, Manu doesn't even recognize their acronym.

Manu watches the program a moment before the bartender returns to the far end of the bar. "Peace talks?" Manu says, lifting his chin to the screen. "Sounds like assimilation talks."

"Alliance bastards'll be coming after New Sarjun next," the bartender says affably. "What are you having?"

Manu orders a draft lager — it always tastes faintly of engine oil here, whether a fault in the dishwasher, the lines, or the brewer, he's never been able to figure out. The scrubbers kick on faintly in the background, and slowly the bar's air begins to freshen.

"Manu, *mon ami.*" Manu turns to see Louis, bright eyes smiling, deep-russet jaw salted with the shadow of his graying beard.

"Hallelujah, how is it?"

Louis's eyes light up at Manu's use of his full name, and Manu gives him a hug. The man smells like old earth and sweat, and a hint of chemical smoke that Manu can't place and probably doesn't want to know about. Manu suspects they might end up on the opposite sides of gunfire if shit ever hit the fan again in Bulari's underworld, but he and Louis struck up a conversation over beers once at a local pub, and over the years they've fallen into an arrangement close to friendship.

Louis hoists himself into a seat beside Manu and the bartender meets him with a bottle of his favorite sour ale. Louis raises the bottle in salute. "Thomas, your baby's better?"

"Yes, thanks! That doctor you recommended was a miracle worker."

Louis flashes a smile, but the levity in his expression quickly fades as the bartender turns away. "So, *mon ami.* You've heard what's in the wind?"

Manu juts his chin at the screen above the bar. "Alliance is taking down another rebel group," he says, though he knows Louis isn't here to talk politics. The way the other man's watching him turns something cold in the pit of his stomach.

"What is it, man?"

"You haven't heard about Blackheart," Louis says. "Her soul's gone on."

The name's like a knife in his gut. Manu takes a long drink. "Not to a better place, I can tell you that."

Louis just shrugs. He's not here to talk religion, either.

"How?"

"A woman who lives by the gun dies by the gun."

"A hit?"

"She didn't die of old age." Louis takes a sip of his beer, watching Manu out of the corner of his eye. "You oughta be happy to see Blackheart go."

"Me and the rest of Bulari. Half my bones still ache when it rains."

"Good thing it ain't rained all year, then."

And good thing Gia isn't half-bad at reknitting severed nerves, Manu thinks but does not say. His scarred left hand has slipped out of sight beneath the bar, clenching on his thigh. Yeah. He's not sad to see Blackheart get her due.

"You hear who did it?" he asks.

Louis purses his lips. "Oh, I heard everybody did it. Local gang on Indira, pissed-off girlfriend, girlfriend's pissed-off husband, secret agents from New Sarjun, rebel terrorists . . ." Louis takes a swig of his bottle, then looks at Manu speculatively. "Your man, of course."

"It wasn't my man."

"Pity."

"Yeah?"

"Just that then I'd know somebody'd made a plan for the mess that's about to come."

"And what would you know about that?" Manu asks.

"*Rien du tout, mon ami,*" Louis says.

"You and everybody else."

Louis just smiles. "I do know the Dry Creek crew put out a call for soldiers this morning."

Sensing a fight among Coeur's splintering crew and looking to pick up the pieces, surely.

"My man's got it covered," Manu says. Does Jaantzen know yet? If so, he'll be throwing his weight behind the most likely candidate to keep Coeur's crew from disintegrating: Naali Hinoja. But they'll need to act fast.

"Jackals scent blood," Louis says simply. "I can't guess where that blood'll come from."

On the screen above the bar, the news program has moved on from the peace talks on Indira to the puzzling phenomenon of luxury vacation homes out in Durga's Belt — a real estate boom on the asteroid belt's dwarf planet chain fueled by the uneasy inevitability of the Alliance gaining control there, too.

Manu lifts his eyebrows to the screen. "Jackals, indeed." His mind flashes to Starla, what she will feel seeing wealthy Indiran citizens descend like fleas on the Belt after her own people had been thoroughly tamed and exterminated.

Louis frowns at the holographic tour of a luxe build-out, every surface bursting with rich materials and ridiculous tech. "Looks like my own private hell," he says. "Give me the sun and fresh air."

"You don't want to go into space?"

"God grant that I die on this rock. You?"

"It would be nice to visit."

Louis tips back the rest of his beer, sets the bottle on the counter. He waves off the offer of a second one, and Manu reaches to pass his comm over the tab before Louis can pull his own out. Louis gives him a sly smile. "One more thing I know," he says. "A certain half-robot soldier's planetside. He caught up to you yet?"

Manu tries to keep his voice neutral, but he can feel the flush touching the back of his neck. "Oriol?"

Louis winks.

"Nah. I ain't seen him yet."

"Want me to send on a message, he comes back into my shop?"

"He knows how to get ahold of me." Manu says it lightly, but he wants to pry. Oriol's back on New Sarjun and hasn't come to see him? For how long? And if he hasn't gotten ahold of him yet, is he even planning to? Manu holds back the questions, though. Oriol's a cat comes home when he wants to, and no bit of prying ever made him come home sooner.

"Gotta get back to work. You be careful out there, *mon ami*," Louis says, and at the tone in his voice, Manu looks up. This is more than a meaningless parting phrase. Louis lays his hand on Manu's shoulder. "Blackheart dead, peace talks bringing Alliance to our rock. Bad winds coming."

"You too," Manu says. He takes a deep breath, leaves his own beer unfinished on the bar. Thoughts of Blackheart and complicated feelings about Oriol have bittered the brew.

He shakes it off.

He needs to get back to Cobalt Tower and talk to Jaantzen. But first he'll have to go see how urgent a message from Cedra about RKE could possibly be.

Geordi Jimenez Space Terminal is more crowded than usual due to the *Maria Elena III*, the Ganesh-class transport lumbering in orbit above them. The crew's mostly on shore leave during the cargo offload, and the city's flooded with tourists. On top of that, everybody and their cousins are flinging cargo haulers into orbit to downtrip goods, regardless of paperwork or the space-worthiness of their ships.

Despite the crowds, Manu normally likes being in the terminal. Even if he's just there to check on a shipment, he still gets that giddy high of possibility, the feeling that he could be about to embark on a journey, heading anywhere else in the system. He loves his work, but damn this city feels like a death sentence sometimes.

Right now, though, he's got other things on his mind.

Ground level of the terminal is reasonably neat, with loiterers trying to look like they have business and soldiers armed with tasers on patrol to make sure no one falls asleep on any benches. Levels A and B, the two floors below, are mainly amenities for crews: hair stylists and dentists and tattoo parlors and bars like Le Comptoir Darna.

But Level C?

Level C hits Manu like a physical thing: the scents, the din, the crush of people. Manu pauses in the entry, taking it all in. The air is heavy with fry grease and engine oil and voices echo off the high ceiling, jumbled so it's hard to pick out anything individual. Warring news and music programs blare from the lunch stands, callers hawk wares as they wander the crowds, and the buskers and street performers only spike the chaos.

The center of the space is a maze of carts and temporary tents hawking food and goods, the wall ringed with lean-to shacks interspersed with doors. Manu sidesteps a woman with a tray of steam buns, ducks past a street performer who seems to be playing both parts of a sword fight.

He finds his destination between the misspelled posters of a fried noodle stand and the sizzlingly graphic neon signs of a porn shop.

Twin Star Salvage.

The door's open. Manu raps on the frame.

It's been years since he's been by — there's never anything that requires a personal visit — and he'd forgotten how tiny Twin Star's office is. It's crowded with tattered cardboard boxes, rolled-up charts, and a few dusty electronics.

Another man might have been lost in the clutter, but the man sitting behind the desk does not easily blend into drab surroundings. He's wearing an orange-and-blue ikat-print lumosilk shirt unbuttoned at the neck, his smooth brown skin and a flash of a gold medallion visible beneath. Strong cheekbones and long black lashes, dark hair stuck out at unruly angles that manage to look tousled in just the right way. He's younger than Manu expected the manager of a salvage company to be, maybe a decade or more younger than Manu himself.

Manu checks the bio Cedra sent over again. Yep, that's the guy.

Manu sets his shoulder on the doorjamb, crosses his arms, lets his weight sink into one hip, easy-like. Territorial-like. The man frowns up at him; one hand disappears underneath the desk. Manu ignores it.

"Benedicto Kulikutan?" Manu asks.

"Just Beto," the man says. "Who are you?" His hand is still underneath the desk. He's got an accent, but it's faint. Manu's not sure how to place it.

"You called this morning. About a shipment for Rosco Kudra Enterprises? I'm here to check it out."

"You're not my usual contact," Beto says, and Manu just nods, eyebrows raised like, Yeah, I know. Beto taps at the screen of his comm. "Okay, so you're — " He breaks off, realizing he's about to give away a name. Good man. "I'll need to see some identification," he says instead.

"Glad to hear it."

Beto clears enough paperwork off the corner of the desk to reveal a sign pad, and Manu saunters up, palms the pad. The desk hums a moment — it's ancient, Manu can see why Beto seems to prefer paper charts — then flashes up an identity on Beto's side. Manu knows what it will read: Manu Juric. Citizen: Bulari, New Sarjun.

Beto frowns at it. "That all?"

"What more do you want?"

"I've never seen an ident card this blank."

"Am I the guy Cedra told you was coming?"

Beto nods.

"Well then."

"And . . . what do you do for Rosco Kudra?"

Curious, this one. Manu approves. "I solve problems," Manu says. "I heard we had a problem."

"Twin Star doesn't have a problem," Beto says, too quickly.

"With the shipment."

"Yeah." Beto clears his throat. He glances back down at Manu's ident. "I need to make a call to my RKE contact. Protocol."

Manu gestures for Beto to go ahead. He likes this operator: unflappable, stands his ground. He scans the room while Beto calls Cedra and verifies Manu's visual and palm print. Along with the clutter of plans, manifests, and schematics there are signs that Beto spends a good amount of his time in his office. There's a pile of cushions in the corner that one might arrange into a bed. Food wrappers stacked for a trip to the recycler, and a few vintage travel posters tacked to the walls, advertising a pristine prewar New Manila.

At the posters, Manu finally places the accent. You

don't hear it much. There aren't that many immigrants from New Manila here, at least not outside the mines. Aren't many from that war-torn country who can afford fare off Indira on their own, and not many indentures earn out their passage to New Sarjun before the mines wreck them completely. He's met plenty of their kids, but by then the accent's gone.

Young, healthy man with a first-gen accent? His parents probably paid a lot of money they didn't have to keep him from being drafted into either the Alliance or the New Manila Liberation Front.

Beto finishes up his call, slips his comm back into his pocket.

"You ready to see the cargo?" he asks.

Back aboveground, Manu sees that Cedra's already got RKE's magtruck driver waiting at the loading dock in the terminal's cargo area; Manu raises a hand in greeting as they walk by and the driver lifts her chin, goes back to reading. A wreath of cigar smoke drifts from the open window.

The storage unit is well-secured with both mechanical and biometric locks, Manu is pleased to see. Beto throws open the door to the container. "Everything looked all right on the initial visual inspection, but our scan showed a plus-one miscount in cargo. I knew this one was to be freight-forwarded without repacking, and I didn't like the idea of someone trying to slip something past a client. So we took a closer look and found this."

This is sitting by itself on top of a ventilator hood. It's a case about the length of Manu's arm, carved with what looks like an old statue of a woman — or a zoomorphic goddess. Like something you'd see in history books of old relics from back on Old Earth, long before the diaspora. He's never before wondered if any such antiquities made it out on the *Ark Matsya*, but it's possible they did, that there's museums back on Indira dedicated to the ancient homeland and packed with cargo precious enough to take the place of supplies the *Ark Matsya* needed for the trip.

Or, more probably, the place of additional people they could have carried away from humanity's dying homeland.

Manu tilts his head, considering the case. "I don't think this belongs in any HVAC system I've heard of," he says finally.

Beto gingerly rotates the case, runs a slim brown finger along the seam. "It looks like it opens here, but there's no latch. And we didn't try it."

"Good call."

"You don't know what it is?"

Trouble, says a voice deep inside Manu. "How'd you get it past customs?"

Bribes is the usual way, and most downtrippers will bill that in as an agreed-upon line item. But Benedicto Kuliku-tan's pause is a touch too long. He swallows to buy himself time. "We have a few false compartments in the *Coldfire*. Our ship."

"You scan all your customers' cargo for miscounts and contraband?"

The briefest of hesitations. "Yes?"

"That's class, thorough. I like it."

The other man's gone all tense again. Manu tilts his head, watching.

"What else do you bring down?"

That flush, creeping into Beto's cheeks. "Nothing," he says, too fast. "We're just watching out for our customers."

"I'm not here to tell you how to run your business," he says. Jaantzen won't care that their downtripping contractor engages in a bit of skimming on the side so long as they're good at it. He turns back to the case. He doesn't want to touch it; something about it turns his stomach. "Send the shipment on, but box that up and have our driver drop it at the main office, care of Manu Juric. And tell your crew to keep this close to heart. You never know who might be out there looking for it."

He starts to turn, to leave; reconsiders. This man's got a good head on his shoulders, and in Manu's experience, it never hurts to have a man like that in the pocket.

He pulls out his comm. "I'm sending you my personal contact," he says. "I don't want to hear about any RKE business — you'll still send that to Cedra. But you got any other business or personal problems, feel free to contact me directly."

Beto frowns at him. "What sorts of business or personal problems?"

"I'm not a fortune-teller, man," Manu says. "With family, maybe. You got a family?"

That hesitation: Benedicto Kulikutan's still judging his character. "A sister," he says finally. "And she's got a kid. How about you?" He's trying to re-level the playing field.

"Keep up the good work out there," Manu tells him with a wink. "I'm sure I'll see you around.

Manu checks his comm as he leaves, but there's still no message from Starla or Jaantzen. Have they heard yet, about Coeur? They would have let him know if they were going to skip the showing today, which means they're probably still with the real estate agent. Either that or they're being sensationally murdered by Jet Park street gangs at this very moment. Manu doesn't care what Jaantzen says — that part of town is *not* up and coming.

Manu slips his comm back in his pocket, hesitates

between the entrance to the terminal and the train station that will take him back downtown.

He's got an hour at least before Jaantzen gets back to Cobalt Tower and the real planning happens. Which means he has time to answer one more pressing question before he catches the downtown train:

Fried noodles from Level C? Or the dry tempeh sandwich he has waiting back at the office.

What kind of question even *is* that?

Manu heads back into the terminal.

3

JAANTZEN

From Julieta's spacious suburb in southwestern Bulari to the northern fringes where the city pushes up against the launch reserve of the terminal: the neighborhood of Jet Park isn't far from Bulari's glittering downtown core, yet it feels worlds away. Sand rushes in whorls outside Jaantzen's window as the Dulciana passes through; the magtrucks that head through the neighborhood from the terminal to the mines northeast of Bulari are equipped with scoops and brushes to sweep drifts of sand off the tracks. One lumbers past them at an intersection. Along with the brush, it's also equipped with bulletproof armor and what looks like a stun bolt array to discourage theft.

Starla gives the armored magtruck a once-over, flashes Jaantzen a skeptical look which he ignores. Jet Park may not be known as a desirable place to visit at the moment, but Jaantzen's banking on the future.

Over the past twelve years, Bulari has become a completely different city. Before, it was a morass of warring crime lords washing through each other's territories like lava flows, burning everything in their path. Now the territories are fairly set, each crew comfortable — and profitable — in their specific vertical. In part thanks to Coeur, who crossed everyone she worked with and ended up uniting former enemies in the process.

With any other crew, the boss's death would cause an annoyance as the organization shook itself out into a new arrangement. But Blackheart's crew has their fingers in enough other business — and such an overabundance of warring ego — that the fallout from an internal squabble could throw the whole city back into turmoil. Jaantzen isn't one to take sides in other families' internal quarrels, but Coeur's lieutenant Naali Hinoja will need his help if she's going to keep control of the crew. And having her in his debt will open opportunities to expand his own influence.

A hated rival dead and her territory opened to prospecting, the same day he moves forward with a highly profitable partnership in his legitimate business.

If Jaantzen believed in luck, he'd consider this a good day; instead he believes in traps, in caution. In backup plans.

Still, he's cautiously optimistic.

The property is only a few blocks past the magtruck line on what was once Jet Park's main drag — and will be again. It's an eye-catching building if you can look past the opaque layers of stasis wrap over the glass facade, and the swaths of colorful graffiti over that. It's three stories tall, windows all the way up. The top story juts out over the street almost three meters, its glass-bottomed floor littered with detritus.

"Pretty cool," signs Starla, letting the Dulciana idle a half-block away so they can take in the view. "Too bad it's not in Tamarind."

"Have faith," Jaantzen signs back.

She just pulls the Dulciana into an alley and into the

docking bay that's been coded to open for the vehicle's signature. Starla docks, lets the spinner's engine purr a moment while the doors close behind them. And then a second longer. Her pale cheek flashes in the dim light as she scans the area around them, then she unfolds gracefully from the driver's seat, silent but for the faint whine of her pistol warming to her palm as she rests her hand on the grip.

The docking bay opens straight into the building, the only light coming from the wall of milky, stasis-wrapped windows to the left. To the right, twin staircases, fronted by a service bar that runs nearly the width of the building, sweep to the second-floor balcony. Behind that is a row of doors, and above them is the full glass floor of the third level.

The first floor is wide-open and empty but for a pile of crates, a gleaming full-chrome motorcycle, and the realtor, Aditi Ciam.

"Hi Starla!" Aditi calls with a wave. She's a short round woman in tight black pants and black leather motorcycle boots, a flash of chrome sparking on the caps of her toes as she shifts her weight, folds her bare brown arms over the front of her gold-and-pink lumosilk blouse. "Your people are already checking the place out."

Starla waves back; still, Jaantzen doesn't move until Starla opens his door, which means she's satisfied with the security herself. He and Starla both tell this again and again to clients of the security firm: breaking protocol is the number one way to get yourself — or someone you love — killed.

He knows this from experience.

"Thank you for meeting us here," he says to Aditi. "I know it's not your usual beat."

"It's not a problem," she says with an airy wave of her hand. "I have a dinner meeting at the terminal after this.

And anyway, I simply *had* to see this up-and-coming Jet Park property for myself."

"I'm certain we'll all be impressed." Jaantzen catches Starla's attention and taps a finger next to his eye with eyebrow raised in question. She nods; her lens is catching Aditi's words.

"Can we turn on some lights?" he asks Aditi.

Aditi shakes her head. "The external security systems are turned on, but the rest of the building hasn't been powered for a decade. I spent half the morning trying to get the power company to turn it back on, but the seller has a backlog of bills they want paid first. Is Mr. Seti coming?"

"He should be here any moment."

The gloom does nothing to hide the building's challenges. It may have been well-used once, but it'll take a lot of hard work to get it back into shape now. In its shoddy abandon it could be anywhere he's ever held a clandestine meeting. Anywhere he's ever heard the echoing of footsteps and the whine of a warming pistol, smelled engine grease and the sharp tang of adrenaline-laced sweat.

He's been in his fair share of abandoned buildings over the years. Think back ten years, and it's the bulk of his security firm's prospecting calls, held off the radar since most of his clients back then still danced on the gray side of the law. Back fifteen years, and it's scare tactics on petty drug dealers edging into his turf. Twenty years — and his mind cringes to go there, back to the man he used to be before meeting — and losing — his wife. Before Starla.

Before going more or less straight.

But this isn't one of *those* abandoned buildings. At least, it won't be once Jaantzen is through with it.

A thud and a familiar muffled curse echo off the walls. Jaantzen turns his head to find the source; the way this place carries sound, it could be coming from anywhere. "El? Toshiyo?"

"Here, boss," comes Toshiyo Ravi's voice. "Checking out the offices."

But it's El Anahoy who appears from one of the doorways behind the service counter, carrying a box overflowing with wiring.

"Looks like the offices doubled as junk parts storage," Toshiyo calls from somewhere behind him. "This place is amazing!"

El sets the box on the counter, tucks a strand of electric blue hair behind his ear with dark fingers. Nods respectfully to Jaantzen. Salutes Starla.

"None of that can come home with us, Ms. Ravi," Jaantzen calls.

"Until we sign paperwork on the place, I know." Toshiyo appears in the doorway with a black smudge on her cheek, a roll of solar paneling under her arm. "There's an early-gen sweeper bot in there that's still in pretty good condition. I've always wanted to work on one of those."

Jaantzen sighs. He'd've liked to say, None of that can come home with us ever, but he's under no illusions that he can control the strange things Toshiyo Ravi brings back to the office. Starla and El are discussing the building's security in fluid gestures, referencing specific terminology he's having trouble following. El laughs at something she's said, the silver ring on his nose glinting in the dim light.

"Let's hear about this place," he says to Aditi.

"Charming, isn't it?" Aditi looks skeptically around the room. The floor-to-ceiling windows are cloudy with graffiti, but at least the stasis wrap has kept the glass intact. Debris is strewn about, evidence of a decade or more of serving as an impromptu home for anyone who could find a way in.

"The structure looks good," Jaantzen says.

"It used to be a luxury Pleiades dealership, back when people actually wanted to come out to Jet Park," Aditi says. "Before Weyerman shut down their mines in the east hills. Well before my time."

"Before all of our times." Jaantzen doesn't have any memories of Jet Park other than cracked sidewalks, broken windows, unorganized street gangs. "But history is cyclical, and the winners are those who see a rising star and grab hold."

"I hope you're right," Aditi says, though she doesn't look convinced. "The seller will practically pay you to take this place off her hands, but for what you'll spend fixing it up I've got some real sweet spots I can show you in the Tamarind, hon. Right on the Ave."

A light begins blinking as another of the docking bay doors starts to rise. Starla shifts subtly to stand in front of him, hand on her pistol. El has taken up a similar position beside her.

If Aditi notices the shift in the energy, she doesn't give a sign. "Hiya!" she calls, stepping past El as Mizal Seti's driver slips a sleek silver Magnata two-seater into the dock.

Mizal pulls himself from the low-slung Magnata with a little *oof*, looks down to button his jacket. He's dressed in a rose-gold suit that sets off his ochre skin. He's a decade younger than Jaantzen, though his dark hair is already going salt-and-pepper and he has sharp lines around his brown eyes, deep furrows on his brow. Mizal Seti aged quickly after his father's murder at Coeur's hand, after the business fell to him.

The civil war that ousted Coeur had aged them all quickly.

Starla stands down; Jaantzen walks over to greet Mizal with a clasped arm.

"Willem!" Mizal says with a smile. "Starla, how are you?" He greets Starla with a kiss on the cheek. She does a little double twist of her wrist with an outstretched hand. It means, Just fine. Jaantzen had taken it for USL until last week when Manu explained it was only the trendy new hand slang kids were using on the street.

"It's so good to see you," Mizal says. "Thank you for meeting us here, Aditi. You can see the potential, can't you?"

"It's promising," Jaantzen agrees. Provided Mizal holds up his end of the bargain and turns this neighborhood into a place people will bother to visit.

"I was just telling Mr. Jaantzen that this used to be a spinner dealership," Aditi says.

"That explains the glass third floor," says Mizal. "Though it makes for a risqué dining area." He lifts an eyebrow.

"You could smoke the glass," says Aditi. She gestures behind them, past the service counter. "And knock down this wall and you've got plenty of room for the kitchen. Slightly more than you currently have at the Jungle, Willem. Which is good because you'll be able to fit more tables, too — especially with the balcony." Aditi shines her flashlight up to illuminate the gently curving second-floor balcony, edged by a railing that would have looked nice if it hadn't been torn up for scrap metal. "Filling those tables with bodies, though . . . That's going to take a miracle."

"A little faith, Aditi," Mizal says with a smile.

Aditi shakes her head and walks towards the back offices. "Don't worry. I know who I'm dealing with. If any other two clients had asked me to scope restaurant locations in Jet Park, I would've laughed them back onto the street."

Mizal claps a hand on Jaantzen's shoulder as she walks away. It lingers; he has something to say.

Jaantzen's got a good guess what that is.

"I'm sure you've heard the rumors," Mizal says, his voice low. "About Coeur." He's got a conspiratorial look on his face.

"From what I hear it's not rumors," Jaantzen says.

Mizal breaks into a grin. "Congratulations to all of us, then," he says. "I always wondered why you didn't kill her way back when."

"I had my reasons," Jaantzen says. "Reasons which still apply today."

The grin fades a touch. Mizal lifts his chin, considering. "If you didn't kill her, who did? I don't have that kind of pull on Indira. Believe me, I've considered it."

"It doesn't matter who killed her," Jaantzen says, though he doesn't believe that. "I've got it under control."

"Good." Mizal squeezes Jaantzen's shoulder and turns to follow Aditi. "And I hope whoever did it raises their hand so I can send them a thank-you gift. Maybe the mystery will be solved at the dinner tomorrow night."

"Perhaps."

Mizal Seti is the reason Jaantzen is interested in this decrepit old building, and the reason Jet Park is on the upswing. Now that New Sarjun's luxury legal, and semilegal, gentech mods industry is starting to pick up, gentech businesses like Mizal's need cheap real estate to house their factories and clinic complexes.

With the influx of new corporate money — and the concern that rich clientele will have to visit the neighborhood — will come the beautification project. Jaantzen can scent it on the air, and a conversation with his contact at city hall confirmed it: there will be excellent incentives on the table for breathing life back into Jet Park.

It's a good business opportunity, but that's not the only reason Jaantzen is here. It's also a good opportunity for Jaantzen to take his place among the truly respected businesspeople of Bulari — earning the respect of all sectors of society, not just Bulari's underbelly. Julieta Yang and Mizal Seti may still run illegal businesses, but both occupy the place in society that Jaantzen has dreamed of since he was a boy in the orphanage. He's achieved their level of wealth, earned their respect as a fighter. Now it's time for them to see him as their equal.

Aditi leads them around the far staircase and stops in front of a wide bay door. It wouldn't look out of place in a transport hangar down at the terminal.

"This is the best part, hon," she says, one fist on one wide hip while she plays her flashlight over the doors. "Already climate-controlled, though the system's out of date. Open the doors and you can have the brewery on view from the restaurant. Or you can seal the space off for security."

"Does this even work?" Starla signs.

"Do the doors work?" Jaantzen asks Aditi.

"The seller assures me that they do," Aditi says. "But I'd hold off coming to a final price until we can get the electricity turned on."

"Gimme a minute, boss," Toshiyo calls. She's perched cross-legged on the service counter, typing into a device he doesn't recognize.

"You're not — " Aditi starts, but there's a faint whine and a *pop-flash* from one of the chandelier panels. The control panel beside the bay doors flickers to life.

Aditi sighs. "If anyone asks, I had to leave early for another showing."

"No one will ask," Jaantzen says.

He nods to Starla's quizzical expression, and she presses the symbol that will open the doors. With a chest-tightening metal-on-metal groan, the doors begin to telescope back into their pockets, the first few segments fitting relatively smoothly before something catches and the whole contraption grinds to a halt. Starla slams her palm on Cancel.

And tilts her head. Her right eye goes mirror-finish, then glimmers as information scrolls past. Her hand cuts away and Jaantzen pulls Aditi back from the door a split second before he hears the sizzle of a pulse carbine. A beam slices through the air where Aditi was standing, sears against the wall.

Starla's in a crouch behind the left door, two shots through the doorway and Jaantzen hears someone fall with a muffled thud. She holds up three fingers, then closes one back into her fist. Two left.

El takes a position at the right door, while Jaantzen ushers Aditi, Toshiyo, and Mizal to safety in an office.

"Who — " Aditi begins.

"We've got it," he says simply, and shuts the door between them.

Starla glances at him when he joins her at the door. Beyond, the room is a jumble of antique electronics, rubber tubing, and sheetmetal. A man lies on his back beside an overturned table, covered in blood and dusted with an iridescent silvery-blue powder.

Shard. They're making shard.

Starla points at a partially dismantled refrigeration unit and holds up one finger, then at the far doorway and holds up a second finger.

"All armed?" Jaantzen signs.

She nods, then frowns at the glimmering green light dancing in her iris.

"More, unarmed," she signs. She points at the far doorway again.

Unarmed? Jaantzen has a sinking feeling about that. He lays a hand on Starla's shoulder; he'd rather keep from putting any more bullets in this place if he can help it, anyway.

"Walk out the door and we have no quarrel with you," Jaantzen calls.

"You ain't takin our stuff." The man's voice comes from behind the refrigeration unit.

Jaantzen expects his main business, Admant Security, to provide him with a competitive edge in these sorts of situations. But today it's years of importing industrial-grade heating and cooling units that's coming in handy. The refrigeration unit the man is hiding behind is a Garachi, an older model in their low-end H series. The insulating walls are barely stronger than foil.

"We won't take your shard," Jaantzen tells the man. "We'll be destroying it."

"You with the Dawn, we paid our dues."

Jaantzen frowns at that. "We are not the Dawn," he says. It's not the first time he's heard the name of the back-country religious cult associated with shard cookers, but it's the first time he's come across one of their operations inside city limits. He files that away for later. "Get out now and be grateful your trigger-happy friend didn't injure any of my people."

In the echoey silence that follows Jaantzen hears the faint whine of a pistol. Conversation over, he supposes. He taps Starla twice on the shoulder.

"Cover," she signs, and slips through the bay doors.

Jaantzen fires a round of slugs into the refrigeration unit. The resulting scream confirms his suspicion that the Garachi H series are just as poor at providing cover in a fire-fight as they are at maintaining a consistent temperature. El fires at the flash of movement in the bathroom doorway, and a moment later the sound of breaking glass comes from the room, muffled swearing, the retreating sound of running footsteps on pavement.

El slips in after Starla to cover the far door; Jaantzen will keep his guard up in the doorway until he sees her sign. But if Starla's scan is correct and there are more people in the far room, they're not showing themselves.

Starla crouches behind the refrigeration unit, hauls the shard-cooker to his feet. He's bleeding from where one of Jaantzen's slugs tore through his knee, shivering in a feverish combination of shock and shard.

Starla deposits him in a chair and he howls.

"How many more of you are there?" Jaantzen asks. The man spits at his feet, but it's desperate malice, not true defiance. This is the sort of man who breaks simply and quickly.

Jaantzen's nostrils are filled with the acrid stench of ozone, seared flesh, engine oil, blood, and fear. Turns out this *is* one of those abandoned buildings from his darker days, after all. The man's glaring at him in a mixture of hatred and terror, and Jaantzen can think of a dozen creative ways to make this interview go the way he wants it to.

Except that Mizal Seti and Aditi Ciam are just outside, and it's Starla standing there with her weapon pointed at the shard-cooker, not one of the brutes Jaantzen used to run with. She meets his gaze, waiting on his command, and he wonders what it is she expects him to tell her. How many steps she'd be willing to take down the path that leads to the bad old days.

He nods at her. She takes aim at the man's good knee.

The man shrieks, holding out his hands. "Please!"

"How many more of you are there?" Jaantzen asks again.

"Nobody," the man spits between chattering teeth. Jaantzen sighs, raises a hand to signal Starla. "No! I mean, no more guards. Just the workers."

Jaantzen glances over his shoulder; El has disappeared through the doorway in a string of profanity. Guards, workers, and shard. Jaantzen's seen this sort of operation before, back when he was working to rid his own neighborhoods of shard-cookers. What El's about to find probably won't be pretty.

"Go help El," he signs. As Starla walks away, Jaantzen fires his own weapon into the man's good knee.

"Do you work for the Dawn?" Jaantzen asks when the howls die down.

The man shakes head, sobbing. "Paid dues," he pants. "Supposed to have. Protection."

"From them, certainly." Jaantzen sets his weapon to stun and fires into the man's chest. Across the room, El and Starla are ushering a trio of dazed workers into the dim light. Two men and a woman, thin and translucent as rice paper. One of the men is reciting what sounds like scripture or poetry, and his voice has got that high-pitched shake, like he's vibrating between planes of consciousness. They're all higher than the stars right now.

"Boss?" El calls.

Jaantzen surveys the scene — a pair of bodies, blood glittering on shattered glass and seeping into powdered shard — calculating the time loss of red tape against the potential cost savings he could leverage from a seller negligent enough to let the squatters in.

"Call our cleanup crew, please," Jaantzen says to El. "Stay with Ms. Ciam and Mr. Seti until they come, then drop off the workers and this one with the police." It's not his favorite move, but the workers need somewhere to go that isn't out on the street.

"You killed him!"

Aditi and Mizal are standing in the doorway. She's pale and wide-eyed; he merely looks uncomfortable. He's the sort of man who hires people — people like Willem Jaantzen, in fact — for things like this rather than wielding his own violence. Jaantzen wonders how much he's slipped in Mizal's estimation — back towards hired gun in a nice suit, rather than business equal.

"He was using slave labor to cook shard," Jaantzen says to Aditi. He slips his weapon back into his shoulder holster and buttons his suit jacket. "But he's not dead. He'll just need to reconsider his job options in the future."

"Boss?"

Jaantzen turns to find Toshiyo rooting through the shard-cookers' equipment. He winces, but at least she's wearing gloves.

"Ms. Ravi?"

She holds up a blue-dusted glass slide with a pair of tongs. "This look like shard to you?"

Yes, it does, though Jaantzen doesn't spend much time around chemistry sets or designer drugs. But he's not one to admit ignorance on any topic.

"What do you see?" he asks instead.

"The tab that goes under the tongue, it's a capsule, not powder. Some sort of gel."

"They do get creative, don't they," Mizal says.

"Tell the buyer we're interested," Jaantzen says to Aditi. "That is, once she cleans this out and sees to her security. We're even happy to help with the latter. You can put her in touch with Starla."

Aditi nods. It's clear she's not sure which part of the scene to find most shocking, so she's attempting to ignore it all. "I'll see what I can do about the price, after all this," she says. "Unless you'd rather I show you that location in the Tamarind?"

"Not at all." Jaantzen smiles. "This place is perfect."

4

STARLA

The temperature drops fast in Bulari after dark, and Starla's starting to wish she'd brought her coat when she climbed up to the top of Cobalt Tower to watch the sunset. With sunset had come the first feeble star struggling through the dusk and Bulari's light pollution, and once she'd waited for the second, a third and fourth were there, tiny pinpoints that could slip out of focus in an instant.

An hour later she's still naming them as they spark into view: that one's Arctas, that one Prixa Minor, then Caba Regina just starting to glimmer on the eastern horizon. Now, shivering in the dark, she's struggling to remember the latest batch she learned, in the Sword constellation. She could power up her lens and ask it to identify them, but she doesn't want to cheat. The name's dancing around the edges of her mind anyway. She taps thumbs against middle fingers absently, trying to jog the memory loose. Aurex, Auror, something.

Something about gold.

A flash of movement in the corner of her eye catches her attention, and Starla glances over to find Manu standing silhouetted against the glittering backdrop of downtown Bulari. She lifts her chin in greeting and takes her feet off the other chair, kicks it back from the table for him.

"Thank you," he signs, lounging back in it. Long, lean legs stretched out and crossed at the ankles, fingers steepled over his abs, dark skin ruddy in the red lights Starla installed on the rooftop to preserve her night vision. Beyond him, faint lights from Bulari's five sprawling slums — the Fingers — snake like dying brushfire up into their respective ravines.

Jaantzen's office building isn't the tallest one in downtown Bulari, but it's got the best view. If only she could drown out the ambient light, one of these days just throw the switch on the main power grid and plunge the whole city into darkness, for just an hour or so, to give the struggling stars space to breathe.

Then, it would be perfect.

Then, it would almost be like home.

Manu's trying to catch her attention.

She switches on the table lamp — also red — so she can see his hands.

"I thought you left for the night," he signs.

She shrugs. "Still working. Well — still work to do." She's clearly not working right now.

There's the thing with Julieta Yang's shipment, of course. It's in a warehouse in Carama Town — the littlest slum finger that spills south into the plains — and Starla has it under surveillance while she plans their move. Yang may be a friend of the family, but Starla's not going in without intel.

Plus, she needs to hunt down blueprints of the abandoned dealership in Jet Park and get back to the seller with a quote on interim security installation — assuming they can get her to agree to clean up the place.

And assuming Seti can clean up the neighborhood. There could be another hundred drug labs holed up in abandoned buildings out there, operated by or paying tribute to one of Bulari's minor crews — or, apparently, the Dawn. They sure do push a lot of drugs for a rural religious cult.

"You hear about the Dawn in Jet Park before?" she asks Manu.

Manu makes a face: Nah. "I didn't think they got into the city."

The Dawn's been recruiting kids to the desert and pushing inferior shard back into the city for years without attracting too much attention. But cooking shard in Jet Park?

"You think that neighborhood's going to get better?" she asks.

Manu looks unbothered. "Mizal is putting in a clinic. Others coming, probably."

"And genetic tourists drink beer?"

"Old man needs a hobby to retire with," Manu signs with a laugh.

"Retire? Are we talking about the same Willem Jaantzen?"

"Maybe not retire. But everybody needs a pet project."

Do they? Starla frowns at that. "What's yours?"

"I like to travel," Manu signs after a minute, though she can't remember the last time he went on a trip that wasn't for work. As far as she can tell, Oriol's the one who likes to travel, not Manu.

"What's yours?" Manu asks.

Starla just raises her gaze to the heavens before meeting

his again. If she's trapped on this rock, stargazing is the next best thing.

A shooting star slashes through the Egret's head just then, crossing in front of the star that forms the constellation's eye. She finds icy Bixia Yuanjin glinting to the south, Indira just setting on the horizon, and she scans along the elliptical by habit. Somewhere out there, fragments of her family's station are still scattered through Durga's Belt. That shooting star could have been part of the debris, the generator core, maybe, or something more personal. Her parents' kitchen unit. Her childhood bedroom.

A light touch on her arm shocks her back to the present. She looks back at Manu.

"The one with the pentagram, what is it?"

Her gaze follows his pointing finger to the Pangolin; she fingerspells the name. It's one of the few constellations in New Sarjun's night sky named for a desert creature, rather than those that flourish back on water-rich Indira. Manu tilts his head to look at her again. He gives her a thumbs-up, raised eyebrows, questioning.

Starla gnaws on the inside of her cheek, considering. *Is she okay?* She's felt off-kilter today, like the whole world is a space station with a gyro gone off and every third step along a supposedly flat corridor isn't quite where you expect it to be.

Beyond the new restaurant and destroying Julieta's shipment, there's that third problem that arose today. A dead one coming back to haunt them all.

Shit. She hasn't even asked him.

"I'm fine. But you: you heard? About C — "

He waves away the name she's about to spell.

"I heard."

She wants to ask how he is, but she feels awkward

forming the question. Manu's always been the older brother. The one who probes, who asks how you're doing, who listens and calms while you rail against the world. They've grown close as family over the years, but she's still fifteen years his junior, and she can't think of a time the unburdening went the other direction.

She was still a kid when her godfather led the underground civil war that ousted Coeur from her stolen mayoral seat in Bulari and sent her into exile on Indira. Only eighteen, she and Jaantzen both still holding out hope that her real family was scattered out there among the stars, that this arrangement was temporary.

They'd tried to keep her out of things, but she remembers tense and wordless meals, remembers unfamiliar thugs in the home she was instructed to give a wide berth to. She remembers hiding at the top of the stairs, watching Jaantzen in the kitchen with his face sooty and streaked with blood while Gia stitched him up and another woman reloaded rifles. She remembers tearless, angry wakes. She remembers Manu, unconscious and floating in the knitting tank while nanos repaired shattered bones and burn marks and sadistic slashes.

And though she's gleaned much of the story since then, she knows she's still very much in the dark — about the true brutalities of the civil war, and about the events that led up to Jaantzen's hatred of Coeur.

She's probed, of course. But the answer she always gets — from Manu, from Toshiyo, from Gia — is to go ask Jaantzen.

How could she?

Ask, hey, remember how you used to have real children, and a wife you loved? A real family? It's silly, and she knows talking about the past won't magically resurrect his wife and children any more than it would her parents. And after fifteen years, she no longer worries that her life with him is a temporary arrangement — nothing he has ever done has made her think it was.

Still, there's a scared girl somewhere inside of her that fears a single word said wrong will send her and her new family ricocheting apart, tetherless into the black.

Manu's still slouched casual-like, but he's barely moving. Barely breathing. Caught in memories of his own. The network of old scars on his left hand glistens red in the light.

Starla touches the back of his hand and he flinches.

"How are you doing?" she asks him.

It's not the right question, but she's not accustomed to being in the role of caregiver, of confidant. And Manu's not one to confide.

She sees the moment he pulls himself back, when he chooses to ignore whatever thoughts had their claws around him.

"Thinking I need a whiskey," he signs with a wink.

She makes a face, playing along: Gross.

"You come from a line of distinguished space pirates," he signs, shaking his head solemnly. "It's criminal that you're such a lightweight."

"More for my friends, I guess."

"Well, let's go toast to the death of a certain gangster. I'll have your shot."

"Be my guest."

The buzzing of her gauntlet breaks the moment, and she triple-blinks her lens back on to read the message. Manu's reaching for his comm.

SINCE YOU'RE BOTH STILL HERE, I NEED YOU IN MY OFFICE.

And here's the real unspoken reason they're both still at work despite the lateness of the hour. Jaantzen had disappeared into his office the moment they came back from visiting the abandoned dealership, and Starla knew eventually he'd be ready to discuss a plan for dealing with Coeur's death. She could either wait around and work, or head back to her apartment and sit on pins and needles for his call.

She switches off the little table lamp and stands, cracks her neck.

RIGHT THERE, BOSS, Manu types.

Starla pauses in the doorway to the stairwell, gives the night sky one last glance. What little night vision she could muster out here was destroyed when Manu opened the door to leave, but she catches one last shooting star. One home already broken apart and scattered through space, she thinks. She won't let anything touch this one.

Jaantzen's office is the lower level of Cobalt Tower's penthouse suite. His living quarters are above, and the offices for his various legitimate businesses occupy the floors below. He's rented out the street-level spaces to an array of shops catering to Bulari's business crowd and off-planet tourists, but otherwise the building's filled with Jaantzen's people. Even if not all of them realize they work for one of his subsidiaries.

Starla has an apartment here, too, though she prefers her little dive on the edge of Nidaly Square, about ten blocks away. Sometimes a girl needs to breathe. Or to bring a boy home without explaining to him why she lives in Willem Jaantzen's tower.

The office is open, a hydroponic garden slicing

through the floor as though someone had slashed through with an axe and a slice of Indira sprang up after in the cleft. Soft holographic witch lights pulse among the foliage.

Jaantzen's standing at a bank of floor-to-ceiling windows so clear it looks like he's perched on the edge of a cliff above the city with nothing to keep him from launching into oblivion. The view is of high-rises and neon canyons, the port pulsing beyond to the northwest, transport ships smearing cinder against the night sky as they shudder into the heavens. Such feverish nighttime activity is unusual; that Ganesh in orbit demands it.

He waves them to a set of electric-blue couches, then pours them each a glass of brown liquor from one of his decanters. Starla sets hers on the coffee table untouched. She's always suspected Jaantzen pours for her out of politeness and simply finishes her drink himself once she's left. Today, Manu gives her a wink and pours hers into his own glass. He takes a longer draft off his glass than usual, and she pretends not to notice. For all his banter on the roof, he's shaken.

They wait for Jaantzen to speak.

"I've arranged a meeting with Naali Hinoja for tomorrow evening," he says finally. He's using the glass in his hand as an excuse not to sign, but he often defaults to speech when he's stressed — it's frustrating but mostly fine; her lens is good with his voice and intonation. And today has been a very stressful day.

Manu shares a look with Starla, clears his throat. "What terms are you offering her?" he speaks and signs.

"My backing and aid in putting down any uprisings within her crew, in exchange for complete control of the Tamarind District."

Manu's lips form a whistle. "Blackheart's crew bring in a lot of income from the Tamarind."

"So do we. Talk me through this."

"Naali's main threat is going to come from Levi," Starla signs. "Is he her only threat?"

"Anyone who's not Levi Acheta and wants to take her down will have to take him down, too," Jaantzen says. "No rising star in Blackheart's crew has that kind of power."

"Are we talking soldiers for an all-out fight?" Starla asks. "Assassinating Acheta?"

She doesn't miss the look Jaantzen gives her at the suggestion. Yes, she can be useful outside of running Admant and handling the occasional beyond-the-pale job for people like Julieta Yang.

"I'd prefer the latter," he says slowly.

"I'll prepare for both."

"Thank you," Jaantzen signs.

"Did she have Coeur killed?" Manu speaks and signs. "Or do you think it was Levi?"

Jaantzen shakes his head. "Neither," he says. "Hinoja kills Coeur and she loses her main claim to power. But if Acheta had killed Coeur, Hinoja'd be dead by now, too. If he was making that play, he wouldn't tip his hand."

"Then who?"

"I don't care."

Manu takes another drink, sets his glass down heavily. It's empty. "Do we need to clear your name?"

"No, let the rumor mill play out," Jaantzen says. He pauses, chewing over his next words. A strange energy crackles in the room; Starla has the fleeting feeling of standing on the edge of a precipice, the sense that one word said right here could send them into safety, another square into the path of a tornado.

Jaantzen swirls the liquid in his glass, watching it catch the light. "We'll learn more from the rumor than if we try to turn its tide. And I don't give a damn whether or not anyone thinks I killed her. I only care about keeping this from destroying what peace we already have."

"Naali is good at seeing opportunity," Starla signs. "When's the meeting?"

"Tomorrow evening at the Oasis," Jaantzen says. "Before the party."

Manu's expression is carefully neutral. "Maybe a call would be better, boss?"

"In person. No weapons, one lieutenant each." He sets down his glass before Starla can respond. "Manu will come with me," he signs.

What? Hell no.

Starla shakes her head fiercely. If her godfather insists on walking into a meeting with Naali Hinoja face-to-face, Manu can protect him. But not like she can. And she's not going to let anyone in this family walk into danger without her at their side. She lifts her hands, but Jaantzen is already moving.

"You'll be dealing with Julieta's problem," he signs.

"I can send El and Simca without me."

"It's for Julieta. I need you to take care of it."

Jaantzen's final sign is sharp and solid, held like a shield against whatever other reasons she might hurl.

Starla narrows her eyes at him; Manu is still and silent beside her. She sits back against the couch.

"I understand," she signs. She shares a little nod with Manu, as though he needs anyone to tell him to bring Willem Jaantzen home alive.

"And I would like you to stay at the tower tonight," Jaantzen signs.

It's a request he rarely makes, and he's hesitant as he does so now. But she understands why. She doesn't have many people on this rock she would call family, and her own heart is thudding in her chest at the thought of letting any of them out of her sight until this mess clears up.

But she won't say any of that. Instead, she pulls on a smile, gives a little roll of her eyes as she gets to her feet, then kisses him on the cheek to let him know they're fine. "Anything to keep your blood pressure down," she signs. "No dates tonight anyway."

He returns her smile, but it's a half second too slow, and steeped in an emotion she can't quite name. The weight of memory, maybe, shot through with the bright, honeyed spark of coming opportunity.

She has the dizzying sense that something shifted today, and it's never shifting back.

5

JAANTZEN

J aantzen hates the fourth floor.

Toshiyo's new lair should be an upgrade from the cramped room where she used to spend her time, back when she first joined Jaantzen's crew, but it's still a tangled warren of wires and cables and monitors, disassembled devices strewn across workbenches, their guts stacked in teetering piles. It's a haphazard system, but a system nonetheless. Or so he's been told. And just as in Julieta's greenhouse, he knows better than to touch anything here.

A bigger space is both a blessing and a curse; it's just given her room to collect more things. And because these days she never has to leave Cobalt Tower if she doesn't want to, she can disappear for ages down here. Though they talk almost daily and work in the same building, Jaantzen can go a week or more without actually seeing her.

He follows Manu, who ducks beneath a low-hanging swag of cables, swivels his hips around an antique holographic projector designed to show vids in an arena. Jaantzen frowns at it.

"Why do we have a holographic projector?"

Manu turns, tilts his head to study it a moment like he's never seen it before. Perhaps he hasn't. "Damned if I know, boss."

"It was free and interesting," comes Toshiyo's voice from somewhere deeper in the tangle of cables. "I was going to use parts from that old military satellite to repair it."

"We have an old military satellite?" Jaantzen pivots, trying to locate the source of her voice. Trying to find a clear path through her chaos.

"It's just behind you."

Jaantzen turns. He doesn't see anything resembling a satellite, though he does see a stack of what look to be spinner nav panels. "I thought we built a meeting room for you so I didn't have to see any of this and raise my blood pressure," he says. "Why do we have so many spinner nav panels."

"I don't know," answers Manu. "And we did build a meeting room. Tosh, ah, she and Starla've got a project going on in there right now."

"The nav panels are for the catering staff," comes Toshiyo's voice.

Jaantzen takes a deep breath. "Naturally."

Yesterday his entire being had been consumed by dealing with Coeur's death, so much so that the visit to the warehouse with Mizal feels like it happened weeks ago. It's such a strong sensation that he's almost shocked his businesses are still going on around him, that the employees who know nothing of his past are still at their desks today, still combing through shipments, still sending messages.

When Manu came to him this morning with word of a strange addition to an RKE shipment, he almost pushed it aside to deal with later. But sitting around waiting for his meeting with Naali tonight — or for the world to crumble around him first — isn't productive.

The world keeps spinning. It continues after Coeur's death, and it will after his, too.

They finally find Toshiyo's desk, and it's as incomprehensibly cluttered as the rest of the space. Three auxiliary monitors, four half-dismantled comms, and a spinning hologram projected above it all.

Toshiyo has her fingers in the hologram's guts, tilting it on the axis to get a better look. She spreads her fingers and the whole image enlarges beyond the edges of the projector, the edges lost in the grainy low-resolution margins.

It's a schematic more than a true-to-life copy, and the colors are odd, a greenish-blue wash that casts Toshiyo's face sickly pale, catches in her glossy black hair.

Manu twines his fingers in one of her long locks, gives it a playful tug. "You find a way in yet, Tosh?"

"Not yet. She's sealed up tight."

Jaantzen leans in, studying the hologram. "What is this?"

"Downtripping crew found a case in an RKE shipment," says Manu. "Didn't match the manifest so they pulled it out and gave us a call."

"There's no clear way to open it, though there's a seam on the side," says Toshiyo. She zooms in on the seam, then switches to a deep scan view. "See these channels running the length of the case? Break either of them and you're toast."

"Boom," finishes Manu. He raises an eyebrow. "Respect to whoever came up with that."

"You can go play with it when it's not in my scanner," says Toshiyo.

"Is your scanner in my building?" Jaantzen asks.

Toshiyo nods. "Then you can play with it when it's not in my building."

"You're both no fun." Manu reaches over Toshiyo's shoulder and switches to a deeper view. A dark sphere is carefully wedged in the cavity. "Here's what we think it's protecting," he says.

"And what is that?"

Manu shrugs. "Tosh?"

"Working on it."

"Does it also explode?" Jaantzen asks.

Toshiyo glances up at him, then tilts her head to study it. "I don't think so? My scan says organic."

"I don't want this thing in my building," Jaantzen says.

"Copy that. It seems like there's a way to get in," Toshiyo says. "But it needs a key, or a code of some sort. I've been trying to crack it, but so far no luck."

"Do we want whatever's in there?"

Both Manu and Toshiyo give him startled looks. It's clear neither has thought to ask this question.

"Was this meant for us?" Jaantzen asks. "Or did we just intercept it thanks to an overly cautious salvage crew?"

"RKE shipments normally go to our warehouse to be sorted before heading on," says Manu. "We package up shipments to our local buyers there, send them out individually. But for nonlocal shipments, we'll sometimes have them packaged at the origin point so they can head straight from the loading dock at the terminal on to the cargo hold of a short-jump ship without us looking at it again. And this case was found in the latter."

Jaantzen nods, thinking. If it was a shipment for Admant Security, that nonlocal destination might be one of the far-flung mining colonies on New Sarjun, like Toshiyo's home region of Ruby Basin. But Rosco Kudra Enterprises has only one nonlocal customer.

"It was headed to Redrock Prison," he says.

"And we weren't expected to open this particular package before shipping it on," says Manu.

"Meant for Ximena Nayar?" Toshiyo asks. "Or one of her crew?"

"Meant for someone who knows how to open it without it exploding," says Manu.

"Who else knows about this?" asks Jaantzen.

"The crew of Twin Star Salvage. The lead down there thought it seemed odd, so he stowed it away where customs wouldn't find it on the downtrip and let us know."

Ah. So their downtripping contractor is good at keeping things out of sight from customs. Good to know.

"Very clever of him," Jaantzen says. "Is he a problem?"

"Nah. He's a pro. He's got a good head on his shoulders."

"Better than two snakes on your shoulders," says Toshiyo.

A chill touches Jaantzen's gut; he turns slowly to look at her. "What did you say?"

"The case, boss."

Toshiyo begins typing on her desk. The hologram of the case flickers once before being replaced by lines of code, snatches of text, flashes of images half-hidden beneath the carcass of a dismantled comm. Toshiyo absently pushes the comm aside, her fingers hovering over the desk like a fisher about to snatch her prey from a pond. They pounce on one bit of data, swiping it into the lower left-hand side of the screen, then another, another.

She palms away the search, then pulls up the articles she'd earmarked, paging through them until she finds what she's looking for. It's a decade-old press release from the Museum of Religious History on Indira, announcing a new exhibit of goddesses. The virtual tour link is still archived on the net. Toshiyo touches it and a series of miniature pedestals rise as projections out of her desk.

She selects one on the far left; the projection swoops in to view it. Then she calls the case back up, zooms out so Jaantzen can see what's etched on the lid.

What's she's found matches the case: a carving of a goddess. A pair of twin snakes sprout from the woman's neck, turned to face each other with fangs bared. One pair of hands are held at her shoulders, clawed to pounce. The other pair cradle the human skull at her waist; a skirt of woven snakes wraps around her hips.

The plaque underneath reads: *Coatlicue; Aztec (ancient Earth) goddess who gave birth to the moon, stars, and the god of war.*

"Boss?" Toshiyo has been talking to him; Jaantzen can't hear her above the roar in his ears.

"I've seen this before," he says finally. "Only smaller, the size of your thumb. Titanium." There's a reason for the metal choice, and he's having trouble saying it without losing himself. But now is not the time to lose himself. He takes a deep breath. "So it wouldn't melt in the blast."

He doesn't need to turn to know Manu has flinched; the man's arm is only an inch away and his energy is suddenly electric, furious. Toshiyo half swivels in her chair to look up at Jaantzen, a stitch between her eyebrows.

"Not . . . ," she says.

"Coeur," Jaantzen says. "She left a copy of this statue as a calling card when she set the bomb in my spinner that killed Tae. To make sure everyone knew it was her."

"Bitch is messing with us from beyond the grave," Manu says. His voice is husky.

"But she wasn't sending this to us," says Toshiyo. "This must have been meant for Ximena."

"And Ximena would know who sent it. Get her on the line."

"Yeah, boss." Toshiyo cracks her ring fingers in unison, spins back towards her desk, and stabs at a control button until the desk fizzles abruptly into black. The room is unsettlingly dark in the absence of its glow.

"And get in touch with our people on Indira. I want to know who thinks they're being funny by smuggling something with my goods."

Manu straightens. "Sure thing, boss."

The goddess may be gone from his sight, but Jaantzen is under no illusion that she's gone from his life.

"And get that thing out of my building before you blow us all to pieces," he says.

But somewhere, deep at the root of his world, the bomb has already gone off.

He knows exactly where it is, though he hasn't opened the box in over a decade. Willem Jaantzen doesn't hold on to too many things; he can count all the mementos he's kept throughout his life on one hand. There's a smooth, round stone Tae gave him on their first date. A pair of children's handprints set in glass. The pocketknife his childhood friend Paz had been carrying the night he died, the night Jaantzen talked him into escaping the orphanage together.

And this: a thumb-sized titanium goddess who gleams

as wickedly as the day Jaantzen found her, in the wreckage of his disintegrated spinner.

The spinner that should have held him alone.

It's like ice in the palm of his hand, its surface just as slippery smooth. The detail of the craftsmanship is incredibly fine — Jaantzen has never examined it so closely before. The snake heads' tiny fangs, the minuscule scales patterning the woven snake skirt, the lines on the palm of the outstretched hands. Coeur'd certainly had a flair for the artistic. If only she'd used her talents to become an art curator rather than a murderous crime lord, the world would've —

Jaantzen stops himself. He doesn't think in what-ifs. He's not that kind of man.

"It's what you do that makes you a good man," Tae told him once. "Not what you did or where you came from."

She told him that she loved him, as though he wasn't a creature of shadows. He's killed. He's robbed. He once made a deal with a demon, who predictably double-crossed him and then made war on everyone he loved when he refused to roll over for her.

He failed to save the ones who mattered most.

Jaantzen brushes a thumb across the figure's relief; each tiny detail feels so unassailable, so final.

Tae had believed he was a good man, but only, Jaantzen has always suspected, because she ignored the rough details of his life, combed through his stories for the narrative she preferred.

He'd bravely escaped the orphanage rather than take on a mining indenture, heroically bringing Paz with him, she told him, only to spend far too many years blaming himself for Paz being killed on the streets. He'd fearlessly carved out a place for himself in the dangerous street gangs of the

Fingers, she told him, only to feel guilt for doing what it took to survive.

He'd broken protocol once, just once, she would say if she were still here. Only to spend the rest of his life blaming himself for his family being in the spinner instead of him.

His comm buzzes in his pocket, jarring him out of a dangerous reverie. It's a message from Manu:

IT'S TIME.

Jaantzen slips the little goddess back into her box and closes the lid tight against the brilliant gleam of her titanium skin.

She has no place here, not when there's so much work to be done tonight.

It's time to call on Naali Hinoja.

6

JAANTZEN

Ajesh Paiman's Oasis is well off the beaten path, on the other side of the main magtruck line from the popular Tamarind District. It makes the occasional list of best places to test your taste buds against Bulari's spicy korris cuisine, but its location far from the glittering tourist core means that it doesn't get much traffic, and Ajesh is more than willing to take private reservations for the whole place if the price is right.

And with a certain segment of his specialty clients, the price is always right.

For decades, the Oasis has been an aptly named lull in the harsh landscape of Bulari's underground — neutral territory where a generation of bosses have met to work out hostage exchanges, treaties, and collaborations over Ajesh's famous pepper sauces. Work and heat are a recipe for heartburn, Gia would tell him, but Jaantzen doubts the tightness in his chest right now has anything to do with his diet.

After he makes his offer to Naali Hinoja, his crew will either be at war with her or at war beside her. He never would have attempted this meeting with Blackheart. Not back in the civil war, and not today. Hinoja, on the other hand, may have worked for Coeur, but she doesn't have her boss's deeply rooted impulse to betray. He'd like to think she's the sort of woman who can see reason, who understands that the only way she remains in power without Coeur is by making an alliance with another crew.

The neighborhood arterials are filled with the usual blend of scooters and electric motos and bicycles and spinners and pedestrians he would expect at the end of a working day. People of the neighborhood, out running their pre-dinner errands, or heading home from work.

He scans the windows of the apartment buildings, the lines of the rooftops, but nothing seems out of place. The sanctity of neutral territory is in theory unassailable; still, Jaantzen isn't letting his guard down.

In the street beyond, a pedestrian shouts obscenities after a bike messenger. Behind him, Manu leans against the parked Dulciana, arms crossed. He looks relaxed, but Jaantzen's familiar with that posture — Manu's left hand's centimeters away from the gun at his side.

"They've redone the facades on this block," Jaantzen says. "Very trendy."

"They're trying too hard for the retro vibe," Manu says, but he's not looking at the buildings, he's scanning for trouble. "Reminds me of old gangster vids my grandma used to watch."

"False nostalgia draws a certain crowd."

"Yeah, Arquellian expats. We're gonna have to find a new korris place."

"I didn't think you minded Arquellian expats."

"I don't mind a certain Arquellian expat."

Jaantzen allows himself half a smile. "Is Oriol planetside? I wouldn't mind having extra muscle around."

"I'll let him know if I hear from him."

Is that a bite in Manu's voice? Not for Jaantzen to probe at.

"Thank you," he says instead. He takes a deep breath. "Shall we?"

Manu takes point through the familiar clean-swept alley that leads to an irregular pedestrian plaza two streets off the main road, a hushed location that seems peaceful or claustrophobic by turns, depending on the company. This whole neighborhood is one of Bulari's first, built when residents were still attempting to copy the aesthetic of old Indira rather than adopting the bolder, more angular look the people of New Sarjun grew to champion. This plaza in particular plays up the Old Indira vibe, from the incense burning in twin shrines on either side of the arched entrance to the knotted mosaic tilework around the dry fountain.

When Jaantzen was first getting into the game, the players were all small-time crew bosses controlling a few square blocks of neighborhood and shoving each other over real estate. You got in with a crew one way or another — as part of the operation, or as one of their customers strung out on the drug of the day.

Jaantzen had come to the game at a particularly bloody time, when there were more gangs than street corners, and even more corruption in the government. Coeur was one of the first to take her crew beyond the quick hits and drug deals. One of the first of the petty crews to start making alliances, though it didn't take long for others to learn that alliances with her came on her terms, and her terms only.

But she had brought stability to her corner of Bulari. She'd pioneered the model of respectability that allowed Jaantzen to follow in her footsteps, allowed him to make inroads to the business community. She'd risen from crew leader to mayor through ballot stacking, and stayed there through sleight of hand: Crime goes down when you rule your city with an iron fist, when you assassinate your rivals, when you murder their families. And the good people of Bulari don't care about a few bodies so long as they're not civilians in the streets.

Blackheart had ushered them into a new era, but she hadn't recognized the signs of change she brought. Others — like Jaantzen — had become stable, too. Julieta Yang and Mizal Seti's father had consolidated their hold on the very rich and their vices. The Demosgas had their agricultural empire and their casinos. The Lordeurs had the deep pockets to fund what needed funding. And they were all getting used to the idea that they could make money in peace.

Thala Coeur learned the hard way that the world had changed around her when she stabbed one person too many in the back — Mizal Seti's father. Enough blood had been shed to oust her from power. Hopefully less would have to be shed to keep her legacy from rearing its ugly head once more.

Ajesh Paiman is waiting for them by the fountain. The short man's bulk fills the bench he's sitting on; he raises a hand when he catches sight of Jaantzen and Manu, crushes his cigarette into a potted fan palm, rises with a jovial smile.

"Willem," he calls, arms wide for a hug. Jaantzen bends to embrace him, straightens with the man's cologne and cigarette smoke clinging to his suit jacket. Ajesh clasps Manu's arm warmly. "It's good to see you, Manu," he says. "How have you been?"

"Giddy with anticipation over your cooking, Ajesh," Manu says, clapping Ajesh's shoulder as he takes in the plaza. Through the open apartment windows above, a man is scolding a child over the sound of clattering pots. A rope creaks in the alleyway as someone hauls in laundry. A cat drops from a stack of barrels and wanders over to investigate the offerings at the foot of the entryway shrines.

"Good, good," says Ajesh, squeezing his arm. "Naali's already here."

Ajesh starts explaining the specials as they walk towards the restaurant, but Jaantzen isn't listening, and the way Manu is scanning around them, he isn't, either. It's a game Jaantzen's played here many times: ignoring the pleasantries while scanning for danger. The Oasis may be neutral territory, but Jaantzen doesn't believe for a minute that couldn't change if someone wanted it badly enough.

Manu follows Ajesh past the Closed sign, Jaantzen behind him.

"I'll take your weapons now," Ajesh says, but his words trail off into an anguished cry. He stalls in the entryway, hand over his mouth.

Manu's weapon is already in his hand, but it's not going anywhere near Ajesh's weapons safe. Jaantzen pulls out his own pistol, gently pushes Ajesh out of the way.

The dim restaurant is empty, as planned. But no sound comes from the kitchen, no banging pots, no chatter from Ajesh's wife and staff. Jaantzen's never heard the kitchen silent, but even without that detail, something is clearly off. A faint, sharp haze stings his eyes. Overlaying the scent of frying garlic and ginger there's a scorch of gunsmoke, body odor, and blood.

Naali Hinoja and her second are sitting at a table in the center of the room. They're both dead, bodies riddled with bullet holes.

Except for the two bodies, the room is empty.

"The kitchen," Jaantzen signs to Manu. He gestures for Ajesh to stay put, then steps into the restaurant. There's nowhere to hide but the far hallway that leads to the washrooms and back alley, and no one's there. Jaantzen shuts and locks the door to the alley, then returns to the restaurant as Manu emerges from the kitchen. He gives Manu the sign for all clear.

"Ajesh, your family is fine," Manu says quietly.

"Mirana!" Ajesh cries, darting to the kitchen. Manu steps aside to let him pass, then heads to cover the front door.

Jaantzen approaches the table in the center of the restaurant.

It's been set for four, though the elegant dining set is now broken into shards. The waiting bottle of wine has been shattered, crimson liquid washing blood from the tablecloth. Hinoja is sprawled back in her chair, thin, pale neck lolling, her knot of fiery red hair pulled free in the violence and twisting down behind her, gentle in the breeze from the open front door. The man in the chair beside her is one of her lieutenants, a man named Chase. He's slumped forward like he's fallen asleep at the table, head resting on blood-spattered hands.

It's Chase's blood, mostly, on the table, sprayed from the single bullet wound to the back of his head, then pooled under his cheek where it rests on the tablecloth. The man never saw the killer coming, or he trusted the killer well enough to have his back turned.

From the angle of Hinoja's bullet wounds, Jaantzen thinks it's a fair guess she was shot seconds after, while the person who took out Chase still stood in the same position. Not enough time to draw a weapon, even if she'd been armed. She was half out of her chair when she fell. Trying to fight back but far too slow, though the killer lost precision with her and squeezed off a spray; Jaantzen counts three bullet holes in her white suit jacket, one through the neck.

She would have seen the killer approach. Which means she knew him.

If Levi Acheta wasn't the one who pulled the trigger, Jaantzen will quit this game.

He lays two fingers on Hinoja's neck. The pulse is gone, but it hasn't been long. Her torso is spattered with blood but for a single creamy envelope tucked into the breast pocket of her white suit jacket after the fact.

His name is written on the envelope.

Jaantzen tugs it carefully free with two fingers; Hinoja's blood seeps into one corner of the otherwise pristine envelope. He slides the card out.

If you think you can get Blackheart's crew to sell out to you so easily, think again, old man.

The scrawled note isn't signed, but declarations of war don't always need to be. Jaantzen hands the note to Manu, then goes to the kitchen. Ajesh is there, speaking in low tones to his family and staff. A ring of faces, which all freeze in varying hues of fear the instant Jaantzen enters.

"Is anyone hurt?" Jaantzen asks. A few heads shake, no. "Did anyone see who did this?"

Furtive glances, then finally Ajesh's oldest daughter raises her hand. "It was her man." She glances at her father, who motions for her to continue. "The one she comes in with sometimes. Tall, dark hair, tattoos . . ." She touches the back of each hand, then the left side of her neck to indicate the placement.

"Sounds like Acheta," Jaantzen says with a glance at Ajesh, who nods agreement. "Did he see you?" The girl shakes her head. "Good, good."

Ajesh is watching him, hands spread. Manu is watching him, too, waiting for orders. "Mr. Jaantzen," Ajesh says, this horrifying breach of neutral territory catapulting them firmly out of first-name address. "What do we do here?"

"I have a team that will take care of it." Two messes in as many days; Jaantzen has a bad feeling about this trend.

"But if it was Acheta — "

"Don't say anything about Acheta to anyone," Jaantzen says. "You never saw him. Or us."

"If the police ask — "

"They won't. But even if they do, you know how to handle it. Don't spin any tales you can't back up, keep your stories simple." He waves his hand around the kitchen. "It gets loud back here, preparing for the dinner rush. Ajesh, you went outside for a smoke."

Ajesh nods slowly, and Jaantzen pulls out his comm. It's not necessary — he trusts Ajesh as an old friend. But it *is* polite. "I'm sending over something to cover the damage," he says, and with a few taps the message to his controller is sent. "And my team will take care of any repairs while they're here."

The money isn't for repairs, it's a severance package. Jaantzen certainly won't be meeting any enemies here in the future, and he doubts any other crew bosses will either, not once news of Hinoja's murder gets out. Good thing the Oasis is in an up-and-coming neighborhood.

"Call the cleanup crew," he signs to Manu, who's already on his comm. "And check in with Starla. She should know what happened here."

Jaantzen takes a deep breath of the familiar scent of carnage. The tang of salt, sweat, and fear laid over smoked chiles and oil. The bouquet of a brief, tragic moment in time, beginning to be replaced by the acrid, earthy scent of rice left on to scorch in the kitchen.

He claps Ajesh on the shoulder — the man flinches — then follows Manu into the other room.

On the bright side, at least now he has a few hours before he and Hinoja are, both, expected at Leone's dinner party.

He'll need that time to prepare his plan for the first phase of war: collecting allies.

Hopefully things are going better with Starla and her crew.

Carama Town is Starla's favorite of the Five Fingers. While some depressed parts of the city — like Jet Park — are clamped down like a bony fist, Carama Town is bustling and open. There's always something going on: parades, street fairs, ball games in the vacant lots. They passed by the preparations for a night market to get here, bright, hand-painted banners strung low over the road to point the way — or to entrap passersby. Starla had barely been able to glide her moto beneath a few.

Carama Town is the shipping hub to the southern mining regions, and a good percentage of its inhabitants are employed in the refineries that dot the southeastern edge of the city. Which are served by the blocks and blocks of warehouses.

Starla slows her moto and checks the address again on her lens. The warehouse containing Julieta's shipment is the last in a long row of them, each stenciled with the name of a mining corporation or shipping outfit. This one is unmarked and crumbling, and if Starla didn't know better, she'd assume it was host to a shard-cooking operation or a camp of squatters fleeing their mining indentures.

It's not, of course. Toshiyo's had it under surveillance since Julieta tossed them this job, and no one has come in or out.

The job's simple: An electrical fire started at the fuse box, expedited by a few poorly stored fuel cells. An abandoned building like this? You never know when it's going to go up in flames.

ALL CLEAR. UNLOCKING THE GATE.

Toshiyo's message crawls across the bottom of Starla's lens. She'll have sent it to the others on the crew, too. Starla glances over her shoulder to see her backup on a pair of motos behind her: El Anahoy and his younger sister, Simca. Neither are on the books as employees of any of Willem Jaantzen's businesses — they're Starla's soldiers, and she keeps them busy enough with odd jobs like this that they don't need to go looking for freelance work during dry spells.

They're also both native USL speakers, having grown up with deaf parents. Starla loves her family, but her work for her godfather has . . . made it difficult to make friends outside the crew. And while Manu is easy enough to talk to, nothing can quite beat the exhale of being around El and Simca.

The gate slides open and Starla and her crew coast in, park near the door to the warehouse. Toshiyo has hacked the monitoring system so anybody watching will see only the last hour's feed on loop. This warehouse belongs to one of Julieta's shell companies, so it's unlikely anyone will be watching — but protocol is protocol.

El's already scanning the area, sidearm in one strong brown hand. Simca touches the button that folds her helmet back — a pair of long black braids tumble out — and carefully opens the explosion-rated cargo bins on the back of her moto. She begins to unload the delicate cargo, stacking cases by the door.

"Glad that's off my bike," Simca signs. "Cargo unloaded," she says for Toshiyo's benefit; her words scroll across the bottom of Starla's vision.

Simca Anahoy is the cheerful antidote to her stony older brother, a compact bundle of muscle and energy whose name on a poster can draw overflow crowds of adoring fans to local wrestling tournaments. She's a good fighter, a fast thinker, and — a benefit — has excellent taste in dance clubs.

Starla shorts the cheap biolocks, and Simca helps her lever the docking bay door up. Julieta wanted them to destroy the building without going inside, but the accidental fire will seem more real if it starts at the fuse box, so Starla's making the call. Julieta wants things done a certain way, she can blow up her own damn shipments.

El gives her a sharp nod, and she and Simca slip underneath the door into a dim, cavernous space lined with shelving units. Only a few dusty yellow strip lights near the ceiling provide any sort of illumination. Starla switches her lens to scan for biosign, slowly turns to take in the space.

It's empty. No one around and no one watching — still, Starla's not about to get too sure of herself. She gives Simca a thumbs-up, and the other woman slips back under the door to start handing cases of fuel cells through. All in, and she returns to help Starla stack them by the fuse box.

"Look for flammable materials," Starla signs, turning to scan the warehouse once more. Julieta told Jaantzen that hers was the only shipment in the warehouse, and Starla has no way of telling whether or not that's true. In fact, they only have Julieta's word that her shipment is here at all. Many of the shelving units are empty, with a larger concentration of pallets and crates near the far end of the warehouse.

What could be so damning that Julieta Yang would blow her whole warehouse to destroy it?

WE GOT INCOMING.

Toshiyo's message blinks insistently on Starla's lens.

ONE PERSON AT THE BACK ENTRANCE.

ON IT, El answers.

"Finish up here," Starla signs to Simca. HEADING TO BACK ENTRANCE, she types into her gauntlet.

She glides through the aisles towards the far wall, pistol in hand. The shelving units near the front are empty, but in the back a row of pallets provides potential cover — or a hiding spot for someone else.

A sliver of light catches her eye, a door opened and closed.

THEY'RE IN, from Toshiyo.

And from El: DOOR'S CLOSED. DO I FOLLOW?

Not yet, not if whoever just entered is waiting to ambush him.

WAIT, types Starla. SIM, WITH ME.

There's a flash of light, playing faintly along the back row as though someone's looking for something. The light's coming from the last row of shelving units, moving systematically. Maybe it's a thief, looking for something interesting to steal. Maybe it's a squatter, looking for a place to spend the night.

Or maybe it's a trap.

Because no matter how much Jaantzen trusts Yang, Starla doesn't have that same rapport with the old woman. Her godfather's mentor lies to get what she wants for a living — not that they all don't, but there's a difference between lying to strangers and lying to your friends. Julieta Yang is so damned paranoid that she'll lie to her friends over nothing.

And someday that's going to get Jaantzen hurt.

TARGET'S OUT OF MY VIEW, writes Toshiyo.

Starla pauses to type. *SW CORNER, LAST ROW*.

She's three rows away when she notices the light has gotten more rhythmic, bobbing like a warning light.

Or like it's swinging alone on a cord.

And if it's the latter, she's walking into a trap.

Starla ducks for cover, knowing Simca will follow her lead, and feels a crackle of energy in the air. A plasma bolt slams into the leg of the shelving unit behind her, which sends two stories of metal listing drunkenly directly above; she feels the grating of metal-on-metal in her chest. The shot came from the other side of the pallet that Starla's now hiding behind, and plasma pistols take five seconds to reload. Starla glances over her shoulder and meets Simca's gaze. She makes the sign for smoke, then pistol, then holds up three fingers. Simca nods.

Simca fires three shots at where the plasma bolt came from, followed by a smoke bomb, and Starla follows the whole mess around the corner with her own pistol ready, crouched low. The haze comes quick, but with her lens on the biosign setting she can see a figure crouched for cover.

Starla levels her pistol.

The figure charges.

It's a sloppy tackle on account of the poor visibility, but it connects and they both go crashing to the floor. Her assailant is strong, but Starla has youth and training on her side. She blocks a blow from the woman's yet-uncharged plasma pistol and knocks it loose; it goes skittering across the floor.

Starla manages to roll them out from behind the pallet stack and into the open walkway where Simca can see them and the smoke isn't so thick. The other woman lands a punch to Starla's kidney in the process, and Starla grabs her by her long, thick hair, jabs an elbow at her throat. It doesn't connect well, but the other woman does lose her grip for a second. Starla uses the hesitation to wrench her hips and flip them both over so she's straddling the other woman's chest.

Starla aims her pistol at the other woman's head.

The woman slumps back, panting.

Her face is covered in blood and distorted by rage, but she looks familiar: dark red skin, fierce black eyes, military cut to her clothes. Starla stares at her a moment, trying to understand where she's seen this woman before. Not from her childhood. Not in Bulari. Which means not on New Sarjun, unless . . .

Shit.

"Friend, I'm a friend," Starla thinks she says, hopes the other woman understands. She clicks her safety on but doesn't take the pistol away from the woman's forehead, not quite yet. She gets slowly to her feet and steps out of range before holstering her gun.

But whether it's her words or her accent, the other woman's eyes go wide. She raises herself to her elbows.

"You're that girl," Starla thinks she says, and a split second later the lens confirms it as the words crawl across her screen. "Jaantzen's girl."

Starla nods.

And this is the woman who helped rescue her all those years ago from Redrock Prison. The requisitions officer —

now COO — that Jaantzen has worked with on and off over the years, though Starla hasn't seen her since that long-ago day.

Major Ximena Nayar.

Thala Coeur's sister.

Starla gestures for her to get up. "Why are you here?" Starla signs, but Ximena just frowns at her. Starla sighs, annoyed, and reverts to baby gestures: pointing at the ground, big exaggerated shrug.

"I'm looking for something. Why are you here?" Starla thanks her lucky stars that the woman's enunciation is clear. What words she's not getting by reading lips, the lens's transcription software seems to read just fine.

Thala Coeur's sister. Looking for something. In the shipment Julieta asked them to destroy.

"Get El in here," Starla signs to Simca; Nayar glances over her shoulder to see who Starla's talking to. Sees the stack of fuel cells near the fuse box, the piles of flammable materials they've gathered.

"You're destroying the building? Why?"

Starla just shakes her head. Not something this woman gets to know.

IT's X NAYAR, Starla types to Toshiyo, not in the mood for a spelling contest. BRINGING HER IN.

COPY.

El's there by now. "Get her out of here," Starla signs, and he nods. "We good?" Starla signs to Simca. "The timer: set it on my signal."

El and Ximena are arguing when Starla turns back.

"I'm not leaving," Starla thinks Ximena says. "Not until I find it."

"What is she looking for?" Starla asks El, who repeats the question.

The major's lips shut tight.

Starla motions for El to interpret. "You're coming with us whether you want to or not," she signs. "So tell us what it is if it's important, or we drag you out of here and let it blow."

Ximena takes a deep breath, then finally leads them back to the last row, where her light is indeed suspended from an electrical wire, swaying back and forth as a distraction. Ximena's scanner is there, too, and with a sullen glance at Starla for permission, the woman picks it up and plays it over the last few pallets.

"This one," she says. Starla and El step back as she breaks it open. Expensive furs and leathers that would fetch a fortune on livestock-poor New Sarjun pour out onto the ground. And in the center, wrapped in a red leather coat, is a silver case about the length of Starla's arm. It looks light; Ximena picks it up gingerly, cradling it to her chest.

Starla frowns at it. The lid is etched with a figure that has the torso of a woman, though two snakes sprout from her neck. It's hideous.

"What is it?" she asks.

"I don't know," answers Ximena. "I only know it's important."

Starla blinks a snapshot of the case, then patches it through to Toshiyo. WE FOUND WHAT SHE WANTED, she types.

BRING IT, Toshiyo writes back. BE SUPER SUPER CAREFUL, POTENTIALLY EXPLOSIVE.

Beside Ximena, El's eyebrows rise as he also gets Toshiyo's message.

Explosive? How in hell would Toshiyo know that? But Starla's never seen Toshiyo's intel turn out wrong.

"Simca's bike is already equipped," El signs.

Starla nods. "Let's go." They've spent way too much time in this warehouse. She taps at her gauntlet. LEAVING NOW, WE ALL GOOD OUT THERE?

Toshiyo's reply comes almost immediately. ALL CLEAR.

COPY. Starla gives Simca the signal as they come around the corner, Ximena still cradling the ugly case, El following behind with his pistol in his hand.

"One-twenty seconds," signs Simca.

Good. Plenty of time to be long gone, and for this mess to be over.

"We've got you some new cargo to worry about on the ride home," Starla tells her. "Toshiyo says it could explode."

"Great." Simca makes a face and reaches to take it from Ximena.

"She'll take the cargo. You're with him," she tells Ximena; El repeats it. Ximena hesitates, and Starla points at the bomb at the fuse box, makes an exaggerated sign for explosion, shrugs like, Do what you want, lady.

Ximena hands over the case.

Outside the warehouse, Starla's helping Simca secure her cargo when Simca straightens, attention on the front gate. Her eyes narrow.

Toshiyo's message flashes on Starla's lens before Starla can ask Simca what's wrong: NEW PROBLEM, URGENT. WE HAVE INCOMING. MULTIPLE VEHICLES OUTSIDE FRONT ENTRANCE. STAND BY.

Simca whirls back to her bike, fingers working the latches on her explosion-rated cargo bins.

2 MOTOS, 2 SPINNERS, 1 TRUCK WITH A HANDFUL OF GUYS IN THE BACK.

Toshiyo's message crawls beneath a steadily falling number. It's blinking red: 0:55.

LOOKS LIKE THEY'VE GOT THE CODE FOR THE GATE.

Starla takes a deep breath, mind racing.

STALL 30 SECONDS THEN LET IN, she types.

"What's going on?" Ximena asks from the back of El's moto.

"Did anyone follow you here?" Starla signs.

A pause as El repeats the question, then Ximena shakes her head.

It could be anyone out there: a local street gang looking for an abandoned building to party in — or who got wind of Jaantzen's people in the neighborhood and are looking to test their luck. It could be somebody after Ximena, somebody after the case.

It doesn't matter.

Starla points at Simca. "I need you running defense; take my bike. We protect the cargo, protect X. I take lead."

FIND US A SAFEHOUSE, she types to Toshiyo.

HEAD BACK THE WAY YOU CAME AND FOLLOW MY DIRECTIONS, Toshiyo writes back.

Starla touches the button that folds her helmet into place, then coasts Simca's moto around the shadows on the right side of the warehouse; the other two follow her. If they're lucky, it's just some street gang who's not expecting anyone else to be here. If they're unlucky and the crew outside the gate is here looking for them, they can at least have the element of surprise.

0:28

"Smoke," Starla signs to Simca.

OPENING THE GATE NOW, Toshiyo writes.

Starla's body has already memorized the path through the gate and out — the way she'll need to shift her weight, the turns she'll need to make — so by the time Simca's smoke bomb goes off in front of the gate she no longer needs sight to navigate it.

GATE'S OPEN THEYRE THROUGH. 2 SPINNERS IN, MOTOS COMING.

0:12

Starla revs her engine, gunning her moto towards the path she's memorized. The first spinner looms shadowy in the smoke and she banks around it, narrowly missing one of the enemy motos and skidding through the gate in a spray of gravel as she turns hard to the left and guns it past the truck. The air over her shoulder sizzles with electricity as a plasma bolt splits the air; a street sign to her right shatters into shrapnel.

0:00

Starla feels the concussion in her gut as the bomb goes off in the warehouse, and her helmet's in-screen rearview goes fiery red with the explosion. She can pick out two other riders flowing out of the flames — El and Simca still on her tail. She lets go the breath she's been holding.

It takes a few more seconds, but other figures leave the flames: the two enemy motos, one of the spinners, and the truck.

1 SPINNER DOWN, Toshiyo confirms.

The row of warehouses is fronted by a wide boulevard, no turns and no cover for the better part of three kilometers. It's a thrillingly open road — the locals hold illegal drag races after dark, Starla's come to them before — but not the sort of place she wants to be caught out in a gunfight.

R IN 2 KM.

Two kilometers? Starla sends Toshiyo a mental stream of curses, then gives the moto everything she's got. The truck and remaining spinner are being slowed by the constant potholes; the two enemy motos are gaining.

They're firing, but none of the bullets and blasts are anywhere close. Another bolt from a plasma carbine rips into the asphalt just in front of her moto, and Starla swerves to avoid it. It pings something in her mind, but it's not until El's message flashes on her screen that she realizes what it is.

THEY'RE TRYING TO STOP US, NOT SHOOTING AT US. THEY WANT HIM AND I OR THE CASE. SIM, STAY CLOSE TO ONE OF US.

"Him and I" is presumably the transcription software's version of Ximena, and as Starla shifts her focus to her helmet's rearview, she realizes El's right. The plasma carbine blasts are meant to derail them, and the motos aren't shooting at all.

Yet.

COPY, LET'S LOSE THEM, writes Toshiyo. R 500M. HIDDEN ALLEY.

Starla guns it.

100M.

Starla sees it, the rough track between two high adobe walls topped with razorwire. One of the motos has caught up to her, she catches a glimpse of a grin and, at his throat, a dove perched on the crown of a broken skull.

Yesterday she would have had to fight for the memory of where she'd seen that image before. But today her memory's already been jogged.

The Dawn? Here?

With guns?

He levels his pistol at her.

NOW.

Starla throws her weight and skids into a turn, revs into the narrow alleyway. A bullet buries itself in the adobe wall beside her; a shower of clay shrapnel peppers her back and shoulders.

El and Simca are behind her, followed by the second

moto, who was far enough back not to miss the turn. The alleyway should be too narrow for anything larger than a moto, but it doesn't stop the truck from charging in, sides gouging roiling clouds of dust out of the adobe walls.

SPINNER DIDNT FOLLOW, WILL KEEP AN EYE ON IT, Toshiyo writes. TAKE NEXT L, HEAD W.

Starla more or less knows this part of Carama Town — it's a warren of makeshift blocks plotted a century ago around squat claims and homesteads rather than through a plan. Streets crash into each other at diagonals and break strangely at intersections. It's residential, but generally shuttered for the night, and only the rare pedestrian jumps out of the way as they blaze past.

This isn't the sort of place Starla'd prefer to be caught in a gunfight, either — but at least they're not sitting targets anymore.

Both motos are back, the one Starla'd lost back at the boulevard overtaking the truck as soon as they reach a street wide enough.

Time to do something about that.

Simca's over her left shoulder. She knows the neighborhood well, since one of the best wrestling venues is here. She'll be their best defense.

Starla signs for Simca to break off.

Simca nods. COPY BREAKING OFF, she says. TAKE YOUR THIRD RIGHT.

When Simca disappears down the next alleyway, no one follows her. El's hunch is correct: they're after Ximena or the case — or both. Good. They can use that.

Starla throws the moto into a hard right turn, suddenly recognizing the road they came in on, draped low with banners for the night market. She ducks and El follows. In her rearview she catches a flash of motion: Simca drifting across the road in a cloud of tire-smoke, two flashes from her pistol and one of the moto riders goes down. The other over-steers and goes into a slide before being bucked off the moto and high into a wall.

Simca disappears into another alley.

The truck comes charging out of the smokescreen, a torn night market banner draped across the hood. One of the riders in the back levels his pulse carbine. Starla swerves as the bolt fells a lamppost across her path.

SPINNER'S BACK. Toshiyo's message blinks.

Sure enough, Starla can see it now in her rearview. It overtakes the truck in a wide part of the road.

"Split up," she signs to El, who nods.

SPLITTING UP, he says for Toshiyo's benefit.

COPY SPLITTING UP, writes Toshiyo. ROAD T IN 100M. BUSY ARTERIAL, CAREFUL.

The spinner is bearing down on them. The passenger fires out the window, aiming for Starla's tires. The driver — a woman with a tight braid of silver hair and a wicked scar down her cheek — guns it until she's only meters away.

Starla throws her weight and drifts into the turn, skidding to the right through the intersection. It's a main arterial on the edge of Carama Town, and despite the hour there's plenty of traffic. Starla's going against the flow on the far shoulder, skirting the edge of a dry canal. The spinner's on her tail. Ahead, vehicles are bolting out of her way.

LEFT AT THE BRIDGE, WATCH FOR EL.

Starla remembers the bridge. There's a blind intersection beyond it, she knows — they passed it on the way to the warehouse earlier. She can see it up ahead, but it seems impossibly far away, and the driver of the spinner is gaining. A spray of bullets chews up the verge in front of her; she swerves to miss it.

Starla sees a space in traffic and takes it, cutting across until she's got two lanes between her and the spinner.

LOST TIME, comes Toshiyo's response. *I NEED YOU FASTER.*

Only a few hundred meters to the bridge. Starla pins it, low over the handlebars as she pushes everything she has into her speed.

ALMOST THERE. A LITTLE FASTER.

Starla charges forward, banks into the left and onto the bridge.

ALMOST THERE.

The spinner is only meters behind her rear wheel; the blind intersection is seconds away.

GUN IT.

Starla pushes her moto past its limits and speeds through the intersection a split second before El and Ximena flash in from her left. In her rearview screen she sees the wide eyes of the silver-haired woman in the spinner as she wrenches on the controls, clips the truck that was chasing El, and goes careening into a lamppost. The truck hits a guardrail and skids out of control, tumbling end over end into the dry canal below.

Starla allows herself a giddy breath but does not slow.

SAFEHOUSE DIRECTIONS LOADED, writes Toshiyo. A map superimposes itself in Starla's helmet screen. Behind her, El falls into formation. At the next intersection, Simca joins them.

FUN NIGHT, Simca says.

Starla just breathes deep. It's not over until they're at the safehouse.

Jaantzen's scattered safehouses include everything from empty apartments in the slums to fancy condos in the tourist district. Some serve as places to put up visiting business partners from Indira, but others are holdouts from the Jaantzen of years ago, the one who pulled daring heists and double crosses and needed a network of places to go to ground when he went to war with people like Coeur.

This one's in a seedy hotel, the sort of place with hearts on the sign and mirrored windows around the reception desk and private underground parking stalls for regular patrons and their discreet lovers.

Starla lets the parking stall door close behind them before she turns on Ximena. The other woman's clutching her helmet; she looks shaken and more than a little green after the wild ride.

"Why is the Dawn after us, and what the hell is this case?" she signs. El interprets.

"I don't know. My sister sent it to me. Thala. She said it was important, but I'm not sure what it is."

"What did we just risk our lives for?"

Ximena shakes her head in exasperation. "I don't know. I'm just supposed to bring it to her."

"Bring it? She's dead."

That look on Ximena's face? That hesitation before she answers? It's not the shock of learning about her sister's death. Starla can tell. It's the moment where she's considering how to break the news to Starla and her team. Ximena knows something the rest of them don't, and Starla has a sick guess as to what it is. Oh, please no.

"She's not," Ximena says finally. "She's alive. She's here on New Sarjun."

And Starla had thought this night couldn't get any worse.

8

JAANTZEN

The last time he was in this particular safehouse, Willem Jaantzen was orchestrating the hit that took out Coeur's chief lieutenant and sent herself fleeing to the Arquellian embassy — and off this rock for good. A noble history for such a sordid place. It should have a history plaque on the door, but no one adds hotels that specialize in mirrors on the ceiling to lists of historic places.

Starla's in the cramped parking cubicle when he and Manu arrive. They've found Ximena and another case, she told them, but he senses there's more to the story by the troubled expression on her face. He's glad he already dressed for dinner. He has a feeling the time he gained not meeting with Naali Hinoja is about to be eaten up dealing with this new turn of events.

"Are you all right?" he signs to his goddaughter, scanning her for injury. She's got a cut over one eye and her knuckles are scraped, but otherwise she seems fine.

"All good," she answers. "How was the meeting with Naali?"

"She's dead," he signs. "By Acheta before we arrived."

Starla's eyebrows rise, but the news doesn't seem to faze her, as if she's in a place beyond surprise, tonight. An uneasy feeling grips Jaantzen's gut.

"That's too bad," she signs. She takes a deep breath, and Jaantzen steels himself for whatever she's about to tell him. "So. Coeur's alive."

Beside him, Manu bites out a curse.

"She's here. On New Sarjun." Starla raises her gaze to the ceiling, points at it with an incredulous expression. "Ximena? She wants us to help her save her. Apparently that crackpot religious cult the Dawn have her. They want whatever was in the case Julieta wanted us to destroy. They tried to kill us and take it, but we killed most of them first."

Starla pauses with one elbow in her other hand, tapping a finger against her cheek, lips pursed to the side as if in thought. "I think that's it," she signs. "You're all caught up."

Jaantzen strokes a finger above his eyebrow, questioning.

Starla touches the cut above her own, rubs her fingers together as though checking for blood. "I got in a fight with Ximena. That's a very nice suit."

It's a cheap deflection, but he honors it; Manu is watching, her people are upstairs. And she's come home alive and safe, just like she has every time before this — though he can't think of a job gone as wrong as this one. Maybe later he'll even get her to tell him the bigger story underlying her nonchalance, or at least hear it from Manu secondhand.

What's important now is that she's fine, that she took care of herself and her people both.

Jaantzen takes a deep breath.

Manu clears his throat. "You found Ximena and another case at the warehouse," he says and signs; Jaantzen knows the speech is for his benefit. "Then you fought Ximena, then the Dawn tried to kill you because they want the case, and now Ximena is saying Coeur's alive and we should help save her?"

Jaantzen's not sure if Manu's repeating Starla's words to ensure Jaantzen catches the nuance, or because it's such an unlikely story he's having trouble believing it himself. The parking cubicle is starting to feel claustrophobic, his collar too tight around his neck.

"The case: does it have the carving of a woman on the top?" Jaantzen signs.

"Snake woman," Starla signs, both hands making the sign for snake as they slither up and past her face. She looks into both of their faces in turn. "What the hell is it?"

"We found one a few days ago just like it," signs and says Manu. "Smuggled in one of our shipments."

Starla's eyes narrow. "Admant?"

"No, RKE. We think there's something hidden inside, but it doesn't look like we can get into it without setting it off."

"Toshiyo said it might be explosive," Starla signs.

"Something like that."

"Cool."

For one brief moment, Starla looks like this night has put her at the end of her rope. Then she shakes her head and her gaze refocuses into action. She blinks into middle distance as though reading something on her lens.

"You've got forty-five minutes to get to the judge's," she signs to Jaantzen. "Do you want to deal with Ximena later?"

Jaantzen shakes his head. He wants to deal with her now.

Starla hits the button on the private elevator, and it whisks them up to the fifth floor.

It opens into a suite that hasn't changed a bit since Jaantzen was last here trying to take down Thala Coeur: a few ragged couches, a dust-covered desk that barely worked then and probably won't even boot up now, a stack of cots in the corner, a few rickety chairs. The lush burgundy carpet and velvet drapes are the only things original to the hotel room — and the mirrors. So many mirrors.

Jaantzen has prepared himself, but it still catches him by surprise how much Ximena Nayar looks like her younger half-sister. Rust-red skin still smooth even as streaks of gray have woven into her pitch-black hair. It's worn military-style in a bun at the nape of her neck, serious and reserved where Coeur was — is; Jaantzen's stomach tightens — bois-terous and joking.

Ximena starts to rise but catches the corresponding twitches from the weapons the Anahoy siblings have pointed at her. She lifts her chin instead: part greeting, part challenge.

"I see my goddaughter gave you as good as she got," he says.

Ximena cracks a smile, touches her split lip. "She's a good fighter. And she's got a good head on her shoulders. You should be proud."

"I am." He watches her a moment, wondering where to begin. With the case, probably. He's not ready to talk about the other bombshell of the evening.

"Wait outside, please," he signs to the Anahoys. He waits until they're in the elevator before walking past Ximena to examine the case on the table behind her. He saw the other only in hologram. Now, he sketches a finger down one of the goddess's fangs.

"I know this symbol," Jaantzen says, keeping his voice light. He pretends he's discussing the weather. "Your sister left it for me when she murdered my wife and children. I can only assume this case is also from her."

The briefest of hesitations. "It is."

"Tell me about it. Is it a bomb? Drugs? What is she sending to you?"

"A business plan."

Jaantzen turns to regard her coolly. "I thought you weren't interested in her business."

"I'm not. But this is different. Willem, this is huge."

He doesn't like being so close to the case, so he crosses the room to sit in a chair across from Ximena. Starla leans against the wall over his left shoulder. Manu settles himself on the arm of a couch to his right.

"Tell me."

Ximena takes a deep breath.

"It's not news that the Alliance has their own secret operations going on at Redrock. Technically we're our own corporation, but Alliance officers come in and ask for something — extra requisitions, prisoners for labor, whatever — we do it. I don't make it a habit to get in other people's business — not my coworkers', not my employers'. I keep the lights on and the kitchens stocked, that's all. Sometimes I put in extra food orders or order equipment I know isn't going to the prison kitchens. Warden asks for it, I do it."

"And meanwhile the Alliance grows rich off New Sarjunian soil," Jaantzen says.

She brushes that aside. "And meanwhile you and Thala grew rich off selling drugs to New Sarjun's poorest." That dismissal of her sister doesn't surprise him — there never was much love lost between the two women. Fierce loyalty, yes. But love? Not in the way he recognizes the world.

He doesn't rush to correct her about how he made his own wealth, if that's what she's hoping for; he's the one on the offense, not Ximena.

"I got a message from Thala," she continues. "Saying

there was some kind of excavation operation going on in the northern hemisphere, near Redrock. She sent me pictures, and at first I couldn't believe what I was seeing."

Jaantzen frowns. "Excavation? Like mining?"

"More like an archaeological excavation."

Jaantzen's gaze shifts beyond her to the case on its table.

"Not that," Ximena says, glancing over her shoulder. "That's . . . That's an old joke of Thala's. No. At Redrock, they're pulling out shit that's a lot stranger than the Old Earth artifacts you see in museums."

She's looking at him like he should know what she's talking about, but his mind is having trouble going there. Behind him, Starla takes a sharp breath.

"As in, artifacts from original colonists?" he asks. It's what she has to mean. "I didn't think anyone landed in the northern hemisphere until much later."

Ximena shakes her head.

Starla signs an unfamiliar word, though he catches something that could be *space*, and the sign for *person*. She frowns, taps at her gauntlet. Jaantzen's comm lights up, and he sets it in the center of the table so Ximena can read, too.

ALIEN?

Ximena nods. "That's what Thala said."

"Alien artifacts?" Jaantzen just laughs. Starla's watching him, a strange, serious expression on her face. A conversation for later, he thinks. "We've been all over Indira, all over the moons, all over the dwarfs in Durga's Belt, nearly all over New Sarjun. If we weren't alone in the Durga System, we'd know by now."

"I'm just saying what I was told. But wherever it's from, they've found some sort of serum that's key to helping them terraform the desert. I've seen it myself. They're growing things up there, and not in a greenhouse."

Jaantzen frowns. "Not . . ."

"You've seen it up there, right?" Ximena asks.

Starla and Jaantzen both nod; Manu shrugs a no. The Jupari Desert band that separates the planet's northern and southern hemispheres is impassible over land, and there's a reason no one goes up to the northern hemisphere except to rot at Redrock. Whereas you could at least eke out a life in the hills to the south, anything north of here is a wasteland.

"I thought nothing could grow north of our latitude," Jaantzen says. "That's what I've always heard."

"And you're right. We have greenhouses to grow some of the produce for the prison, but there's nothing like the fields you can plant down here. At least, there wasn't."

She slides her comm across the coffee table; Jaantzen tilts the comm so Starla can see. He can feel Manu watching him, evaluating his reactions.

The valley he sees could be in Indira. It's about two kilometers across, and filled with green. Rows of what looks like soybeans. Squash, maybe. Probably corn.

Jaantzen hands the comm to Manu; his eyebrows rise a fraction.

"You saw this in person?" Jaantzen asks.

Ximena nods. "I took these images. Willem. Imagine if the northern hemisphere could support actual settlements? Or imagine if the southern hemisphere could grow more of its own food? Stop relying so much on Indiran exports?"

"Imagine if we didn't need the Indiran Alliance," Manu says.

"Start exporting that food to the Belt planets," signs Starla. "Then they wouldn't need the Alliance, either."

Manu nods, still thumbing through the images. "New Sarjun could support a bigger population, and all those refugees from New Manila and Corusca and Teuça could have somewhere real to go."

"This is quite a bit of imagining," Jaantzen says. "But if it's true, I can see why the Alliance would want to keep it quiet." Feeding New Sarjun and shipping food out to Durga's Belt is a huge business already. Control that business, and you could control entire planetary economies. The idea is incredible.

"They're keeping it under wraps," says Ximena. "Secret supply requisitions. Disappeared prisoners doing the work. Communications blackout. The whole bit."

"Then how did Coeur know?"

Her expression closes for a fraction of a second; she's preparing to lie.

"I can't help you — I can't help anyone — if you don't tell me the truth," Jaantzen says. He says "anyone" because he's not ready to acknowledge that her sister's still alive, not yet. But Ximena takes his meaning and nods solemnly.

"There's a cult that started at Redrock," she says finally. "By one of the prisoners there who says he's some sort of prophet."

"The Dawn," offers Jaantzen.

"They have this obsession with death, and purifying the world for the end times. Or something like that. Anyway, they figure this same serum that the Alliance is using to help terraform the desert can transform humans, too. They wanted to get their hands on it, so they paid Thala to steal the samples the Alliance had taken to Indira and ship them back to them on New Sarjun."

Jaantzen sighs. "And let me guess. She figured she'd take their money, then ship it to you instead, and then make her own money off it."

"Old habits die hard," says Manu.

"She didn't tell me that part — I learned it the hard way when the Dawn started coming after me. Thala said it was the Alliance taking advantage of what should have rightfully been New Sarjun's."

"That sounds suspiciously altruistic," says Jaantzen, and Ximena shoots him a dark look.

"She had a business plan," she says. "And she didn't think much of the religious folks who were footing the bill. So, no, she wasn't here to save the day."

"And you were going to go along with her?"

"Of course not. I have a perfectly good thing going at Redrock." Ximena laughs sadly. "Had. While I was waiting for her shipments to arrive, I got a frantic message saying she was in trouble, and that I needed to run. I got out just as some psycho cultists came after me, and I figured I'd try to find this shipment before they did." Ximena taps a finger against her split lip. "And I guess you all know the rest of that story."

"Not quite," Manu says. "How did you find the shipment?"

"Tip-off. Thala was using a friend of hers to ship it in, some smuggler named Yang. She contacted me to let me know where it was."

Julieta had asked him to destroy the shipment, then told Ximena where it was so she could salvage the case first? Something about this sits very wrong with him.

"My house is yours for as long as you need it," he says.

She looks up at him, too quickly. "Even if my trouble's with the Alliance?"

"You wouldn't be my first Alliance refugee," he says mildly.

Her gaze flickers to Starla.

"And Gia, of course," he says, to see if she winces. She

does, which he takes as a sign that she's still got at least part of her soul. Her sister had never felt guilty about her role in selling Giaconda Áte off to rot in Redrock Prison.

"And if I don't want to stay?"

Jaantzen leans forward, steeples his fingers. "I would like you to be my guest for now," he says. "Though you're not a prisoner. So long as you agree to tell me the truth about everything."

"Not a prisoner, but I can't leave."

"I think you'll find we can both help each other quite a bit."

Ximena looks like she's about to argue, but instead she sits back, pressing her lips into a thin line.

"There is one more thing," she says. Her gaze shifts between Jaantzen and Starla, as though wondering how much Starla's told him.

"How do you know your sister's alive?" Jaantzen asks.

Ximena's shoulders relax as though in relief she didn't have to break the news. "Her captors contacted me with proof. They wanted me to find the case and bring it in trade for her life."

"The Dawn."

"I assume so. They didn't say. Willem, I need your help."

"I'm not giving them anything."

"I'm not suggesting that. Those bastards have my sister, and I have to help her."

Jaantzen watches her coolly. "Years ago, I promised you I would cease my vendetta against her life, and for fifteen years I've watched her thrive. Now you're asking me to *rescue* the woman who murdered my family."

Ximena takes a deep breath. "When you came to me for help freeing Starla, my price was hard for you to bear — but you did it. With grace. Now I'm coming to you for help, and I know there is no parity here."

"I see that."

"But I am in your debt. And Thala will be in your debt."

"The idea of Thala being in my debt unnerves me," Jaantzen says, then raises a hand before Ximena can respond. "If I help you rescue her, it's not to set her free. It's not out of obligation and friendship to a business partner. You're both trading one captor for another."

"But I trust you. Far more than them."

"If I rescue your sister, it's because I see the value in what she's stolen from the Dawn, and I don't want them — or anyone — to have her as leverage. I want you to know that."

"I understand."

Jaantzen doesn't look over at Manu; he can sense his lieutenant's cold, reproachful gaze, feel the tension in every angle of his pose. I'm so sorry, Jaantzen thinks.

"I'll help."

Ximena closes her eyes, a brief flutter. "Thank you."

Jaantzen stands, buttoning his suit jacket. He holds out a hand to Ximena, who rises to meet it. Her hand is ice cold, but her grip is firm.

"I'm late for an appointment," he says. "Starla, will you drive me? Take Major Nayar down and inform the Anahoys. We'll follow in a moment."

Manu doesn't look at him until the elevator doors close.

"Manu — "

"You can't be fucking serious." Manu is still, a single vein pulsing in the hollow of his neck. "Tell me you're not serious."

"I don't like it. But we can use her."

"*Use* her? Nobody *uses* her. Blackheart uses you." His

expression is dangerous, deadly. "Or have you forgotten what she's like?"

"I haven't forgotten anything. We control her, or we let the Dawn do it. Or, worse, they let her loose to take her old territory back, only this time she has an extreme advantage."

"Control her." Manu bites the words out.

"If she's truly still alive, I want her where I can see her, not hiding in the shadows." Jaantzen leans forward, locking his gaze on Manu. "And she will see justice, Manu. I promise you."

Manu takes a sharp breath at that, reining in whatever else he might have said.

"I need you tonight. I can't afford to be down my best man, but it's worse for us all if you go when you shouldn't. You have to tell me if you can do this."

Manu's always warm eyes are flint. Three breaths, and decision made. Manu nods.

"Good. Go with the Anahoys. Take Major Nayar and her cargo back to Cobalt Tower. Find out what she knows about where her sister is being held and make a plan for as soon as possible." To rescue Coeur, he does not say. But the muscle twitching in Manu's clenched jaw tells him the message is clear.

"On it, boss."

Manu stands stiffly and goes to pick up the case. As he walks past, to the elevator, Jaantzen stops him, a hand on his lieutenant's shoulder. He keeps his grip light; he's seen this arm laid open sinew and bone on Gia's operating table.

"Manu. I'm sorry."

After a long moment, Manu meets his gaze. "I know," he says, a slow, tired breath. "I think we're all going to be sorry."

9

JAANTZEN

"I should go in with you."

Starla's stopped the Dulciana just shy of the steps to Leone's home so that the passenger door will open into a thornbush. It's a clear sign she's not ready to let Jaantzen out without giving him what's on her mind; he wills himself to relax.

He's not in the mood.

"Things aren't normal right now," she signs. "I need to make sure you're safe."

"No," Jaantzen says, then lifts his hands. "No seconds at dinner," he signs. "It's tradition."

An exasperated look. "I'm not a second. I'm — " Starla's fingers pause in midair and he hasn't a clue what sign her hands were on the verge of forming. "Your daughter," she finally signs, the sign clipped and fast, the hesitation in it unacknowledged.

"If I bring you — " He's trying to speak and sign, and in his frustration he doesn't have the energy. When he's this close, her lens mostly transcribes his voice better than he can sign anyway.

Yet it's a crutch he uses too often. He forces himself to speak her language, scowling at the clumsiness in his hands.

"If I bring you, the others will insist on bringing their seconds. Or their heirs." He doesn't know the sign and fingerspells it, pushes himself past her sudden stillness at the word. "Go home. Get some rest. You'll need it for later tonight."

Her lips quirk to the side. "You trust these people?"

Jaantzen lets out a sharp breath. He isn't in the mood for this conversation.

"These people are my . . ." He spirals his hands, trying to think of the sign. "Friends."

It's not the right word, but he's not sure what is. If he were speaking, he would have said associates, but even that word doesn't have the right connotation. What does one call a pack of disparate predators in uneasy alliance? A coyote, a jaguar, a cobra, a scorpion, a lion standing back to back?

Certainly not friends. And he doubts most in that home tonight would consider him their peer.

"Julieta Yang." Starla tips a skeptical eyebrow at the woman's namesign. "She told us to blow up her shipment, but also told Ximena to go get it?"

It's been gnawing at him, too.

"They accept you when you're useful," Starla signs, and there's a deep bitterness in her face that he doesn't expect. "They don't know you, they don't know me, and they don't want to."

He lifts his hands, but he's far too slow.

"All these society people see is where you come from."

"Starla — " he says.

"And that's their mistake."

"Thank you," he says. Then, in sign, "Keep an eye out; I don't plan to be long. I'll call."

Starla looks for a moment as though she'll argue, but she decides against it. "Fine," she signs, the gesture sharp and deliberate.

She moves back to the controls, but he touches the back of her hand.

"Tonight," he signs, "this thing with — "

She cuts him off with a sharp gesture. "You need me."

Jaantzen lets a smile touch the corner of his lips. "That's what I was going to say," he signs.

Starla's skeptical side-eye softens and she gives him a faint nod, lets the Dulciana roll forward, presents the chief justice's rising staircase to him like the opportunity it is. Jaantzen rests his hand on the door handle. For a man brought up without parents, he thinks he's done a decent job with the daughter he inherited. In fact, inheriting a daughter already broken and raging had been liberating where raising his own children from pure blank slates had been a source of crushing anxiety. He remembers watching his son and daughter play as though he were a voyeur, hand over his mouth in case a wrong breath was enough to destroy their happy, fragile lives. Celebrating each of their few birthdays with a growing sense of dread, knowing they were one year closer to understanding him. Judging him.

He remembers lying in bed at night listening to Tae breathe, knowing that at least they would have their mother — once they grew old enough to realize the kind of man their father truly was. Because surely by then she would have realized, as well.

Would he have allowed his natural-born children to be involved in the darker sides of his business? Would *Tae* have allowed it? Certainly not.

He tries to picture the laughing three-year-old girl of his memories, all grown up and pointing a weapon at an already-bleeding shard-cooker while she waited unbothered for him to order her to pull the trigger.

Waited, unbothered, for him to ask her to cross a line he does not want her to cross — a line he assumes she has not crossed, though admittedly he can't be sure.

Starla may not have been the child he created, but she is the one given to him. And sometimes — a stab of guilt at the thought — the universe knows best.

His hand is on the handle and his heart is pounding as he wills himself to say one last thing. His hands learned the sign nearly fifteen years ago, but they still balk every time he tries to form it.

Who do you think you are, a voice from inside seems to ask. What right do you have to say it?

He takes a deep breath.

"I love you," he signs.

And Starla's fierce expression softens, the corner of her mouth quirks up into a reluctant smile. She gives him an amused little shake of her head, then leans across the seat to kiss his cheek. He catches a lingering whiff of perfume, wonders what prompted her to wear it today.

"I love you, too," she tells him. "Be careful in there."

Chief Justice Geum-ja Leone greets him with a clasped forearm and kisses on both cheeks that she pulls him down to receive. She's grown shorter and boxier each year he's known her, silver hair shorn tight against her scalp, expensive Coruscan opal earrings hanging heavy from her pale ears. He hasn't seen them on her before, and trade with Corusca has been almost impossible since the Alliance cracked down on a rebellion there five years ago. Probably a gift from Julieta, then.

For a New Sarjunian supreme court judge, Leone has expensive tastes. If pressed, she'll say she's handled her family's existing assets well, but Jaantzen has padded her pockets with enough of his own funds to know where the money is coming from. Everything on this planet is decided in the end by the judiciary, and having a good — if expensive — relationship with someone like Geum-ja Leone is the cost of doing business in this town.

Some of the biggest business deals and most lucrative alliances have been made at her dinner parties. To get an invitation is to get access to a tier of society a street kid like Jaantzen never could have dreamed existed. His friendship with Julieta ushered him into the fringes of Justice Leone's social circle, and his role leading the fight to oust Coeur had earned him a standing invitation to those dinner parties. Starla's right — he's always suspected most here still see him as a street criminal brought to heel. But tonight he's not here for their approval. He's got bigger problems on the horizon.

"Willem!" Leone says. "It's been too long."

"It has, Madame Justice."

She accepts his proffered bottle of wine with a little gasp of delight. "I've had my eye on this vintage," she says. "Have you been spying on me?"

Jaantzen smiles.

"Julieta has the spies," he says. "My secret is simply attention to detail."

Leone just laughs and holds out her elbow to usher him to the sitting room, moving her attentions to a light banter on the weather.

Jaantzen's mind isn't in the right place for pleasantries. In general, but especially tonight. As a younger man, he hadn't understood the point of small talk, or how much negotiation occurs in who remembers children's names or the host's favored wine varietal. Now he understands it, he just doesn't get the same delight the others seem to.

Julieta may have schooled him to take away some of his roughness, but there's still a fundamental divide between those who were born to the high-society game and those who wear it like a second skin over ingrained habits. He sometimes wonders if they can't see his feral nature in his eyes, or if they just choose to ignore it.

Let them look down on him. Which of them would've survived a childhood in the streets with him and Coeur?

Leone plucks two glasses from her waiter's tray, presses one into his hand. "You must try this aperitif," she says. "The liqueur is made with plants gathered wild on Agate Ridge, I think it's just splendid."

She sips, then watches him taste; it's surprisingly refreshing, light and bubbly with just the hint of herbs he can't put his finger on. "It's wonderful," he says.

"It's from a new distillery. I met the owner recently and was impressed. She's from Carama Town; what she's built from nothing is really quite commendable."

Jaantzen gives her an encouraging smile and waits for the pitch. Leone has always had a soft spot for a slum kid with a can-do attitude.

"And I thought," she continues, "wouldn't a cocktail like this just be wonderful on the Jungle's menu? You two must meet."

Jaantzen takes another sip. It *is* delicious, and he has a soft spot for slum kids, too. "Forward me her contact and I'll set up a meeting with my bar manager," he says.

"Perfect," says Leone, patting him on the arm. And whether a kickback, a promise of shares, or simply another in a long string of favors owed, Chief Justice Geum-ja Leone has made another payday.

The sitting room is already filled with familiar faces; he can hear more voices coming from the dining room beyond. A full house tonight, it seems. Casino tycoon Phaera D is doing harried business over a call in the window seat. She keeps talking, gives him a look of faux warmth with an apologetic tap at her earpiece: her practiced businessperson's way of saying he's clearly the most important thing in the room, though she regretfully can't come say hello. Aging banker Teo Lordeur wields his new wheelchair like a throne while trade commissioner Youssef Tabari leans in conspiratorially.

Julieta is already there, holding court with Mizal Seti and agricultural heiress Lhasa Demosga from the grand settee. Mizal looks up as he enters, gives him a wide smile that seems meant to imply no shift in feelings following the incident at the dealership in Jet Park.

"Willem," he booms. "Just the man I wanted to see." He stands to shake Jaantzen's hand. "I was just telling Julieta and Lhasa about the developments in Jet Park."

"You've *got* to come up with a better name for the neighborhood," calls Phaera from the window seat before going back to her business.

Mizal shoots her an irritated look; they've clearly had this conversation before. "Aditi just told me the buyer's agreed to your terms. Congratulations!"

"Thank you," Jaantzen says; negotiations on the property in Jet Park have been the furthest thing from his mind today, but he recalls now that he has an unanswered message from Aditi Ciam waiting on his desk. "I'm looking forward to getting the work started."

"I'm so glad you're on board," Mizal says, clapping him

on the shoulder. "It'll be a boon to have a man like you in the neighborhood."

Jaantzen smiles back, judging the words. A man like him? A guard dog to keep out the worse riffraff? Muscle the shard-cookers won't mess with?

"The more respectable business owners we have on board, the better chance we have of getting attention from the city," Mizal continues, and Julieta gives him a wink. Jaantzen raises his glass to her, then turns to the young woman beside her. He and Julieta will have business to discuss later.

"Lhasa, it's good to see you. How's life on the family farm?"

Lhasa Demosga rises to shake his hand, launching into a discussion of the price of triticale that he merely nods along to. He hasn't had many business dealings with the Demosga family, beyond a few aboveboard contracts through RKE to outfit the restaurants in their opulent orbital casinos. He's certainly never paid attention to the agricultural empire that built their original wealth. But now he regards Lhasa with new scrutiny. Whatever he decides to do with Coeur, the potential of the terraforming technology she's dropped in his lap is incredible. If he acts on it, the powerful Demosgas could become allies — or rivals.

"Jaantzen, Lhasa, good to see you both." Phaera has finished up her business and cuts in on his conversation with Lhasa; Lhasa's expression smooths into polite greeting, a thin smile a few socially acceptable degrees above ice. The two women exchange fleeting kisses and, after a flutter of false pleasantries, Lhasa excuses herself. Never friends, there.

Phaera slips her earpiece into the pocket of her body-skimming jumpsuit. It's raw silk, its color shifting in the light from teal to ink blue, a natural effect Jaantzen has seen mimicked by woven-in holograms in the more tawdry dresses of Arquellian women on holiday from Indira. It sets off her pale complexion and sharp, magenta-streaked bob. Phaera must be doing well for herself these days.

When she shakes his hand there's teeth behind it, but Jaantzen has learned it's just her way. Despite her expensive suits and real estate deals, Phaera is more like him than the others: she's still a woman more comfortable ordering a shot after a bar fight than a 500-mark bottle of wine. She earned her first small fortune playing the odds until that bit of coin allowed her to invest in the upscale casinos she runs now, but Jaantzen will be damned if she's not still willing to get a little blood on her suit.

He certainly hopes she is.

She jerks her chin at the cocktail in Jaantzen's hand. "Are you biting?" she asks. "Leone already talked me into a hundred cases for the casino."

"It *is* good."

"Help out a friend, et cetera." Phaera glances at a message on her elegant gold wrist cuff. "So," she says. "I hear you didn't do Blackheart in."

"Word gets around."

"It was Hinoja, then? I suppose I can ask her when she arrives." She leans in conspiratorially. "Unless you've already worked your coup on Blackheart's gang." From her teasing expression he can tell she's prodding for his plans, not revealing intel she already has. But she's sharp. She knows how he thinks.

"Not quite," he says quietly. "There's been an upset in Blackheart's crew, but that may lead to opportunity for like-minded businesspeople."

She lifts her chin, considering. Her casinos border

Blackheart's territory; she's squabbled with the crew for years. Jaantzen knows she'd welcome a chance to end that fight for good, and her resources could help turn the tide if it comes to all-out war with Acheta.

"What happened?" Phaera asks. Jaantzen's fully aware of the hush that falls over Julieta and Mizal. Geum-ja Leone, off to check on dinner, has paused in the doorway.

"Naali won't be making it tonight," Jaantzen announces, and Leone turns, brow furrowed. Apparently *this* word hasn't yet spread. "She's dead."

Phaera's jaw drops. Leone lets out a stream of unjudicial swear words under her breath, and for a moment Julieta's face shows pure terror before she gets herself under control. One hand lingers at the brooch at her throat.

Silence, then: "Did you do her? Or are you two-for-oh?" Phaera asks lightly, earning a sharp glare from Julieta.

"No, I did not." Jaantzen takes another sip of his cocktail.

"Levi?" Leone says, and Jaantzen turns to confirm her guess when he realizes she's looking past him, into the hallway.

Oh, the nerve.

Levi Acheta is dressed for the occasion, in a well-cut suit and what looks like a real leather coat with a gold-trimmed collar and cuffs that frame the tattoos on the backs of his hands and his neck. The clothes are nice, but the way he fidgets with them betrays a man more comfortable making his point with his fists.

"Sorry I didn't let you know ahead of time, Madame Justice," Acheta says. "But I'm here in Naali's place." He pauses; another feral one unused to niceties, but without the benefit of Julieta's tutelage. "For good," he says, finally.

His gaze lands on Jaantzen, holds for a moment, before returning to Leone.

He holds out a slim package. He's brought a gift, at least; the man knows that much. "I did what I had to do, Madame Justice. Thank you for hosting."

Leone gives a gracious smile, then steps forward as though to take the package. But the way her fingertips brush the jeweled cuff at her wrist, the step out of her doorway is something more. Jaantzen's team at Admant upgraded her household security two years ago, reinforcing external security, but also adding TR-X 17 partitioning throughout the home. The right sequence entered in her cuff, and force-fields slam shut throughout the house, shearing anything in their way. Levi Acheta is still standing firmly on the outside of the sitting room.

"You're welcome, honey, of course. But I won't have any trouble in my home."

Acheta bristles, reins it in.

"With Blackheart gone, Naali didn't have what it takes to keep things together," he says. "Things would have gotten out of control, under her. I did this city a favor, and I'll be bringing true prosperity back to Blackheart's crew." Acheta smiles tightly. "You know how it is," he says to Jaantzen, and there's a familiarity there that kindles a fire in Jaantzen's blood.

"I'm not sure what you mean," he says, but he keeps his tone light.

Acheta can't be working on his own, Jaantzen thinks. He doubts Acheta could hold Hinoja's half of the divided crew without help, any more than Hinoja could have held Acheta's half. He's allied himself with someone — possibly someone attending here tonight, though Jaantzen can't sense Acheta's attention going anywhere but directly to him.

The room is filling behind him, Acheta's arrival and the electric energy between him and Jaantzen drawing spectators like moths to a flame.

Leone clears her throat, reclaiming Acheta's attention. "We've lost some good people these past few days, son," she says. "This isn't how regimes are changed. Not these days."

Acheta lifts his chin; the words sting. "It's how they changed," he says. "Whether it's by the rules or not, it's the new reality." He's looks back at Jaantzen as he says this.

Leone follows his gaze, meets Jaantzen's eyes herself.

"We do business with Coeur's crew, no matter who runs it," she says, a rebuff to any objection Jaantzen — or anyone else here — may have. "You're welcome to join us for dinner tonight. May I offer you a drink?"

She leads him through the crowded sitting room to the dining room. He steps close to Jaantzen as he passes, shoulder to shoulder, invading his space. Jaantzen doesn't flinch.

"You got my message?" Acheta murmurs with a cold smile.

"I see you made your move before Hinoja could make hers," Jaantzen says. "Who'd you find to hold your hand?"

Acheta's face darkens. A question that hits close to home, then.

"Naali would have given up our crew to you," he growls. "I'm making alliances to make us stronger. Watch out, old man." His shoulder jostles Jaantzen's as he pushes past, stalks after Leone into the dining room.

"The nerve of that child," murmurs Mizal Seti as soon as Leone and Acheta are out of the room.

"Nerve is a good trait," says Julieta. "Anger is not."

"I'm not sure I like his direction," Mizal says firmly, to Jaantzen, and there's an unsubtle depth to the words. There are murmurs of assent around the room, and Jaantzen notes the split. Some, like Lhasa Demosga and Youssef Tabari, are carefully excluding themselves from the conversation. From his wheelchair, old Teo Lordeur gives Jaantzen a solemn nod, and Jaantzen makes a mental note to call on him soon. What Teo and his sister lack in armed strength they make up for in bankroll.

"Dinner is ready," Leone calls from the doorway. Slowly, the room begins to empty.

Phaera lifts her glass to him. "I always appreciate an opportunity to work with like-minded businesspeople," she says with a small, private smile. "Let me know what you need."

"I'll be in touch."

"I look forward to it." Phaera clinks her glass against his, then turns to rib Mizal as they follow the others into the dining room.

Jaantzen holds out his hand to Julieta. "Shall we?"

But Julieta's watching Phaera walk away. "I always thought you two would get on well together," she says after a moment with a speculative smile. "She's a strong woman. She'd be good for you."

Jaantzen clears his throat. The back of his neck prickles with unexpected heat. "We were discussing business."

"Ah. Well, maybe I'm not as good at identifying a 'come hither' look as I used to be." Juliet takes his hand and gets stiffly to her feet, then lays her hand on his arm. He covers it with his own; he can feel the bones, the fluttering pulse. It's like holding a bird.

"I was afraid, when you said Naali was dead," Julieta says quietly. "That it was part of the same mess Thala involved me in. But it was just Levi." She's walking slowly, holding him back from the rest of the group. "It seems there was an electrical fire at one of my warehouses earlier tonight," she says before he can answer that thought. "Accelerated by poorly stored product. I'll have to have a conversation with my warehouse provider."

"I hope your loss wasn't too great."

"I'd been paid," she says. She pats his hand. "It's nice to have people you can trust."

He's sure it is. But can that trust go both ways, after what he's learned from Ximena? "That shipment. Who was it going to?"

"Thala's sister in Redrock."

"Have you heard from her recently?"

She gives him a sharp look, tinged again with fear. "No. Is she dead now, too?"

"No, she's fine."

Julieta's fingers relax; they'd been digging into his forearm. Jaantzen releases the tension he's been holding in his shoulders. Julieta can lie with the best, but that reaction was pure fear. She's not the one who tried to get Ximena killed by sending her to the warehouse tonight.

"Having that shipment destroyed is a weight gone, Willem, you have no idea. How's that jadau branch I gave you? Has the wound healed?"

"Not quite yet," Jaantzen says, though in truth he hasn't thought about the damn thing since he brought it home. But he's guessing it's too early for it to be ready for rooting, and Julieta makes a satisfied noise that says he guessed right.

"By early next week, I would think. It's a shame about Naali. I liked that girl," she says. "But what a tragedy, taken out by her own lieutenant. It makes me so grateful for my Aster and the others, as you must be for your daughter."

"I am," he says.

"And I am grateful for you, Willem. You're a wolf with the cunning to act like a house pet when it suits you," Julieta says. "I fear our new addition is a desert hound without a thread of domestication in him."

Coming from one of the others, he would have found the comparison offensive. But Julieta has never flinched away from the darkness within either of them, never lied to herself and told him it was a virtue. Instead, she meets his darkness with her own.

"I agree," he says quietly. "Can I count on you?"

"You never have to ask, Willem."

He settles her in her chair, then kisses her hand. "I have another appointment tonight," he says, and she smiles at him. "I'll be in touch."

At the other end of the table, Levi Acheta is gamely holding his own with Lhasa and an Arquellian politician Jaantzen hasn't met. Acheta spares a look for Jaantzen, who ignores it, instead works his way out of the room making excuses and shaking hands. He claps Teo Lordeur on the shoulder — "Let me know what you need, boy," Lordeur says — and meets Leone in the doorway.

"I'm so sorry to leave before dinner," he says. "But I have other business that can't wait."

Her gaze flickers past him to Acheta; there's displeasure in it, and Jaantzen can't tell if it's aimed at Acheta for his disruption or at Jaantzen for his early departure. She'll assume he's leaving to avoid the other man. It's true in part, but he's also achieved what he needed. Acheta can work this room all he wants, Jaantzen knows who's on his side.

"Oh, honey, how disappointing! I'll be doing this again soon, though, and I *won't* have you miss it next time." That last has the bite of a command, and Jaantzen makes a mental note to make this right with her as soon as possible. The last thing he needs is to cross Geum-ja Leone.

"Thank you," Jaantzen says. "I'm honored."

He leans down to kiss her cheek, then slips from the dining room and messages Starla. Her response comes through immediately, and he sinks gratefully into the passenger seat of the Dulciana, feeling the weight of the unfinished evening settling on his shoulders.

"Let's get home," he signs, but she doesn't move to take the controls. The way she's watching him fills him with dread. "What is it?"

"I saw Acheta," Starla signs. She hands him her comm, open to an image. "And you're not going to like who he was with."

"It's definitely her," Toshiyo says, speeding back through footage from Starla's helmet's rearview camera on one half of the conference table, with the image Starla showed Jaantzen at Leone's doorstep displayed above the other half. He and Starla are back in his office with Toshiyo and Manu; in the downtown ravines surrounding them, all but the late-night neon clubs have blacked out their signs for the night. The city seems eerily dark, unsettlingly calm. A storm's coming in, the horizon smudged with dust clouds; the desert beyond Bulari's skyline is briefly luminous with lightning before flickering into darkness again.

Jaantzen zooms in on the image. It's a deep blue and silver two-door spinner dropping Acheta off at the front door, a silver-haired woman driving. Toshiyo stops the helmet footage, comparing the driver who tried to take Starla out earlier in the evening with the driver of Acheta's spinner. In the second photo, her hand is bandaged.

"She's not one of Coeur's crew," Jaantzen says. He would recognize anyone Acheta trusted enough to be a driver, and he's never seen this woman before.

"I've been running searches since Starla sent that over," Toshiyo says. "She's got a record."

She pulls up an ident card. "T.J. Meijer. Served time in Redrock, was released just a couple of years ago. Most often seen with this guy."

Jaantzen does recognize the face on the new ident card she pulls up. Shaved head and ice-blue eyes, jagged scar slicing through his tanned cheek.

"Bennion Zacharia," he says. "The Dawn, right? Their prophet?"

"Not their prophet, just the local boss," Toshiyo says.

He's never met Zacharia in person, but he's heard the name associated with this organization — especially since they began diversifying in recent years from passive recruitment to their cult and cooking drugs to actively proselytizing their religion and pushing those drugs. From what Jaantzen's heard, the man is intensely private, reportedly preferring to spend time in meditation and isolation rather than be hands-on about the day-to-day operation.

Jaantzen stares into those ice-blue eyes. They're not the eyes of someone who spends much time in meditation, he thinks. They're the eyes of a killer.

"So she's switched sides and joined our man Acheta," Manu says and signs. "Or Acheta's working with the Dawn."

"I'd guess the latter," Jaantzen says and signs. "Puts himself in the Dawn's debt, then shows up with a gift for the judge." Both fingers and tongue stutter over the words like they always do when he tries to speak two languages at once. It's late, he tells himself, though in truth he needs to get back to his practice.

"Like a cat bringing in a dead lizard," Manu says.

Starla laughs. "Mine did two just yesterday."

"Your cat's a badass," Manu signs back.

Manu picked up USL like he picks up everything else: with enough charisma and graceful bravado you never see the fierce study beneath it. Fifteen years since Starla crashed into their lives, and he's a natural — to Jaantzen's eyes, at least. For Jaantzen, adapting to Starla was more than learning USL, which he took to like an arid desert cat would take to Julieta's claustrophobic greenhouse. He'd gone from mourning a pair of toddlers to raising a teenager, without the years of acclimation normal parents get to ease the transition. And from scorching his heart black after his family's death to peeling back the scar tissue and finding, unexpectedly, unlimited space for a broken child.

Jaantzen hasn't made it this far without knowing when and how he needs to start shifting his stripes.

And that time is now.

"Blackheart's crew and the Dawn," Jaantzen says. "I don't like it."

Toshiyo lets out a sigh. "Then you're really not going to like where Coeur's being held."

She begins to tap at the table, but the lift's arrival flickers the lights and she looks up instead. Ximena Nayar stands in the doorway. Food, a shower, and a few hours of sleep in a real bed have worked their wonders, and she's as polished as he's ever seen her. Her long black hair's tied back in a sleek bun, and though she's wearing civilian clothes, they do nothing to disguise the decades she's spent in the military.

Jaantzen beckons her over to the conference table. "We're finalizing plans. We need everything you know."

Toshiyo pulls up a map of the city, zooms into Dry Creek, the thumb of the five slums, on the northern end of town. A beacon blinks deep in the heart of Dry Creek crew territory.

"That old smelter north of the city," Toshiyo says.

"So the Dawn is working with the Dry Creek crew, too?" asks Jaantzen. "Lovely."

Manu pinches the bridge of his nose. "I hate this woman so much." At Ximena's frown he flashes her a smile, cracks a knuckle on his scarred left hand.

"How do we know this is it?" Jaantzen asks.

"They gave me this address as a rendezvous for after I got the case," says Ximena.

"So I looked into it." Toshiyo zooms in on the location. "And between people on the ground and my surveillance, they brought a prisoner in yesterday and no one's come back out."

"How convenient for us that you know the address," Jaantzen says to Ximena.

"It's probably a trap," Starla signs. "Hoping whoever has their precious case comes for Coeur."

"Then they'd be right. Now that we know we're walking into a trap, let's prepare for that eventuality."

"They may not expect us to act so soon," Ximena says. "We'll have the element of surprise on our side."

"And we took out a bunch of their crew earlier," Starla signs.

"It won't be as easy for us to get out fast as in other neighborhoods," Jaantzen says to Ximena. "This city's sliced up. There are parts where it's not prudent for my people to go."

"Willem — "

"I'm not saying we won't do it. I'm saying there's an increased risk, above and beyond trying to break into an enemy's jailhouse."

Ximena lifts her chin. "Name your price, I'll pay it."

"I'm not taking your money. There's not enough money in the universe to convince me to rescue Thala Coeur."

She searches his gaze for a long moment, then nods. This debt is more complicated than money for services rendered, runs deeper than favors exchanged.

"We'll do it," Jaantzen says. "We just need to exercise extreme caution. The Dry Creek crew will recognize most of our people."

Starla catches his eye. "The good news? There's not a lot of security."

"Then it's definitely a trap," Manu says and signs.

"Then we'll be smarter than them." Jaantzen stands, buttoning his jacket. "Have a doctor standing by for when we return."

Starla makes Gia's name sign, lifts an eyebrow.

Jaantzen lets out a long, slow breath. "Ask her to recommend someone."

Starla's comm vibrates on the desk and she thumbs through a message.

"El," she signs. "It's time."

When Jaantzen was coming up, the streets were sliced block by block, and you knew which ones you could go on and which you couldn't. That world had felt constricting, like the too-small coats and shoes Jaantzen suffered through in the orphanage. He'd never been a small boy, and during his growing years he shed sizes like a snake sheds skin.

On the streets, finding the right-sized clothes had been easier — once he joined a crew, most necessities were there for the taking so long as you knew where to look and who not to cross. But the streets themselves? Walk twenty paces and butt up against an invisible boundary. No one telling you you couldn't step across, but you knew there was a bullet in it for you if you tried. He remembered the rich folks in their fine spinners back then, slicing through the streets without a care to wherever their path took them. To be rich was to have freedom, in more ways than one.

But money alone doesn't open up all streets. Some take warfare and diplomacy, and some, like Dry Creek, you just write off for good.

It's been years since Jaantzen has been in this neighborhood, and he doesn't know the intersections, the way they crash into each other at odd angles, the way the streets gently bend. There's some arroyo or canal running through it, a dark slash in the map that's forcing the streets into odd patterns. Dead ends and misdirections. Starla's following a map superimposed over the windshield, navigating as easily as if she grew up here. Haze from the coming dust storm sparks against the windshield.

The target is in an apartment building, once factory housing for a manufacturing corporation which has long since shut down. The smelter had required enough workers to fill three of these apartment buildings, taking up approximately a city block each; now only one still stands below the burnt-out remains of the smelter's chimneys. To its left is a square of rubble. Across the street, only the facade of the third building. Behind it — beyond the smelter's chimneys — the wall of the ravine juts into the night sky.

The road is littered with broken rocks and the husks of burnt-out spinners. Starla approaches the apartment building from the back, parks in the shadows in front of the smelter. Three stories of windows gape above them, many broken out over the years, but some kept clean or boarded up. This building's original residents may have moved on, but it seems squatters are making use of the space. The Dry Creek crew has run anyone who can afford to move out of the neighborhood in the last few years.

Starla cracks her window and slips her hand through. A matte black drone the size of a cockroach unfurls in her palm and lifts into the air.

"Airborne," Toshiyo says through their earpieces. Light dances in Starla's eye as Toshiyo's transcription comes through. "Visuals look good. Stand by, I'm going in."

A glint on the other side of the building is El's two-door spinner, a green dot on the map overlay. Both that and Starla's four-door stretch model were designed to be nothing to look at, but stocked with military-grade armor and plenty of firepower. It's an advantage the Dry Creek crew aren't likely to have — or expect.

"I have eyes on the inside," Toshiyo says. "Only three guards: one at the main gate, two at apartment six. Sending locations to map."

A trio of red dots blink up on the screen.

"Looking more and more like a trap," Manu says.

"Agreed," says Jaantzen. "Let's make this fast."

"On it," Simca says. "Going in." She cracks her knuckles, slips from the back seat, and begins to scale the back side of the building, Manu on her heels. They disappear through a broken window on the third floor.

The waiting is always interminable, and Jaantzen uses the time to replay his moves in his mind. In through the bedroom window of apartment ten, on the ground floor, then out into the courtyard using the play structure as cover. Wait for the sign from Toshiyo, then one shot, two shots. Then through the door of apartment six.

"At the window," Simca says, and Jaantzen motions Ximena out of the spinner.

Outside, Jaantzen hands her a rifle. "Every one of my crew has been instructed to shoot you if you try anything," he says. If that bothers her, she doesn't show it.

"Understood," Ximena says. "I know the plan."

Simca's already working on the window of apartment ten by the time they get to it. She removes the security bars easily, then unlocks the window and stands back to let Jaantzen and Ximena climb through. Jaantzen's problem right knee protests at the contortions; he ignores it. He turns back to help Ximena, but she lands like a cat. Desert dust billows up around her feet from the ancient, gritty carpet.

This room's empty, and the next, holes torn into the walls where scrappers have salvaged appliances and wiring, the floors littered with mouse droppings and used shard tabs. It reminds Jaantzen of the places he squatted in his youth, furnishings already stripped out and sold by junkies, bold rats initiating miniature turf wars in hopes of stealing some of Jaantzen's shoddy crew's meager food.

Jaantzen shakes off the image. No time for a trip down memory lane.

Jaantzen finds Manu crouched by the front door.

"The guards," Manu signs. He indicates their position on the other side of the play structure; Jaantzen can just make out their feet through the bars. The rest of the complex seems empty.

"Front door guard?" Jaantzen signs.

"At the gate still."

Jaantzen motions Simca and Ximena to skirt the right of the courtyard, follows Manu around to the left, clinging to the shadows and trying not to crunch in the piles of broken glass that glitter in the moonlight.

They've hit their mark, just on this side of the play area, with clear shots of the apartment guards, who are engrossed in a game of two-card hawk. Simca and Ximena should hit theirs at any moment.

"Now," says Toshiyo in his ear.

Jaantzen's bullet hits the first guard in the back of the neck. Manu's takes out the other. Across the courtyard, they hear a scuffle that must be Ximena and Simca taking out the front gate guard.

"Clear here," Jaantzen says. "Going in to apartment six."

Simca's voice: "Copy, clear here."

Toshiyo's drone is hovering outside the door to apartment six, faint light playing over it. "Someone's alive inside," she says. "Biolocks. I don't sense any weapons."

"We're good here, Tosh," says Manu.

"Copy. Heading to the sky." The drone zooms skyward and disappears against the black night.

Manu yanks up one guard's arm to press his hand against the cheap biolock. A pair of quiet *thunks* sound as the lock opens. He shares a look with Jaantzen, one hand on the door.

Jaantzen nods. Manu shoves it open.

Apartment six is dark and cloying with the thick stink of age and disuse, tempered by human filth, blood, and sweat. In the faint light through the doorway he can just make out a spotlight on a stand, directly in front of him.

Jaantzen switches it on. In the center of the room stands an interrogation desk with two chairs in front, one chair behind. The room's lone occupant is slumped over the desk, hands wrenched in front of her and bound in cuffs. A cascade of black braids hides her face, but there's no mistaking who it must be.

Jaantzen stops at the door, weapon at the ready with a view of the courtyard in case anyone else is here. Behind him, he can hear Manu sweeping the rest of the apartment. The woman at the table makes no noise.

Manu appears at his elbow. One sharp nod: the apartment is clear.

"Get me keys," Jaantzen signs, and Manu slips back out the front door, stoops to rummage through the guards' pockets.

Jaantzen takes a tentative step towards the desk. Coeur hasn't moved. At first he's not sure if she's alive or dead, but then he sees the gentle rise and fall of her shoulders. The spotlight gives him clear view of her, but if she looked up he would be framed by light, impossible to see.

As he gets closer, the light isn't kind.

Coeur's hands are swollen and black with bruising; he realizes with a lurch that they've been broken, and not recently. When she finally hears his step and groggily raises her head, one eye is swollen shut. She rolls her head to look at him, and for a long moment she doesn't seem to register who he is.

"Thala," he murmurs.

She laughs when she hears his voice, her own deep and hoarse.

"You here to finish me up, Willem, make it quick," she whispers. She coughs, a wretched hack that has her doubled over and hissing in pain. When she looks back up at him she has blood on her lips and she's grinning like the devil.

For a long moment he's staring at her throat, the fragile bones there he could so easily crush with his fingers, tell Ximena he found her like that, and by the time they got to help it would be all over. Or, what the hell, just shoot her and say the guards did instead of let her be rescued. Or shoot her and don't even bother hiding the fact, let Ximena go on to her own troubles without him.

He glances back at the doorway; Manu gives him a faint nod, a blessing on whatever choice he's about to make.

"The front is secured," Ximena says through the comm. "What's your status?"

"Still searching the apartment," Manu responds.

Jaantzen switches off his comm. Coeur's wild grin widens.

"I thought these asshole cultists were going to kill me," she says. "But I'd much rather it be you." She coughs again; he has the impression all he has to do is wait and nature will take care of his problem for him. Just one thumb in her already sunken suprasternal notch, held just long enough for the light to leave those already fading eyes. His fingers flex.

"If you're not here to kill me, what the fuck are you here for?" Coeur snarls, and there she is, the Blackheart he's always known shining fierce and feral through her one good eye and bloodied teeth. "I'm not going to beg. Just do it."

Before he can second-guess himself again, Jaantzen switches his microphone back on. "We're good," he says. "Can you walk?" he asks Coeur, and her good eye squints in disbelief. And then the sound of running footsteps across the courtyard, and Coeur's gaze slides over his shoulder as Ximena enters. Jaantzen hears the other woman's sharp gasp.

Manu hands Jaantzen the key, and he passes it over the interrogation desk. The cuffs fold back with a soft click and a savage curse from Coeur, then Ximena is at her side, gingerly lifting her sister's arm over her shoulders.

Coeur's knees buckle as Ximena tries to pull her to her

feet, and Ximena tightens her grip around her sister's waist. Coeur's a skeletal rag doll in her sister's arms.

Jaantzen should go to them, help Ximena. They don't have much time, and his pride could be the thing that gets them killed if he just lets Ximena struggle.

Jaantzen takes a deep breath of stale, putrid air and shoves aside the memories it conjures.

"Let's go," he snaps.

He turns and walks out of the room.

He doesn't watch them exit the apartment, but he does see the expression on Simca's face slide to horror at the moment Ximena and Coeur must have come out.

"Help them," he signs to her. He doesn't want Manu anywhere near the bitch.

Toshiyo's voice chimes in his ear. "Movement on the north side of the building," she says. "Three people maybe."

The window Jaantzen and Ximena came in through is on the west side of the building, which means they may still be fine with the original plan.

"I see them," El says. "Confirm three, starting to climb."

It's starting. Now to see if luck and planning will be on their side.

Jaantzen clears his throat. "Starla: meet us at the window."

And that's when he hears the first gunshots ring out.

STARLA

Starla sees it first, the shadow slinking within shadows down at the far end of the block.

Your 9, she messages El, sees him turn his head from his position at the wheel of the second spinner. He flashes her a thumbs-up.

Tosh, what do you see?

Toshiyo's reply takes a moment, and in that moment the shadows go dark and still once more. Starla isn't sure she didn't just imagine it.

Nothing in the immediate vicinity, responds Toshiyo.

Thought I saw something in the north alley.

Copy.

Starla drums her fingertips against the controls. She and El are idling at far ends of the block, giving them a three-quarter view of the surrounding area. Toshiyo's drone is filling in the gaps, and apart from the three guards inside the building, there's been no sign of life in this neighborhood.

Something is coming.

Something has to be coming.

Jaantzen and the others have been inside nine minutes when Starla sees the shadows shift again. This time it's a clear figure, a child peering around the corner.

Starla sits up straighter.

KID IN THE ALLEY, she messages to Toshiyo and El.

I SEE HER.

This is definitely the sort of neighborhood where unattended children could just be wandering by themselves — but the more likely explanation is the kid is a lookout for someone a bit more intimidating.

MOVEMENT ON THE NORTH SIDE OF THE BUILDING, Toshiyo says. It's on the common channel, so Manu and the others are getting it, too. THREE PEOPLE MAYBE.

I SEE THEM, responds El. CONFIRM THREE, STARTING TO CLIMB.

Seconds later, a message from Jaantzen appears on her lens. STARLA: MEET US AT THE WINDOW.

El's headlights glare to life at the same time Starla hits her own ignition switch; the spinner shivers to life around her.

And a spray of bullets slams against the glass of her rear window.

El's headlights flash and Starla banks out of his way just as he fires a pair of plasma blasts at whoever was just firing at her. Her rearview screen flares with the explosion.

HEAVY FIGHTING AT WINDOW, she types.

ANOTHER FIVE HEADING TOWARDS THE FRONT GATE, says Toshiyo.

Starla maneuvers her armored spinner to cover the window Jaantzen and Ximena went in through, then takes aim at a half-standing wall that seems to be providing cover for a pair of shooters. Direct hit — it explodes into rubble.

WE'RE TAKING FIRE AT APARTMENT TEN, Jaantzen says. *MEET US AT THE FRONT GATE.*

COPY, Starla types.

She's still taking fire from behind; flashes from El's spinner farther down the block tell her he's taking care of business there. She fires a missile rearward at her attackers, then guns it to the entrance.

The entrance is a miniature war zone. Jaantzen and his crew have taken cover at the gates, gunfire flying thick in both directions as they keep back an attack from across the street that's using the burnt-out facade of the other apartment building for cover. Her people are holding on, but just barely. And not for long.

She picks off two of their attackers with a spray of bullets, and another falls from a shot from Manu. Then another spray of bullets strafes the gates and the guardhouse, spitting out chips of brick and sparking against the metal. There's no way her crew can bridge the distance to where she is now.

Starla sidles her spinner closer, ignoring the scraping sensation of the security bollards meant to prevent vehicles from entering the walkway. They're only plastic, no match for the reinforced frame of the spinner. She rams them a second time, feels the spinner lurch free and edge into place between the shooters and her crew.

She hits the button that opens the back doors on the apartment side, and a bullet hits the spinner's center pillar and ricochets to bury itself into the headrest of the passenger seat. The initial three attackers El saw climbing the north side of the building must have gotten inside and are firing on Jaantzen's team from the other side. Manu has ducked into the guard booth to return fire while Jaantzen crouches in front of Starla's door, using the spinner for cover while still trying to hold off the attackers outside the complex.

EL GIVE COVER FRONT GATE, she types.

COMING.

A wave of human stench hits Starla like a fist. Ximena Nayar and Simca are crouched low, carefully helping a woman who's seen better days into the back of Starla's spinner. Starla catches only a glimpse of a face behind the shifting shadow of black braids, but even were it more badly beaten, she'd know it in a heartbeat.

Ximena shouts something to her, then disappears; the impact of the bullets around them is messing with her lens's ability to transcribe.

They can hold on, just another few seconds.

She can't see how many are attacking from inside the complex; more worrying is that the dozen originally at the front of the apartment building has grown to two dozen. They're surrounded, and even if they can get the rest of the crew in without any losses, they'll still need to get through the crowd. Starla cracks her window, fires twice, then flinches back as a blast from a plasma carbine scorches through, singeing the spinner's headliner; the acrid burning smell is a welcome relief from Coeur.

She cranes her neck to look for the shooter and sees something much more alarming.

A man holding a shoulder-fired short-range missile launcher.

She yells at Simca, who sees the launcher and ducks inside the spinner just in time. A bright flash hits between the side window and the windshield, sending rippling waves of heat over Starla and scorching an oily rainbow discoloration in the tempered glass.

Warning lights light up the control panel. They can't sustain another one of those.

The man with the missile launcher stoops behind a concrete planter to reload.

"Distract him," Simca signs from the back seat.

Starla cracks her window again, peppers the man's hiding spot with bullets. The instant she stops, the man rolls from his hiding spot, missile launcher aimed. Simca's a fraction of a second faster. A bullet from her rifle strikes the launcher and the whole thing explodes.

When Starla's vision clears, the man is lying in the street, one bloody arm outstretched towards the launcher. Another half-dozen bodies lie around him, taken out by the same blast. Simca slams her window up against another hail of bullets and shoots Starla a grin.

While Starla'd been focused on neutralizing the man with the missile launcher, Manu slid into the passenger seat. Blood slicks his neck and cheek, but he gives her a thumbs-up. Jaantzen fires one more round over the roof of the spinner, then turns to pull Ximena in with him.

The spinner rocks with a thud Starla can feel in her chest.

At first she thinks she's been hit by another missile, but then she sees him: a huge man had dropped from the apartment windows above the spinner, landing on the roof and rolling off to the passenger side. He flings Ximena out of the way and reaches in to grab Coeur.

Starla draws her pistol and unloads the clip in his chest. He staggers back.

And charges again.

What the hell?

Ximena tackles him from behind and he growls as though annoyed, twists out of the spinner to grab her by the throat. He raises himself to his full height just outside the spinner, Ximena's feet dangling above the pavement. Blood soaks the man's shirt front and back; a bullet has torn through the bicep of the arm that holds Ximena.

None of them have a clear shot, not with the way the giant is holding Ximena in front of him.

"She's an Alliance officer," Jaantzen says, but if the man recognizes the words, he doesn't make a move.

"Be ready," Manu signs to Starla. She nods. He places one hand on the door handle, and Starla's grip tightens on the controls, waiting. For a merciful moment, the sensory overload of sparks and shuddering as the hail of bullets rains down on them is silenced. Manu holds three fingers out. Two. One.

And flinches back from the window; the huge man's head disappears in a fine red mist.

In her rearview, Starla sees El disappear back into his sunroof, sniper rifle in hand. Jaantzen pulls Ximena into the back seat of the spinner and slams the door shut.

Starla hits the accelerator.

12

JAANTZEN

"I'm too old for this," Jaantzen says.

His right knee aches more than usual, his shoulder blazes with pain whenever he lifts his arm above shoulder height, and he suspects tomorrow he's going to find sore muscles he didn't even know he had.

Manu cracks his neck, rolls his shoulders. "I wasn't going to be the first to say it."

Despite how they all looked on their return to Cobalt Tower, most of the crew have cleaned up fine. Manu needed a couple of stitches on a gash behind his ear, Ximena had only a few scrapes, and Starla is going to have a good bruise on her cheek in the morning. Simca Anahoy is preternaturally chipper and seems unharmed; if El's tired or injured he's not showing it. They had the element of surprise and coordination on their side. That won't work the next time they encounter the Dawn.

They were smart; they were lucky. Jaantzen isn't going to let that go to his head.

"That was an awful lot of firepower for a religious cult,

even if they're backed by Dry Creek," says Manu, like he's been reading Jaantzen's mind.

"Find me everything you can about them," Jaantzen says. "I want to know everything about Bennion Zacharia: Who he does business with. Where he came from. What his favorite restaurants are. Where he sleeps and with whom."

"On it, boss."

Jaantzen stretches his shoulders, considering. In the old days, he'd expect retaliation to arrive later, after his enemies had had a chance to lick their wounds and consider how to hit him where it would hurt the most. But the Dawn, that's a blind spot.

The Dry Creek crew is petty and vicious, running drugs, prostitution, protection rackets, trafficking — all preying on the weakest in the city. But they keep to themselves, apart from occasional clashes with Coeur's crew where their territories butt up against each other. The Dawn mainly makes headlines when they manage to convert some rich kid with influential parents, and the feeds all scramble to run salacious details of their religion: the weeklong, shard-fueled rituals, the catastrophic end-times prophecies, the fact that their prophet is a prisoner at Redrock. All accompanied by static photos featuring the cold, blue-eyed stare of Bennion Zacharia, who no one seems to know a thing about.

After a while, though, the rich kid either comes home or the story goes stale, and the Dawn goes back to sweeping up street kids and pumping shard into the city in obscurity.

Except now they seem to be making a move. Aligning themselves with the Dry Creek crew on the one hand and Acheta on the other. But to what end? Business, Jaantzen can understand. Purity and preparation for the end times?

It's on a completely different wavelength from the rest of Bulari's underworld.

"We need to know who else in this town is doing business with the Dawn. We need to know what deal they made with Acheta."

"I've already put out feelers."

"And no one learns about Coeur."

"Of course. Security clearances for floor twelve have already been updated to you and me only. Anybody else gets a one-time code authed by one of us, or comes in with us. I'll debrief the Anahoys and Elian when they're out."

Jaantzen blinks a moment at the second name. Ah, yes. The medic Gia sent over. A graduate of her training school, one she trusts and thought would be well-suited to the sorts of things Jaantzen tends to need emergency medics for.

"Good," he says. "Tap two others you trust for general guard duty on this floor — they don't need to know who they're guarding."

"Already done."

The twelfth floor of Cobalt Tower has two secure medical suites like the one they're standing in now: a small waiting room with one-way observation glass, an operating theater with no expenses spared on the latest medical technology. And tonight one of those suites also contains a ruined but ferocious Blackheart, Ximena beside her, El and Simca standing guard at the doorway while Gia's hand-picked medic edges around them to examine Coeur's hands.

"I had a room prepped for Ximena down the hall," Manu says. He's got his back to the glass, but the tension in his shoulders says he's fully aware who's behind him. "You want her there now, or?"

"I want to talk to them both first."

A twitch in Manu's cheek. "Could be that waits till morning," he says.

"We need what she knows sooner rather than later."

"Understood. Do you want . . ."

"Take care of the security."

Manu's shoulders loosen.

"On it."

He gives Jaantzen a sharp nod, then walks past him to make arrangements. After the first stiff couple of steps down the hallway, Manu's stride evens out into his usual liquid saunter, exhaustion showing only in how he holds his shoulders, rubs the back of his neck.

Jaantzen straightens his cuffs. Even if this could wait until morning, he'd never be able to sleep, not with the devil in his house.

Coeur's staring at the screen in front of her. At first his mind can't make sense of the image. Then, with dawning revulsion, he realizes the image projected there is from the medic's scanner: Coeur's hands, formed now of fragments of bone lined up in stuttered columns.

She's studying each crack and shatter as the medic — Elian — scans them. Jaantzen wants to look away, but he forces himself to watch with her. There's a break on every finger, and almost every metacarpal.

She'll never box again. She may never feed herself again.

She spares him a look when he slips into the room, then goes back to examining her bones. "What are my options, doc?" she asks.

"You'll need surgery, of course. A good surgeon can put plates in, rebuild the structure." Elian clears his throat; he knows exactly who his patient is. "We'll need to rebreak a few. It'll take some time to heal, and I can't promise they'll be good as new."

"What's fastest?"

The medic's frowning. "Fastest to heal?"

"Fastest I can kill the assholes who did this to me."

"Fastest would be to hire someone," Jaantzen says. "Look at them. You're never fighting again."

Thala Coeur gives him a look, head tilted to the side, eyes bright with a gold spark of banked fury that's not directed at him, though he's borne the brunt of it in the past.

"You need a skilled surgeon," Elian says. "We should call . . ."

Jaantzen shoots him a warning look, and the medic trails off. There's no way. He's trying to figure out how to phrase it when Coeur laughs.

"Don't bother Giaconda for me," she says. "Call Naali. She'll have someone she trusts."

"Naali is dead," Jaantzen says.

Coeur's eyes close, a flutter of something that in another woman might be grief, but with Coeur looks like resignation. "Was it Ratham?" she asks.

"Acheta."

"Acheta." There's a speculative chill to the way Coeur tastes the man's name. Levi Acheta's not long for this world if Coeur gets near him.

"You left a troublesome crew when you died," Jaantzen says.

A sly smile touches the corner of her bloodied mouth. "That's the nicest thing anyone's ever said to me, Willem."

"I'm sure it is." He turns away. "Go speak with Manu," he signs to Simca and El.

El frowns. "Starla said . . ."

But El trails off at the look on Jaantzen's face, just like

the medic did. Back in his younger days, Jaantzen had thought that expression of uneasy deference on his crew's faces was a measure of how much they respected him. He's learned since that actual respect is based on trust, not fear — but apparently he hasn't lost the ability to silence someone with a glare.

Coeur brings out the best in him.

El and Simca give him a salute and leave. Starla will be furious with him, but he's safe as he's ever been here. He trusts Ximena not to do anything stupid, and Coeur isn't attacking anyone with her hands like that. Elian is bandaging them now, in a parody of the wraps she used to wear in the boxing ring. Jaantzen would like to think saving her life would have earned him some protection from her, too, but he's not naive.

"Is she stable for the night?" he asks Elian, who is clearly expecting to be dismissed next.

"There's nothing more I can do tonight. I'll give her a dose of sedat — "

"No, pup," Coeur says. And her jaguar's smile stops the medic cold.

"Show me," Jaantzen says, and Elian points out the controls on the medical monitor. His finger hovers over the arm restraints tab, and Jaantzen reaches past him to press it himself. Wide straps snake up and over Coeur's arms, binding them to the armrests. She growls out a curse of pain.

"Go talk to Mr. Juric," Jaantzen says. "Then get some rest. I want you on call, but don't come in here alone, even if it looks like she's dying — this bitch will try to murder you. Bring a guard."

The medic nods, checks a few last settings on the monitor, then slips out of the room.

And Coeur leans back with a sigh of relief. "It was getting claustrophobic in here. Your muscleheads breathing up all the good oxygen. And that jumpy little lamb couldn't possibly be old enough to have a medical degree. Is he one of Gia's?"

"My apologies on the lodgings," Jaantzen says. "I would put you up in one of the guest suites, but I don't want your blood on my nice sheets."

"And these beds come with restraints," Coeur says, waggling her swaddled, bound hands as though she thought she'd get any sympathy from him.

"I'd prefer not to need them." Jaantzen pulls a stool from the corner and perches near the foot of the bed. Out of reach; even in her current state he's taking no chances. "But I don't trust you."

Coeur's always-lean frame is now skeletal, her rust-red cheeks sunken and bruised, her collarbones edging like knives from the neck of her hospital gown. Now that the medic's gone, Ximena dims the lights; even in the lower light Coeur looks half-dead.

"So," Jaantzen says. "I see you're bad at making friends on Indira, too."

"People everywhere are unreliable, Willem. It's a shame."

He inclines his head. "I find it's not difficult to get good help if you're not trash yourself."

Coeur smiles at that. "Are you upset that I haven't thanked you yet?"

"I don't want your gratitude. I want to know what the hell is going on."

Coeur laughs, the sound hoarse and ending in a wet cough that she buries against the shoulder of the arm that's not attached to the IVs. When she can breathe again, she sighs deeply and slumps against the pillows.

"I'm a lucky woman," she says. "Ending up here in a room with the only two people in the world I can trust."

"Excuse me?"

"You're uninteresting, Willem. Not in the ways most others are, but in your predictability. That took me way too long to understand. I can trust you'll tell me exactly what you think of me, and I can trust that you'll keep your word no matter what. You kept your agreement with my sister tonight. A lesser man might not have."

A secret smile spreads across her face; she knew exactly what he'd been thinking in those moments before he called Ximena. She saw the strength of will it took not to just end her then and there. And apparently she's not going to say anything to Ximena. Not yet.

"I've kept my promises," Jaantzen says. "But now you're dead and Bulari is breathing a sigh of relief. So explain to me, Thala. Why should I reverse that gift the universe has given us all?"

Coeur closes her eyes for a moment, long enough that Jaantzen begins to wonder if she's finally passed out from the incredible amount of pain she must be in. But then her lids flutter open once more and her face cracks into a shadow of her old million-mark smile. She's missing an eyetooth.

"You remember back when we were both just kids?" she asks. "You were running a crew out of that apartment building down on Fifteenth. You had that lieutenant, what was his name?"

"Kai."

She lets out a gentle sigh. "Kai. He was a shit pick for a lieutenant."

The betrayal no longer stings; he had been a terrible pick. "It happens."

"That Manu, though." Her smile turns wicked. "Mmm, he was a delicious catch."

Cold fire blooms in Jaantzen's belly, and it's not until Ximena moves to stop him that he realizes he's half out of his stool, fist balled to do damage.

Coeur laughs through split lips. "Don't leave a bruise, Willem," she says.

"Thala," snaps Ximena, and to Jaantzen's mild shock, Coeur looks chastened. "Stop being a bitch or I'll lose my temper myself."

Jaantzen forces himself back onto his seat, but it takes him longer than he would like to calm himself down; he can't afford to let exhaustion dull his edge. Manu had been a catch for Jaantzen, certainly, but the word's double-edged. It conjures up an image of Manu's spinner in a ditch on the outskirts of town, one of his soldiers' throat cut in the driver's seat. Three days of waiting for the demand that finally came: a dozen of her soldiers for his lieutenant. In the end Jaantzen had acquiesced.

A full day had passed without word before, early one morning, a body found in a playground in Jaantzen's territory. Badly mangled, beaten and bloody. But alive. Jaantzen and Gia had gotten there well before the city's first responders, and as expected, as hoped, as feared, it had been Manu: half-dressed and destroyed, his face barely recognizable, his left arm and right ankle at impossible angles, his breath coming shallow and wheezing as though a lung was pierced.

His body a message for the gathering neighborhood crowd: this is what happens to those who side with Jaantzen.

He'd been unconscious until they transferred him to the stretcher, until a bad jolt had woken him suddenly, horribly, with a scream that brought the rest of the neighborhood running. Jaantzen remembers Gia's techs on him with their full weight to hold him down, her left hand on his forehead like a vise, her right jabbing him in the neck with a sedative.

Jaantzen remembers ordering a cleanup crew to stay behind and rid the playground of all traces of the blood that had soaked into the concrete, splashed on the play structures, smeared glossy on the grass. He remembers how, back home, Gia had taken it one excruciating step at a time, cutting away Manu's clothes to reveal a chest blackened with bruising and clotted with blood, left shoulder and elbow dislocated, left wrist and hand mangled, burn scars on his calves and feet, his right tibia and fibula each broken in three places.

Now Jaantzen's fighting flashbacks of standing in a room not dissimilar to this one, staring at Manu's ruined body, Gia up to her arms in his blood, the sound of him choking on the breathing tube, the sweet and saline perfume blend of sweat and whatever luminous blue fluid Gia had used to fill the tank Manu was lying in; she's calmly reassuring Jaantzen that it will stabilize Manu even though it looks for all the world like he's drowning. Threads of pink twisting out into the currents from wounds too small for Gia's attentions. Manu wakes again with a panicked start to thrash against the glass, and Jaantzen's USL back then is so limited compared to what Manu and Gia and the others have picked up, but he knows enough to sign "You're safe, you're home" over and over until the sedative kicks in and Manu's eyes close once more.

The memory is here and gone in a flash, and Jaantzen is still face to face with Thala Coeur.

She's not smiling any more. "Are you ready for another civil war, Willem?" she asks. "Naali and Levi didn't like each other, but they both knew they couldn't hold my crew on their own. If Levi had the balls to kill Naali, that means he has a patron. Would've gone the other way, too. A smart man in your shoes would've made a move on Naali."

She lifts an eyebrow, considering. "You planned to, hmm? Too slow, I guess. Though it's hard to be slower than Levi . . ." She trails off, slow realization dawning. "Shit."

Jaantzen watches her, waiting; her eyes smolder.

"Zacharia got to him, didn't he?" she says. "He would've had all the time in the world to make the sale, what with knowing ahead of time I was going to be dead."

"Tell me about Bennion Zacharia," Jaantzen says. "What would his cult want with your crew?"

"Distribution for his shitty drugs. When did they say I was dead?"

"How long did the Dawn have you?"

"Three weeks," Coeur says, and there's poison seeping through those words. If the Dawn knew Coeur the way he did, they would have killed her. Instead, they forged themselves a vicious rival. He doesn't envy them.

"You only died yesterday," Jaantzen says.

"How'd they say it happened?"

"Shot in the back of the head on Indira. News feeds say it was a break-in."

She makes an offended noise in the back of her throat. "A fucking stupid way to go."

On the surface, the alliance between Acheta and the Dawn makes sense. Whereas Naali Hinoja had always steered Blackheart's crew towards diversifying their business and creating something sustainable, Acheta had preferred the quick, volatile cash that came from the crew's drug trade. He would want an agreement with the chief suppliers of those drugs — and the Dawn would fear losing one of their biggest distributors if Hinoja took control of the crew.

But Coeur's original tiff with the Dawn wasn't about drugs.

"Tell me what's in the case," Jaantzen says.

"A business proposition," Coeur says. A strained roll of her eyes takes in her older sister, who's standing stiff as a soldier at her shoulder. "How much did Mina tell you?"

"Pretend I don't know anything," Jaantzen says evenly.

Coeur coughs, winces. "Fair. Let me tell you about the Alliance."

"I know about the Alliance."

"No, you don't," Coeur snaps. "Big man up here in your fancy suits and glittering tower. You might as well be them, now."

She's trying to goad him again; he doesn't know if it's to make a point, or if it just comes as second nature to her. "If you're done with conversation, I'll go speak with my crew about what to do with you," Jaantzen says. "Your call."

The fierce expression on her face smooths. So it had been instinctive after all.

"I didn't know, either," she says, and it's as close to an apology as Jaantzen will ever get out of her. "I was a kid when all those countries on Indira signed the Eyes of Durga Treaty, so I never knew what the planet was like before Alliance rule. I just saw their propaganda, same as anyone else."

Jaantzen has seen it, too, he remembers the unification videos shown at the orphanage, he remembers seeing images of kids just like himself in poverty-stricken countries, the before-and-after shots of their shacks turned into modern homes, their clothes clean and tidy.

He remembers wishing the Alliance would take over New Sarjun, too.

"But then I'm living there, right?" Coeur says. "Thanks for that. And it doesn't take much looking to see that under the propaganda vids, Indira's still falling apart. What land overpopulation hasn't fucked has been bombed to ash to beat down resistance fighters, or torn up by wars they're pretending no one's fighting. They're still exporting food to us and Durga's Belt because we can pay for it, unlike people from New Manila or any other country on Indira that's not Arquelle. When you first shipped me over to that rock there were riots every few months. Now it's every week. Mina show you those photos? Open fields in the desert?"

Jaantzen nods slowly. "So if the Alliance has found a way to reclaim the land they've destroyed . . ."

"Or to grow crops at scale on New Sarjun and ship them back."

That all makes sense, but something still isn't sitting right.

"What does the Dawn want the tech for?" Jaantzen asks.

"Same reason anyone would," Coeur says. "It turns dirt into gold, Willem. The Alliance needs food, and you and I? We're going to give it to them and get rich doing it."

A business proposition. Working with Thala Coeur. He wants to laugh at the absurdity of her offer, but this night has gone on far too long for laughter.

"The serum, or whatever it is in the case," he says. "It makes land arable."

"Correct."

"And I have it in my possession. So what do I need you for?"

"You don't know how to use it. The research is top secret."

"And you have this research?"

"I can get it."

That false bravado in the pursing of her lips, that little shrug. Coeur doesn't know where this research is any more than he does. Quiet beeps and hums fill the room around them, cut through by the rasping of Coeur's breath. Jaantzen rolls his shoulders, considering.

"I've been made better offers," he says finally.

She lifts an eyebrow, conceding. "True. But you saw the fight you're up against with the Dawn and their new pet crew. You started a war with them tonight. Can you afford to be at war with my crew, too?"

She has one real offer, they both know it. And it's the last thing he can consider.

"Put you back in power," Jaantzen says.

"You need me right now. This city needs me."

Jaantzen's heard all he wants to tonight. He gets to his feet as gracefully as he can, willing his tired body not to betray any sign of the injuries he's sustained.

"I'll see you in the morning, Thala."

"Do you have to talk it over with your masters first?" Coeur asks with a cold smile.

"Thala," snaps Ximena.

"You know what your problem is? You see everything through their perspective. What will Geum-ja think? What will Julieta think? Let me tell you my little secret for success: I don't give a shit what other people think."

"You're looking very successful right now," Jaantzen says. He can't deny the truth in her words: he's spent years learning the rules for success, only to fall short not because of how he played the game, but because of where he came from. Coeur, on the other hand, has never bothered to learn a single rule. It may have shot her all the way to the mayor's office, but it also sent her into exile without a single true ally, even within her own crew.

"I remember you before you wore such nice suits," Coeur says. "Back when you spent all your energy railing against the very society you're so desperate to join today."

Coeur's laugh turns into a cough. It's painful to listen to, and Ximena tenses; he wonders if there's fluid in her lungs, wonders at what point he should call the medic back in. He's reaching for the button when she spits blood onto the floor, shoos one stiff, bound hand at him.

"I'm fine," she says. "Let the cub be."

Jaantzen's finger hovers near the button a moment longer, but her cough seems to have gone down. "We play the game differently," he says. "And one of us is a fugitive in a hospital bed, while the other is a respected member of society."

"Fortune's wheel spins quick, Willem. Don't get cocky."

"That's excellent advice, Thala." He turns to the medical monitor, presses the button Elian had shown him. "Good night."

Coeur takes a sharp breath, glassy eyes sparking with fury. "Dammit, Willem. Fu — "

Her eyes flutter shut.

Ximena collapses onto the cot beside her sister's bed, exhaustion etched into the lines of her face. When she meets his eyes, her expression is troubled. Of course, she's never actually seen him with her sister, and who knows how long it's been since they've seen each other in person.

Maybe Ximena truly had no idea how much pain Thala Coeur has caused.

"Willem. I'm — "

"Don't," he says, because he's not ready to stomach any more complicated emotions from this particular bloodline. If I had a family, he almost says, but he stops himself. Because, of course, he does have a family. "I would move heaven and earth for my family," he says instead, and her shoulders slump as though she has just received a benediction.

Jaantzen buttons his suit jacket; he's not in the business of blessings.

"You're welcome to sleep here, or we've set up a guest room on this floor. You'll be under guard either way."

She nods. "What are you planning to do with me?"

"That depends in large part on your sister. Good night, Ximena. Let my people know if you need anything."

———

The lights are already on in Jaantzen's penthouse suite, Starla and Manu at his conference table, a decanter and three glasses between them. Starla's got both elbows on the table, one hand holding a glass of ice to her cheek. Manu's feet are kicked up in the chair beside him, his fingers steepled over his stomach. He's staring at the ceiling. They don't appear to have been talking, and neither glances up as the elevator doors open, though Starla reaches to pour whiskey in the third glass.

On the eastern horizon the finger slums are dark, but a line of dusty pink rims the plateau they claw into. As though triggered by the realization of the time, a wave of exhaustion crashes into Jaantzen. He pushes it off, lowers himself gingerly into his chair at the head of the conference table.

"It's been a few years since I saw this side of the sunrise," he says. He drains the glass of whiskey Starla poured.

Starla glances at him, brow furrowed and eyes clear, and he belatedly realizes she's taken out her lens.

"I haven't been up this late for a while," he signs.

She makes a tired face. "It's way more fun when you're out dancing," she signs.

"I'm sure it is."

Manu's rolled his head to watch them; now he drops his feet to the floor and sits up, reaching for his own glass.

"Floor twelve's secured," he signs when he's set his glass down. It's empty. "El and Simca are getting some rest, and I've tripled security on this building. Calls out in the usual places for soldiers, for when we need them."

"We'll need them," Jaantzen signs. "We just declared war on Dry Creek. And the Dawn. I need to know what their strength is."

Manu nods slowly. "What about Acheta?"

Jaantzen refills Manu's glass, stalling. Tops off his own, trying to think of a way to say it. Manu's watching him, exhaustion slowly replaced by understanding, then anger. He's shaking his head by the time Jaantzen begins to sign again.

"Coeur thinks she can control her crew if we put her back in power," Jaantzen signs.

Starla's eyebrows shoot up. "You can't be serious."

"Option one," signs Jaantzen. "We plunge this city into another civil war with one of the biggest crews in Bulari, who's allied with a cult that has a lot more firepower than we understand. Option two. We install her as a puppet back in her crew, keep her busy fighting the Dawn and Dry Creek, and deal with her when they're contained."

Manu arches an eyebrow. "A major problem with both plans," he signs. "Coeur murders us all and everyone we've ever loved."

Jaantzen nods, tired.

Manu holds up a finger. "Solution? We murder her first."

Starla laughs, but Jaantzen can see in Manu's expression that it's not a joke.

"It's not so easy as that," he signs.

Manu shrugs. "Or, it's actually super easy, because she's just downstairs and she can't fight back. We load her up in a plane, push her out over the desert."

"And Ximena?"

"If we charter a big enough plane — "

"We're not killing Coeur," Jaantzen says, cutting in, then he switches back to USL. "Not until we have a clear understanding of what we're up against, and whether or not we can handle both the Dawn and Acheta on our own."

Manu's nostrils flare slightly, but then he gives Jaantzen an easy nod. "Sure thing, boss."

"But this is not something we do lightly. Once she's done being useful, she's gone."

Manu raises an eyebrow. "Just like that?"

"Find me the thing we need to control her. Her kill switch."

"We can't blackmail her."

Jaantzen shakes his head. Of course they can't — there would be no faster way to find themselves on the opposite side of her knife.

"Just find me leverage."

"You got it, boss," Manu murmurs. Jaantzen can already

see Manu's mind racing. Where Jaantzen tends to keep his social circle tight, Manu has collected friends and favors in corners of Bulari's underground Jaantzen probably hasn't even heard of. If anyone can find the leverage they need to shut Coeur back down when they need to, it's him.

Starla snaps her fingers for their attention. "We're missing another option here. We dump this thing on the doorstep of the *Bulari Sentinel* and tell them the Alliance found mysterious terraforming technology on New Sarjun that they're not sharing with us."

"Probably Coeur still murders us all," signs Manu.

She rolls her eyes at him. "This doesn't belong to her, or to us. People are dying of starvation. And if we don't take it from the Alliance, they'll use it against us."

Jaantzen shakes his head. "We're not going to the press."

"Your government contacts, then."

"Not until I know what's going to happen."

"You can never know that." Starla takes a sharp breath, and her hands pause mid-sign before she lets them fall in her lap, deciding against whatever she was going to say.

"We need to control it. Let it out the way we want."

Starla's hands snap back up. "That's just what the Alliance would say. That it's not good for the public; we should control it."

He brushes off the sting. "We're all tired," he signs, or thinks he signs. In his own exhaustion he may have used the sign for *angry*. He supposes either works in this context.

"They'll use it against us," she signs again, insistent. "You can't trust the Alliance."

"Of course I don't trust them," he says aloud, irritated. What he wants to say is that she has to get over her prejudices, that everyone's lost someone to the Alliance. Although that's not entirely true, is it? The only thing the

Alliance has taken from him is Thala Coeur, and they sent her back with compliments. He holds up a hand to forestall any more argument.

"No one is killing Coeur or going to the press tonight."

Jaantzen stands, buttons his suit jacket. The planet's dawn is brightening the sky above the horizon now. He's feeling it like a vise gripping his temple.

"Both of you get some sleep," he says. "Starla?"

"I know, I'm staying here."

"Thank you for putting an old man's mind at ease."

Manu gives him a tired salute, but Starla slips her cool, smooth hand into his big rough one, lacing her fingers through his. She gives his hand a gentle squeeze, then turns and leaves.

13

STARLA

Starla loves the fourth floor.

The lingering bitter ozone scent of solder, the feeling of solitude, the inspiration of infinite possibility as she walks through the clutter of half-finished projects and salvaged equipment, fingers trailing through piles of miniature screws and coils of wiring and stacks of circuitry as if by feel she'll make a connection and solve a particularly thorny problem.

She comes here when she can. It takes her back to a childhood spent in the engineering level of Silk Station, up to her elbows in engine grease and salvaged bits of machinery, tinkering on projects of her own or helping Silk Station's chief engineer, Deyva, with some repair job or other.

Starla can't think of anyone more unlike Deyva than Toshiyo, though. Where he was taciturn and content to work for hours without conversation, Toshiyo is a constant stream of jokes and observations. She's never picked up much USL, but her fingerspelling is lightning fast, and she seems to understand most of what Starla tells her. It's not the easy conversation Starla has with Manu or with her few friends outside the crew — other deaf USL speakers she's met in Bulari. But it works.

Today, though, with Ximena in the conference room, Toshiyo is almost entirely verbal, Starla reading along as well as she can as her lens transcribes.

They're at the far end of a long faux-marble desk. It's equipped with state-of-the-art visual and computational technology, but at the moment it's serving merely as a work-bench for a surveillance satellite Starla and Toshiyo have been trying to restore for months. The satellite's strewn across almost the entire surface; still, Toshiyo has managed to clear a bit of space to serve as conference table.

There, a silver case the length of Starla's arm sits alone.

She finds it vaguely comforting. She's not sure if that's because she's seen the goddess etched into the top before, or because it, too, reminds her of home. Little household gods used to grace the corridors and quarters of Silk Station, each branch of her sprawling family with their own totem depicted in relief or paint, draped with fabric scraps and other offerings.

All those gods, now drifting broken in Durga's Belt, trailing behind the dwarf planet chain in a path of wreckage.

Ximena's hands pause over the goddess's snake heads before she gently wedges the tip of each thumb into the small depressions under both chins.

Toshiyo cracks her ring fingers in unison.

Starla takes an involuntary step back.

With the tips of her thumbnails, Ximena presses into the case, and after a pause, it finally gives, shifts. Ximena lifts off the invisible faceplate covering the upper half of the case.

From there it's simply a code entered in the keypad, no biolocks keyed to Ximena, nothing intricate at all. Ridiculously easy, if you can just find the way to the keypad.

HOW DO YOU KNOW THE CODE, Starla types into her gauntlet; she taps a fingernail on the words where they appear on the conference table so Ximena notices.

"It's always the same code with Thala and me," Ximena says. She's working the lid off the case now. "Though I suppose that'll have to change."

Starla shares a look with Toshiyo. They haven't told Ximena or Coeur that the other case has come into their possession as well, and now it seems they don't need Ximena to open that one.

Ximena lifts the lid off and sets it carefully aside; Starla takes a breath of relief. So far, they've managed not to blow Cobalt Tower to bits. All things considered, today is going pretty well.

"That's the serum everybody seems to want?" Toshiyo asks.

A round glass bubble filled with clear liquid is nestled perfectly into a bed of molded foam. A few air bubbles are trapped beneath the surface of the glass, but otherwise it's filled to the brim. There's a small hatch at the top, sealed shut.

Toshiyo runs her scanner over it. "Let's see what this magical stuff is," she says.

After a moment, her scanner blinks with the results. Toshiyo makes a face, passes it over to Starla.

"What is it?" Ximena asks.

"Some kind of joke," Toshiyo says. "I mean, I'll do some more testing. But it's just fertilizer."

Starla reads through the ingredients: available phosphate, soluble potash, urea nitrogen, ammoniacal nitrogen, nitrate nitrogen, chelated iron, manganese, zinc.

A helpful popup on the scanner informs her that the closest known substance with that exact chemical makeup is commercial-grade liquid fertilizer, with a 99.7 percent probable match.

Starla hands the scanner to Ximena.

"Fertilizer," says Toshiyo. "I mean, yeah, that'll definitely help your plants grow. But I can buy this stuff down at the store. Julieta probably has barrels of it over at her greenhouse."

IF ONLY SHE KNEW IT WOULD MAKE HER RICH, Starla types, SHE COULD GIVE UP HER LIFE OF CRIME.

"There has to be something more," Ximena says.

Toshiyo shrugs. "Sure, there's got to be. I'll take a sample and run tests. Can I — do you think I can pull this out?"

"I don't see why not."

Toshiyo gently prises the glass sphere out while Ximena holds the foam down. It pops free; Toshiyo cradles it in her palms.

"Heavy," she says, holding it up to her face to take a better look. "Oh, hey. There's something else in here. At the bottom."

Starla leans in to take a better look. An object exactly the size and shape of a black-eyed pea floats near the bottom of the glass, drifting peacefully along the curved surface as Toshiyo turns the sphere in her hands.

"Maybe it's a super bean," Toshiyo says. She sets the sphere in a stand on the conference table, then scans it again, concentrating on the bean. Frowns at her scanner. "That's weird."

Starla raises an eyebrow: What is?

"Nothing. I mean, it's just not registering it."

"Maybe whatever it is, is meant to grow in the fertilizer solution?" Ximena asks.

"I have no clue," Toshiyo says. "I can pull this case's support systems apart, put it back together, and build you a better one. But this biology stuff? Not my deal. We could take it to Julieta."

Starla shakes her head. Jaantzen trusts Yang, and Starla trusts Jaantzen, but until they know for sure what this thing is and how Julieta Yang is involved, the old woman's staying on Starla's list of suspicious characters.

"This stays inside our crew for now," Starla signs to Toshiyo.

Ximena's nodding as she watches Starla sign, though Starla's not certain how much she understands. "The fewer people who know about it, the better," Ximena says. "People are getting killed over this and we don't know why." A muscle twitches in her cheek. Starla wonders if she's thinking about her sister, broken and laid out upstairs because of this thing.

"Figure out what it is," Starla signs to Toshiyo. "I want to have something we can tell Jaantzen when we meet this evening."

Toshiyo nods. "I'm on it, but if this thing is a plant, we might be screwed." She points across the conference room, where a limp brown spider plant hangs in the window, spindly leaves crisp as charred paper.

Starla remembers when Julieta gifted it to Toshiyo with the reassurance that it would be deathproof against Toshiyo's brown thumb.

"You were supposed to water it," Starla signs.

"It's impossible to kill spider plants," Ximena says. Starla smiles at her.

"I forgot it was here," Toshiyo says. "But that's not the point. The point is if this little bean is some sort of plant, I'm maybe not your woman." Her fingers move to the seal at the top of the sphere.

Starla waves her hands. "What are you doing?"

"Gotta get it out," Toshiyo says.

Whatever this substance is, people are dying for it. Starla does *not* want it splattered all over the conference table.

"Not yet," she signs. "Or not here. Let's just learn some more about it before we expose ourselves to whatever's inside."

Toshiyo frowns at her. "Fine. But we're gonna have to open it eventually."

"We'll figure it out," Starla signs. "I'll do some research."

On whatever the substance could be, of course, but also on who might know a thing or two about plants — and isn't Julieta Yang. If what Coeur told them is true and this fancy fertilizer can transform the deserts of Northern New Sarjun into arable land, it's worth a fortune. And if they're going to do anything with it, they can't go into it half-assed. Starla may not know much about plants, but she's learned a thing or two about running a business since Jaantzen put her in charge of Admant Security. They're going to need experts, scientists. The best in their field.

"I know I'm just here to open the case, and I respect that," Ximena says, the words blinking across Starla's vision, breaking into her thoughts. Starla turns to her. "But can I offer you some advice?"

She's looking at Starla as she says it. Starla lifts her chin in assent.

"The things Thala said about terraforming may sound fantastic, but I can tell you it's happening. I've seen it myself. And with what she went through to steal this serum and ship it here, I'm sure it's valuable. But I wouldn't take anything she's told you at face value."

Starla gives her a look like, No shit, and Ximena holds up her hands.

"I know, I know. You don't need me to tell you that. But you've all been fair to me, and more than generous to my sister. She may not care about that, but I want you to know that I do."

WHAT ARE YOU SAYING? Starla types.

"I'm saying that I want to see this used the right way. To help people. I'm not sure what Thala's plans are, but helping people isn't usually at the top of her list. If there's anything I can do, please ask."

UNDERSTOOD, Starla types. *THANK YOU.*

Ximena nods. "Thank you." Her shoulders rise and fall with the depth of her breath. "Can I help?" she asks.

Starla considers a moment. Her first instinct is to escort Ximena back to her secure quarters on floor twelve, but she is being helpful — and actually not bad company for somebody who's spent most of her career working for the Alliance. And so long as she isn't left alone with Toshiyo, Starla can keep an eye on her. She'd been planning on heading back to her own office to research, but they *do* have a nearly new, perfectly functional, state-of-the-art conference table she could use right here.

She clears a space for Ximena, creates a secure guest login, and indicates for the other woman to sit.

YOU REALLY WANT TO MAKE A DIFFERENCE? Starla asks. *COPY THE PHOTOS YOU TOOK INTO THIS ACCOUNT, THEN WRITE DOWN EVERYTHING YOU KNOW. THE MORE DETAIL, THE BETTER.*

Ximena hesitates for only a moment, then pulls out her comm and sits down.

Starla clears another spot for herself, logs in to her own account, and pulls up an academic research search portal. They're going to need an outside expert for this one.

"Work party!" Toshiyo exclaims. She pulls up the Jungle's menu, scrolls through the daily empanada specials. "Who's hungry?"

14

JAANTZEN

Twice, Manu has hired a housekeeper and cook to work personally for Jaantzen.

Twice, Jaantzen has shuffled that person off to somewhere else.

The first was a matronly New Manilan refugee who could make rice taste like heaven, and whom Jaantzen recommended to Julieta Yang after only three days. The second was a young woman from the Fingers with exquisite skill for combining sweet and savory. She now works as sous chef at the Jungle; Jaantzen politely got her a job there at the end of her first day. Jaantzen doesn't care how well-vetted they are, how much Manu trusts them. He can never get comfortable with someone else in his home.

Jaantzen pulls a textured protein ration bar from a box in his bare cupboard and eats it while he makes himself a cup of green tea. He prefers coffee — coffee is a delight — but leaves the beans in their jar. They can't cure his exhaustion: even one cup after a sleepless night and he'll be ablaze with nervous energy, and he can't afford to be jittery today. He needs a clear head.

And it's after lunchtime already. How the schedule flips when problems arise.

Fast broken, cup of tea in hand, he sits to meet the messages pulsing on his desk.

There's a report from the medic, Elian, on his unnamed patient's health. Looks like she's not dead, so Jaantzen swipes the rest of the message away unread. A note from Starla: she's with Ximena and Toshiyo on the fourth floor, will have an update at dinner. From Manu: he's gone out this afternoon, chasing a lead. From Teo Lordeur, inviting him for lunch this week; from Leone, a veiled barb about leaving her party early buried in a cheerful note passing on the name of the woman who makes the herbal liqueur.

On the surface, the communications all seem so mundane. Offers of support that don't explicitly mention the fact that Willem Jaantzen and Levi Acheta have tacitly declared war on each other and are dividing loyalties around the city. Notes from his crew reporting progress without mentioning what they're making progress on — or acknowledging the enemy sleeping under their roof.

There's another class of messages on the channel his secretary has access to, which he glances at only briefly. There he finds a flurry of notes between his secretary and Aditi Ciam, the real estate agent, finalizing the deal on the old spinner dealership. Eventually it will require signatures, handshakes, attention. But not yet.

Everything changed yesterday, but nothing feels changed. In the pedestrian plaza below, the citizens of Bulari are sitting through the afternoon work lull, arguing with their children, catching lingering glances across cafes, all unaware that something fundamental has shifted in the world just below their notice.

It's Jaantzen's job now to keep their illusion from shattering.

He swipes the rest of the messages aside and calls Julieta. It takes a long time before she answers, but he lets the connection request keep ringing. She doesn't like to be disturbed by voice calls; he knows from experience that she will answer eventually if he is patient enough.

A sudden change in the quality of silence in his earpiece. "Julieta?" he asks.

"Yes, Willem." He hears the rustling of fabric, the quiet rise and fall of her breath, the whisper of wind. She's walking. "What is it?"

"I learned something last night. Acheta is working with the Dawn." He'll gauge how much to tell her as the conversation goes on; likely, her spies have told her almost as much as he knows. "I'm not sure what their relationship is, but my guess is that Acheta got into bed with Bennion Zacharia a while back and has just been biding time."

There's a silence on the other end of the line; either she didn't suspect at all, or she already knew. With Julieta, he'll always suspect the latter.

"We've also learned that the Dawn have a lot of firepower. Probably from the Dry Creek crew."

A sharp intake of breath, now. "Is everyone all right?" Julieta asks.

"We're all fine."

"Good," Julieta says. "And I know they've been growing in power. I've been watching them for some time."

That's not a surprise. The taproots in Julieta's information organization stretch far and drink deep of whatever they find — her network of spies and information gatherers have their fingers in the topmost tiers of society as well as the slums. Threats — and opportunities — can come from anywhere.

"How long have you known about Acheta and the Dawn?" he asks.

"Only since this morning, Willem," she says, a chiding note creeping into her voice. "My Aster has been building contacts over the past year, but it's still in the early stages of paying off."

"Ah." Sending her own daughter to rub shoulders with the Dawn. Jaantzen can't even think of Starla in the same room as Bennion Zacharia and his band of religious extremists. But Aster has the temperament to weather such things politely; Starla would slay them all with one of her incredulous looks, then toss a grenade of scorn over her shoulder as she walked out the door.

The thought makes him smile.

"Do you know what offer Zacharia came to Acheta with?"

"The drugs, of course," Julieta says. "It's smart to marry production and distribution."

"Of course."

"But Zacharia sweetened the pot. Apparently his merry band of dark chemists have developed a new drug, one he's promised to share with Levi alone." In the distance beyond Julieta's quiet breathing he hears a bird call once, twice. "He promises it will make Levi's soldiers invincible."

An image fills Jaantzen's mind's eye: an improbably large man blotting the light through the spinner's door, torso jerking back against a round of Starla's bullets, then lunging forward again with unabated strength. A drug that could boost someone's adrenaline and banish pain, he could believe. Oriol has told stories from his days in Alliance special ops, and Jaantzen has seen vids of impossible Alliance soldiers, smuggled out of countries the Alliance is keeping pacified.

But special drugs or no, no one keeps fighting after a bullet to the heart.

"Willem?"

"I think there's some truth to that," he says.

A pause, the crunch of gravel. "What have you seen?" she murmurs after a moment.

"A man who kept fighting when he should have been dead. Julieta, where are you?"

"Walking, Willem. It's good for the health. But don't worry, the bodyguards Aster hired are nearby."

"I'd feel more comfortable if you stayed inside your compound until this all blows over."

"You both would," she says curtly; it's a dismissal of his concerns. "I'll see what else I can find about this new drug. I should have fresh information this evening."

"Thank you."

"Of course. Anything I can do to help."

The line goes silent, the faint chirping of birds and rustling of desert shrub replaced by the distant sound of sirens and traffic. The latter is familiar, and it should be comforting, but Willem Jaantzen's skin is crawling.

A drug that makes soldiers invincible.

Manufactured by the Dawn and shared with Levi Acheta and Blackheart's crew.

This war could get very bloody indeed — though he does have his own secret weapon. His own woman who keeps fighting though she should be dead.

Last night, he'd assumed that by the light of day the thought of reinstating Coeur and letting her loose against the Dawn and Dry Creek would seem ludicrous. But it's starting to make more sense than ever.

So long as he can cut off Bennion Zacharia's ability to make supersoldiers before Coeur gets hold of it.

God help them all.

15

MANU

Manu trails his fingertips through the condensation on his glass, beads of water pooling heavy in the heat before tracing swift paths down to disappear into the self-cleaning bartop. He's simultaneously antsy with the long wait and about to drift off; the stim tab he slipped under his tongue an hour ago either isn't working or has worn off already.

The bar is low-ceilinged and character-free, but it's still attracted a healthy crowd of early-afternoon drinkers. Including the two women at the far end of the bar who've clearly been goading each other into working up the courage to come talk to him.

He catches the eye of the one with the braids again, gives her a smile, takes a sip of his ice water. The glass is almost empty. The bartender's already refilled it once.

He's trying to make sense of a note about fertilizer from Toshiyo when the woman with the braids finally takes the leap. Manu looks up to find her slipping into the seat next to him.

"Water?" she asks. "You going back to work?" Her own drink has a faint orange hue; her breath smells like cherries.

He clinks his water glass ruefully against her cocktail. "Afraid so," he says.

"Hopefully not too quickly."

"No, but I am waiting for someone." She looks disappointed. "Just for business," he says.

"I haven't seen you around here." She takes another sip of her drink.

"That's because I've never been here before. This your local haunt?" She's pretty, but not overdone in the way of a professional trapper, and the way her girlfriend is watching them with open delight suggests neither of them are regulars at picking up a stranger at a bar.

"Off and on." She taps a neat, unvarnished fingernail against her glass. "I'm not a lush, though — this is actually my nightcap. We just got off a twenty-four-hour shift at the emergency center down the road."

"The Sulila one?"

"Yep. You know it?"

He makes his smile light. "Been in trouble there a time or two," he says. Her gaze drops to the latticework of lacerations and surgery scars on his left hand. "Moto accident. You must be beat after a twenty-four-hour shift."

She gives him a flirty one-shoulder shrug. A braid slips off her dark shoulder. "That depends on the company. How long is your business going to take?"

He takes another sip of his water, considering. Today isn't the sort of day he can disappear from for an afternoon, but a few minutes of mundane conversation with someone who knows nothing about him — a few minutes pretending that he's no one at all — would be liberating. And who knows what it might lead to further down the road, when things have calmed and Manu can afford distractions once more.

Manu opens his mouth to say, Not long, wait for me? But before he can say a word a burly man is at his shoulder.

"If you're not too busy," the man says with a pointed look at Manu's companion. Even in plainclothes the man looks and sounds like Alliance military; it could get him killed in certain parts of town. "He's ready for you."

Manu just winks at the woman with the braids. "Maybe you'll still be here when I'm done," he says.

She gives him a once-over as he stands, her gaze so brazen he feels heat rising in his cheeks. "You worth waiting for?"

"I absolutely am."

He gives a farewell nod to her girlfriend, giggling at the far end of the bar, then follows the Alliance guard into the back.

The pat-down in the back hallway is polite and thorough, professional hands extracting the pistol from Manu's shoulder holster and knife from his dress boot. The guard shoves the weapons into his own waistband and gestures Manu through a far door.

The storeroom is just what he'd expect given the dingy bar out front: the same low ceiling and lack of character, stacked with crates of booze, jars of garnishes like science experiments, and an industrial rehydrator standing by on the off chance someone takes a look at the bar and decides it's the sort of place they'd like to order food.

Alliance Deputy Chief of Mission Marquez ó Lauris sits by himself in the single chair, a paper book held open with leathery, copper-colored hands, one knee crossed primly over the other, pearl-white shoes gleaming. He looks up as Manu enters and Manu catches the faint flicker of dilation in the other man's lenses, the adjustment of focus from near to far. It's followed by a spark of green in the left pupil as ó Lauris's lens feeds him information about Manu.

There's nowhere else to sit, so Manu leans shoulder blades against a stack of crates, crosses his ankles, hands in pockets. The Alliance guard has taken up a position in the doorway, arms akimbo, one palm on his sidearm. The only other exit is a high window, but it's locked shut — and looks to be a tight fit even for Manu's slim frame.

Talk your way in, talk your way out, Manu thinks. And the way the old dignitary's just watching him, it looks like Manu gets to go first.

"They say Blackheart killed everyone who'd ever seen her weak," Manu says. "You look like you're still in good shape, though."

A ghost of a smile touches ó Lauris's lips. "I must say, my nerves have never quite recovered from our little encounter." His Arquellian drawl is melodic, disarming.

"She can have that effect on people," Manu says.

"Of course. Though you seem to have weathered her storm all right in the end, as well."

"I guess what they say about her is wrong, then."

"I wouldn't go that far." One fine eyebrow arches up; ó Lauris re-crosses his knees, right over left. "My apologies for the rustic meeting location. But as intriguing as I found your note, I can't have Willem Jaantzen's people showing up at the Alliance embassy and sparking gossip."

"I completely understand. Thank you for agreeing to see me." It had been a long shot, but Manu doesn't mind taking those. And from what he's heard about the old dignitary, his strongest vice is curiosity. Manu had crafted an inquiry to pique that.

"I find the underbelly of your planet's politics fascinating," says ó Lauris. "And I don't think many of my current contemporaries at the embassy understand the political import of Thala Coeur's death."

Ó Lauris's career had taken a boost ten years ago after the way he handled Coeur's request for amnesty. International politics isn't Manu's forte, but he's familiar with the look of ambition blooming now in the old man's eyes. Knowledge is power — that's the common denominator in both of their games.

"You said you had a question for me, Mr. Juric."

"I know Coeur went to the Alliance embassy hoping you'd help reinstall her as mayor, and I know she fought you deporting her. And I know you won. I wanted to ask how."

"Ancient history." Ó Lauris's fingers drum on his thigh, impatient, but that tilt of his chin and narrowed gaze say he's intrigued. "Are you writing a book?"

Manu just smiles. "I'm gathering interesting information."

"The Alliance had something no one on New Sarjun did," ó Lauris says. "Something we realized she valued more than anything."

Manu's pulse kicks up a notch and he forces himself to relax; ó Lauris is watching him with interest. That spark of green flares in the left pupil again, and the man's pale brown eyes refocus for a moment on whatever his lens is telling him. Manu is good at reading body language, but who knows what Alliance ops tech can tell its wearer about biosign.

"If Coeur were alive," says ó Lauris slowly, "I'd tell you to find her sister. Major Nayar."

Manu's eyebrows shoot up, he doesn't try to hide his disbelief. *That's* the missing piece of the puzzle, why Coeur finally agreed to be exiled from New Sarjun?

"You threatened her sister?"

"Threatened?" Ó Lauris shakes his head. "I don't have a death wish. We ordered Major Nayar to talk sense into her. The major's a level-headed woman, and she seems to be the one person Thala Coeur respects. But I doubt she'll be much help in talking sense into her crew."

Manu can't believe what he's hearing. "Just like that."

Ó Lauris laughs, genuine pleasure at the memory of a tricky job well executed. "No, not 'just like that,'" he says. "It was a delicate, diplomatic business, and we made certain Coeur knew her options for leaving New Sarjun were far more pleasant than her options for staying. But what finally put her over the edge was a stern talking-to from her sister."

It couldn't be that easy, could it? The way to control Thala Coeur was to control her sister? Ó Lauris was smart — he could have blackmailed Coeur into behaving by threatening Ximena, but he had guessed, and rightly so, that would be the fast track to Coeur's list of people slated for elimination.

Ó Lauris stands, adjusts the pleats of his dress pants, tucks his book under his arm. "It sounds like you and Mr. Jaantzen have some interesting things planned for the Blackheart crew." Ó Lauris lingers carefully on the conclusion of the sentence; Manu gives him a slight nod of confirmation. Blackheart's crew, sure. "Would you please facilitate an introduction to your employer? Something discreet."

"Of course."

Manu shakes the old diplomat's hand; his grip is firmer than Manu would've expected.

"It was a pleasure to meet you, Mr. Juric. Please give your employer my regards. I look forward to meeting him."

And with a slight Arquellian bow — Manu returns it

belatedly, awkwardly — ó Lauris is gone. The guard hands Manu back his weapons and follows after.

Manu gives the diplomat and his guard a few moments before heading back out to the bar. The two women are gone, their place at the bar taken by an ancient man nursing a half-empty beer glass. Manu allows himself a pang of disappointment, then brushes it off. He hadn't truly expected her to wait, he tells himself. And anyway, it's probably for the best now that he stinks of adrenaline sweat and needs to get home to tell Jaantzen what he's learned.

The ancient man at the bar catches his eye and pats the counter beside him. "You got a minute, kid? You never see any new faces in this bar."

Manu shakes his head. "Sorry, man. Gotta get back to work."

"Young people, always running off to the next thing," the old man says. "No time to sit and share stories. It's a shame."

"Keeps the lights on and the little ones fed, yeah?" Manu says. Seems like the sort of thing an old-timer in a working-class bar like this one would want to hear.

The man gives a satisfied bob of the head. "Good for you, son." He holds out his hand, and Manu glances around; nothing about this man screams danger, he's just an old drunk at the bar. Manu clasps the offered hand, feels paper press against his palm.

"Thanks, man." Manu swipes a few marks to the bartender. "His next beer's on me," he says.

"God bless, son."

Manu waits until he's at his moto before slipping the scrap back out of his pocket. He's expecting a number from the emergency center worker with the braids, but instead it's a familiar scrawl that makes his stomach flip.

Meet me for tandoori?

Oriol.

Manu checks the time: ninety minutes until he's set to meet Jaantzen for dinner and report on the day's events. Texts his secretary, Lo. I'M GOING TO BE ANOTHER HOUR. AT ANJALI'S IN SURQUILLO IF ANYONE NEEDS ME.

He kicks his moto into gear and peels off the curb.

Surquillo Market is just on the western edge of the Tamarind District, close enough in to be a draw for Indiran tourists — though those mostly cluster in the trinket and brand-name knockoff shops near the colorful main entrance or in the aisle of spicy korris stands, each more garishly decorated than the last with holograms of flickering flame and dancing chile peppers, every single one advertising itself as the famous local favorite, though no one born and raised in Bulari would ever be caught eating there.

Surquillo's more crowded than usual, the influx of crewmembers from the Ganesh transport lumbering in the skies overhead creating a party atmosphere around the city. But the crowded tourist aisles give way to local produce and household goods stalls, and deep in the heart of Surquillo Market, those stalls give way to a row of sit-down restaurants with handwritten menus and surly locals giving stray tourists sideways glares. Anjali's Cafe is at the end of the row, its bright pink-and-green facade with the faux-grass fringe over the windows meant to evoke Teuçan architecture, faux hibiscus shrubs framing the doors.

Inside it's well-lit and smells like liquid gold and coconuts.

Oriol is sitting in their booth, the one facing the door.

The table is filled with fried rice, clay pots of curries and tandoori seitan, naan.

Oriol's skin has lost the golden glow it gets from the New Sarjun sun — he always comes back from a long gig in space looking wan and depleted. He's roughly dressed and unkempt, but he's still the most eye-catching thing in this place. Old T-shirt snug over muscled arms, worn fatigues that fit just right. A cut above the eyebrow, but otherwise Manu can't immediately spot any new injuries. If this trip went like any of the others, there'll be plenty of scrapes to find once those clothes come off. It's a game they play every time they come back together: What happened here? Who did this?

Oriol looks up. Smiles.

"Looks like I rescued you from a meeting," Oriol says when Manu reaches the booth. He doesn't rise, only pours a second cup of coffee from the carafe and sets it in front of Manu's place, scans past Manu as though making sure he wasn't followed.

So they're having a casual reunion today, after eight months apart — either Oriol's got bad news he's trying to break easy, or he's brought home trouble. Manu tamps apprehension down and slips into the booth across from Oriol, trying and failing to match Oriol's indifferent posture.

"Do I look like I need rescuing?" Manu takes a sip of the coffee. It tastes Indiran and expensive, all caramel and smoke. Oriol's springing for the good stuff.

"You're just wearing a damn fine suit," Oriol says. For a moment, his smile becomes real before it fades and he begins to scan the restaurant once again.

"I had people to impress."

Oriol's accent today is faint and lilting, distinguishable

from that of a native Bulari resident only by native Bulari residents. Sometimes Manu can tell who Oriol's spent those long months with based on how the accent has shifted, the slang he's picked up, the deepening of his own long-buried Arquellian drawl.

Manu should be on those missions; Oriol says it every time. Come, explore, travel, see the system and get rich quick.

The last a joke; Oriol's bank account is always hovering near empty, while Manu hasn't wanted for anything since he started working for Jaantzen. He hasn't left the planet, either, and Oriol has never stayed for long. Slinks off like a cat whenever it suits him and comes back the same.

"Hope you're hungry," Oriol says, gesturing to the food. "I ordered already."

"I see that," Manu says. He isn't, but it smells delicious. He spears a cube of seitan, can't quite take a bite.

Oriol takes another helping for himself. "I was starving. I haven't been able to access my accounts since I got back."

"Ah." Manu takes another sip of the expensive coffee. "So I guess I'm picking up the tab."

Oriol winks, tears a piece of naan in half and tosses one half on Manu's plate. "You know I'm good for it. Unless you found somebody new this time around?" And, at Manu's raised eyebrow, an appreciative look. "You must not be trying very hard. Or wearing that suit often enough."

"It's slim pickings in Bulari. And I've been busy."

"Your man keeping you running around, yeah?"

"When he needs me to. Things are a bit off-balance at the moment."

"I've heard that." Oriol's fork stills in his right hand; his left is flat against the table and pressing forward, as though he might reach across and take Manu's.

Manu picks up his cup of coffee, cradles it in both palms. "Where are you staying?"

The intensity in Oriol's gaze fades, a caginess setting in. Head back up and scanning the restaurant, but that rhythm his fingers are tapping against the table is professional readiness, not deceit. One part of Manu tightens in vigilance while another part relaxes. Oriol's not staying with a new lover, that's not what's got him on edge.

"Tell me," Manu says quietly.

"My last contract, it went bad." Oriol's not looking at him, he's watching the door for danger. "Real bad."

Manu frowns. "The security one on the supplies transport?" They'd argued bitterly about it — "If you want to be bored out of your skull for a year," Manu'd said, "why not do it on this rock? Starla can give you a job with Admant guarding shipping containers."

"Nah," said Oriol. "That one finished early and I got bought for something that sounded more interesting."

"Is that right." Of course he did.

Oriol only gives him a lopsided smile. "That's right. Anyway, I'll get to the short of it. Don't want you missing too much of your day."

"I've got time," Manu says, his tone sharper than he meant it to be.

Hands raised: Fine, fine. "Job was on the *Dorothy Queen*," Oriol says, and Manu's eyes widen involuntarily; he doesn't normally bother keeping a guard on his expressions when Oriol's around, and his body's relaxed into old habits even though he's got red flags going off in his mind.

"Robbing the place?"

"Nah, thank god. Robbing a person."

Oriol launches into the story in his easy way, even his short version including a bit of the local color, the slowly growing tension, the inevitable fights and adventure. Manu listens, constantly scanning past him to keep an eye on the restaurant.

A word catches his attention.

"Dawn?" he asks.

"Yeah, seems this Sister Kalia woman was trying to get to the goods before the Dawn could. Didn't make sense at first, until I started looking into them." Oriol leans forward. "You ever heard their prophecy?"

"Prophecy?" Manu has a vague idea that the Dawn don't have a holy scripture like what his grandma used to follow, that instead they listen to some nutcase locked up in Redrock. But he hasn't paid much more attention than that. Didn't realize he needed to, but he won't be making that mistake again.

"Basically, they've got this idea that humanity will come together as one people or whatever, with no more strife and war."

"Sounds nice."

"Sure. But they think it'll happen because of some plague that wipes out ninety percent of us scum and turns the rest into superhumans. And from what I can figure, the ring I stole apparently teaches them how to create that plague." Oriol's fingers brush his sternum, protective, and now that Manu's looking he can see the shadow there. Oriol's wearing the ring around his neck.

"Superhumans?"

"Cultist bullshit. But apparently the plague can also transform the earth and make it grow food. Which seems infinitely more useful."

"Plague. So, a virus?"

Oriol shrugs. "They keep calling it 'the gift of the Fallen.' Some kind of serum."

"Sure." Manu pulls out his comm.

"Manu. Hey."

Tosh stop whatever youre doing with case.

"Hey! Who the hell are you messaging?"

Manu hits Send.

"Tosh. Why didn't you come straight to me?"

Oriol's golden eyes narrow. "I needed to make sure. They've got spies everywhere."

"Who?"

"The Dawn."

Manu blinks at him, incredulous. "You worried I'm a spy?"

"Nah, man. But your man, the way he's always looking for that next business deal . . ."

"Not with the Dawn."

Oriol shrugs, scans the restaurant. "You never know who your business partners are connected with."

"But you think that Jaantzen would — "

"No, Manu."

Oriol takes a deep breath now, eyes half closing in exhaustion. He leans back in the booth, smiles for real this time, slides his foot forward so his calf is pressed against Manu's. Electricity follows.

"I'm sorry, I'm on edge. But I've had just about the shittiest few days and I wanted to make sure I knew the lay of the land before I got myself killed."

Manu allows himself a breath. "And what's the lay of the land?"

"Perilous. But it seems I'm not the only one now who's got problems with the Dawn. I figured it was probably safe to get in touch since it seems like they've got it out for me and your man both."

"Is that the word on the street?" Manu asks. Oriol flashes him a nod. "We need you right now."

"Just so happens I'm looking for work."

"Then stay at my place tonight."

For a moment Manu's afraid Oriol will say no, that he'll disappear back into the depths of the city and show back up only when he's ready again. But, "My code still work?"

"Of course."

"Then I'm going to take a shower. You got a full day?"

"Meeting with Jaantzen in twenty-five." Manu leans forward and slides his left hand into Oriol's right; Oriol's thumb rubs absently over the scars. "But I'll get back as soon as I can."

"I'll be waiting. And you should change your security codes when I'm not here."

There's such a look of concern on his face that Manu laughs. "I do. Don't worry about me."

Manu leans across the table; Oriol tastes like coffee and earth. Manu scratches his fingernails in the stubble along his lover's jawline. "Your razor's still there, too," he says.

"You don't like my space scruff?"

"So long as it keeps everyone else away from you." Manu's fingers slide down Oriol's neck, catch in the chain hidden just below his collar. He hooks the tip of his ring finger under the chain, gives it a faint tug. "You gonna let me take this?"

"Please do."

Oriol breaks eye contact to look back out over the restaurant. The scant other diners are paying no attention to them, and he undoes the clasp, sets the ring and chain both in Manu's palm. Manu puts it around his own neck.

"What else have you heard about the Dawn?" he asks. "Anything about their leader?"

"Their prophet?" Oriol shakes his head. "Still locked up at Redrock as far as I know."

"Nah, the man they got here in Bulari. Zacharia."

Oriol's guard is up again, all sense of playfulness erased from his face. "Not much. But apparently he's got puppets everywhere. Whether he talks them into his religion or gets them with greed."

"Like Levi Acheta?"

"Yeah, I heard about that. Manu. Listen." Oriol leans elbows on table, fingers steepled in front of his mouth. "Acheta isn't the only one around here's gotten into bed with Zacharia. I've been chasing down threads, and they're leading to some pretty unsettling places."

"Who?"

"If I give you a list, you gotta promise to read it before letting anyone else know about it," he says. "I don't care how much you trust them. You have to see how far their influence extends for yourself."

"Of course."

"Even your man."

"Of course, Oriol."

"Good."

"Do you have the list on you?" Manu asks.

Oriol nods and slips him an archaic paper notebook — a quirk left over from his Alliance special ops days. It's scribbled with notes in Oriol's jagged hand, near-illegible even if you do know the code, as Manu does.

"In the back," Oriol says, and Manu skims through dates and times, interview notes. There, written more carefully than the rest of the scribbles, is a list of about forty-five names.

As he scans the coded list, Manu recognizes a fair amount of them, from politicians to street lieutenants of minor crews. Marquez ó Lauris isn't on it, he sees with relief. But one name turns his blood cold.

Yang.

He pulls out his comm again, sends a message to both Jaantzen and Starla.

I NEED TO TALK TO YOU. NOW.

"Hey," Oriol says, snatching back the notebook. "I told you not to go off half-cocked before reading the whole thing."

Manu breathes sharp.

"Forget the shower," he says. "Come back to the tower with me. We need to talk."

"Jaantzen ain't gonna let me in all scruffy," Oriol says, but it's only partly playful; he's on to Manu's tension.

"Shit's happening," Manu says. "You're coming with me."

He glances at his comm. No response. He pings Jaantzen on a call: no answer. He calls Lo, his secretary; she answers almost immediately.

"Hey, is the boss in a meeting?" Manu asks. "I'm trying to get ahold of him."

"No . . . Hold on." In the background, he can hear the sound of people in her office. The moment goes on interminably long; his pulse is rising.

"Manu?"

"Here."

"Yeah, he took off about half an hour ago. To see a friend about his garden?"

To see Julieta Yang.

"Thanks, Lo," Manu says, but the comm's already halfway to his pocket and he's not sure she hears him. He swipes credits from his comm onto the table. "We gotta go," he snaps. "Now."

16

JAANTZEN

The humidity in Julieta's greenhouse rolls over him like a damp curtain, clinging to his face and the backs of his hands. Behind him, Starla sneezes.

"Julieta?" Jaantzen calls. His voice is muffled in the foliage, soaks into the earth around him. There's a faint whine, like that of a plasma pistol warming, and Jaantzen spins, heart jumping. But it's just the control panel for the misters, and with a breath all around them comes the faint spray. Starla holds her hand under the nearest, watches the water pearl on her fingertips.

"She's in the back," Aster says.

Jaantzen has never seen Julieta's youngest daughter enter the greenhouse before, and she does seem to have a certain distaste for it, the way she holds herself away from the plants, pivots to keep the palm fronds from brushing against her suit, keeps her hands pressed together to avoid touching anything organic.

She has always been fastidious, picky, even as a girl. When Jaantzen first brought Starla to visit, he'd hoped the two would become friends, but Julieta's youngest and his own daughter are like night and day. To Aster's secretive reserve, Starla wears her heart on her sleeve. Alongside Aster's obedient efficiency in helping with her mother's business, Starla is a tornado whose energy and enthusiasm can be harnessed, but never aimed.

And whether it was the personality differences or something deeper in the mysteries of teenage girls, they hated each other from day one and never grew closer — though they have at least grown more civil.

"Julieta?" he calls again.

"To the left, I think," Aster tells him, and he takes a left at Julieta's potting table, where she apparently paused in the middle of separating orchids, a trickle of potting soil spilling from a pot. One of the orchids — a showy, venomous-looking bloom of livid purple spotted with yellow and black — is tipped over on its side.

Jaantzen tilts his head to look at it, a flower carelessly placed, and the feeling that's been nibbling at the back of his mind since they stepped into Julieta's greenhouse finally becomes clear.

"Something is wrong," he signs to Starla.

He reaches for the orchid, trying not to bruise its roots with fingers more accustomed to violence than nurturing, sets it carefully back upright.

"Let's go. She's waiting," Aster says impatiently behind him.

"Of course," Jaantzen says, and as she turns to prod them farther along, he slips Julieta's sharp potting knife into his sleeve.

"I have something to show you relating to the new drug," Julieta had messaged him. "This afternoon?"

And he'd decided that Starla could brief him on the case in the spinner on the way over, that Manu could catch him up on whatever he'd found when they got back. Divide and conquer, acquire whatever information they can.

Never once did it cross his mind that a call from Julieta could be a trap.

He keeps himself calm. Betrayed by his oldest friend? Or is his oldest friend facing a betrayal of her own?

The misters click off, and in the sudden silence of the greenhouse he hears a muffled scrape, a quiet thud.

"Aster," he says quietly. "What's going on?"

But when he turns back to her, she's got a pistol in her hand. It's aimed at Starla's head.

"Keep walking, old man," she says.

Julieta's at the far end of her greenhouse, bound and gagged in a chair, straps tight on her stick-thin wrists. She glares up at him and he sees no fear, only unmistakable fury.

Fury directed at her daughter.

"Sit," Aster says, indicating another pair of chairs. And when Jaantzen hesitates, she jams the barrel of the pistol against the back of Starla's head.

Starla looks nearly as angry as Julieta does.

And half as angry as Jaantzen feels.

He lowers himself into the chair, calculating. Aster will have to get close to him to tie him up, will have to lower her weapon on Starla at some point. He can trust his goddaughter to take the opportunity when she sees it, and he forces himself to stay relaxed, to think. Lets Julieta's potting knife slip forward under his palm, hidden beneath his forearm as he rests it on the arm of the chair.

"Aster," he says. "What are you doing. Your mother — "

"I'm taking my birthright," she says. "And I'm not interested in a lecture."

"I'm not offering you a lecture," Jaantzen says. "Though I can guess your mother would like to."

Starla's watching him calmly, waiting with breath steady and shoulders loose. Behind her, Aster's face is a mask of fury.

"Don't presume to know what my mother would want," Aster hisses. "You've been a curse on our house long enough. You may have fooled her, but just wait. All our true selves will be revealed in the end, and everyone will see you've never been anything but a street rat in a fancy suit."

Aster's words have a tinge of rehearsal to them, a taste of propaganda. But it's the venom of pent-up fury that shocks him.

"Is that truly how you feel?" he asks quietly.

Starla lifts an eyebrow at him: Now?

"My sister and brother and I? All forgotten once my mother's new protege came along," Aster says. "We worked our asses off for her for years, but I wouldn't be surprised if you're at the top of her will."

"Your mother respects your work," Jaantzen says quietly. "She and I are only dear friends."

"That doesn't matter, now," Aster says. "None of *these* bodies matter now. The end is coming for all of us, and maybe it's petty, but I *will* make sure you go through the trial first so my mother can finally see what you're truly made of."

Jaantzen frowns. "The trial?"

"You'll find out soon enough." She shoves Starla forward a step with the point of her pistol. "Tie him up," she says over Starla's shoulder. "Do you understand?"

Jaantzen catches that little annoyed eye roll at the question; Starla's lens must have transcribed Aster's words, but she doesn't move to obey.

"Tie. Him. Up," Aster says, louder, as if that will make Starla less deaf.

"It seems your mother was right to be disappointed," Jaantzen says.

And Aster's attention, her fury, shifts to focus on her mother.

Jaantzen lifts his chin.

Starla spins to her left in a pirouette, raised left elbow shoving Aster's gun arm out of range and locking it to her side, open right hand smashing into Aster's nose to snap her head back. Starla steps a foot behind Aster and shoves her hard, stripping the pistol from her hand as she falls. She steps back out of range, gun pointed at Aster's bleeding face.

Jaantzen lets out a breath he didn't realize he'd been holding, then stands up with potting knife in hand. "Keep an eye on her," he says to Starla. "I'll free Julieta."

"It's okay," he tells Julieta as he slips the potting knife under her thin wrist, oh-so-carefully to avoid cutting her fragile skin. Though it's clearly not going to be all right. Her daughter has just turned on her. Surely the rest of her children don't feel the same way — Aster's words had held a tinge of the apocalyptic fervor he's read in some of the Dawn prophet's writing. She'd been spending time with them, Julieta had said. Had she gone over to them?

He can find answers to those questions later. Right now, he needs to get Julieta out of here.

But before he can cut the first bond, Julieta's gaze slides past his and her eyes go wide, this time with fear.

Jaantzen slips the knife even farther under her bonds and her bony fingers close over the handle to hide it. He pats the back of her hand.

"You're very skilled, Starla Dusai," says a voice behind

him, touching the back of his neck like ice. He's heard that voice before, though only in police interview vids. "That was well-done."

Jaantzen straightens. Turns.

Bennion Zacharia is standing behind him in the diminishing light of the evening, holding a plasma carbine aimed right at his chest.

And he's surrounded by a half-dozen well-armed crew.

"I've been meaning to set up a meeting with you, Mr. Jaantzen," Zacharia says. "Is now a good time?"

17

STARLA

Of course that was too easy, Starla thinks. Prissy little Aster holding a gun to her head was a joke. Thinking that Aster had overpowered her own mother was surprising only in that she would have had the guts to do it, not what little strength would be required. Starla wouldn't try, personally — she's sure Julieta Yang would fight back like a hellcat if cornered, talons and teeth and all. Probably poison needles in all those gaudy rings.

And if not — and if they survive this — Starla will work with Tosh to make sure there are.

She's never seen the man heading the goon pack in person, but she recognizes Bennion Zacharia from the profile Manu passed her way after Leone's party. There wasn't much in the file, just a few stills and a police booking vid from over ten years ago, when he was still young and missing that nasty scar down his cheek.

Beyond that, they'd found nothing. Just the misdemeanor charge, and not one mention of his name in any of the news coverage of lawsuits against the Dawn by parents wanting their children back from the cult. Those only talk about someone called the prophet, some bearded old man holed up for life at Redrock.

She does recognize one of his crewmembers, a well-toned woman Jaantzen's age with a thick mane of silver hair braided down one side and shaved up the other, and an angry red scar slicing from ear to elbow. The woman who'd been driving the spinner that tried to take her out after she and Simca and El bombed Julieta's warehouse.

Meijer, her name was, though Starla's forgetting her given name at the moment. Facing down a half-dozen weapons will do terrible things to your memory.

Starla lifts her chin in greeting to Meijer, then lets Aster's pistol spin on her index finger. The other woman steps forward to disarm her.

"You can get up now," someone says — she doesn't see who, only sees the words crawling along the bottom of her lens. Aster gets up gingerly, more out of care for her expensive suit, it seems, than out of any injury sustained. She dabs her fingers delicately against her nose; it's gushing a satisfying amount of unladylike blood.

That look of indignation on Aster's face when she sees the blood, Starla almost expects Aster to step up and slap her now that she's got muscle at her back. But Julieta's baby girl has the decency to look embarrassed at her performance, to step aside, damming the flow of blood from her nose with a dainty silk handkerchief.

Meijer pats Starla down professionally for any other weapons and finds the telescoping baton in her boot, the belt whip, the penknife in her pocket.

Another of Zacharia's crew takes the long, slim blade Jaantzen had been about to use to free Julieta from under the old woman's arm. It'd been worth a shot, Starla supposes. The old woman's fingers twitch over his hand, but her assailant doesn't writhe screaming into death. Starla's really going to have to get her some poison-needle rings if they survive this.

When they survive this.

Her lens doesn't pick up what the next person says to her, but she doesn't need to read lips to understand that a scowl and a jab with a plasma carbine barrel means Sit your ass down in the chair so I can tie you up.

Starla looks to Jaantzen, waiting for his order.

"Sit down," he signs. "Let me talk to him."

The chairs are very Julieta, some sort of woven reed and bamboo that's probably quite popular back on Indira. Possibly even brought over from New Manila by her grand-mother or great-grandmother, or whoever it was came over, Starla hasn't heard her tell that story in years.

She sits, and a man binds her hands down tight into silence, wraps a strap around her waist. Fuck these people, Starla decides.

They're patting Jaantzen down now, too — jacket off and shoes checked all to satisfactory standards. He wasn't armed, since they were coming to see Julieta and he's far too trusting of her.

"What do you want?" Jaantzen asks as they bind him in his own chair; it's uselessly far from hers.

Starla doesn't catch all of Zacharia's answer, his lips stiff and pulled back by his scar, her lens barely any help due to the glitchy humid transcription.

But she does see a name she's learned to recognize over the years by the length of the vowel sounds and effort it takes to say.

Some people rush through it like a curse word, accom-panied by a superstitious sign against evil. Some give it the same brief hesitation and reverent gravitas normally reserved for humankind's worst atrocities. Some, like Jaantzen, say it with forced ease accompanied by an unconscious tick: nostrils flaring, the jaw tightening, a knuckle cracking.

Zacharia says it like a benediction.

"I want Coeur," Zacharia had said.

Starla's sure that's what he said.

But.

Why the hell would anyone want Coeur?

18

MANU

Almost all of what Manu wants to say boils down to one thing:

"Why the fuck didn't you come to me sooner?"

"Where do you think they've been looking for me?" Oriol shoots back. He slaps a palm against the thigh pocket his notebook is in. "Besides. The Maid of Heaven didn't just appear to me and hand this over — I needed the past few days to collect these names."

He's walking more stiffly than usual as they hurry through the parking garage under Cobalt Tower, and Manu wonders if his prosthetic is acting up again. For such an expensive piece of Alliance tech, it does require a lot of maintenance.

Or maybe Oriol's stiff and sore because he's been on the run and crashing in some flophouse or alley these last few nights while Manu's been enjoying a nice, comfortable bed. Maybe Manu should cut him some slack.

And maybe Oriol should have come to him sooner.

Manu keys open the private elevator, the one he uses when he's coming in late at night, or with a discreet client, or bloodied up. All the front desk staff in the Cobalt Tower lobby are his people, but workers for RKE and the other legitimate companies also use the main elevator. He doesn't need them asking any questions.

"How did you get these names?"

"Bit of everything. Asked some seedy friends who owed me information. Followed people around. Stole somebody's comm. Threatened an indentured delivery guy to tell his boss about his drug habit. Helped an old lady across the street. Ate a live snake."

"Wait, what?" Manu frowns at him; he's been messaging Lo, asking her to get ahold of the Anahoy siblings and have them meet him in the conference room, and only half listening.

"I'm kidding. You know I'm not nice to old ladies."

"Tell me what you know about Julieta Yang," Manu says. He hits the button for the fourth floor; he needs to see Toshiyo.

Oriol pulls his notebook from his pocket, flips it open to a page of what look like nonsense marks. "Yang . . . Yang. Here. Word is she's a, quote, Honored Acolyte who will pass through the purification fire as a result of works, lucky her."

"What does that mean?"

"One thing I have figured out is that you're either born with a soul that can withstand the purification fire, or you rack up some good works to help skate you through. Seems like Yang is the latter category."

"And one of those good works was calling Jaantzen into a trap?"

"You don't know it's a trap."

"Of course it's a trap." With Manu out of the building, kept away by an urgent message from —

Manu stops the lift.

Oriol tilts his head to watch through narrowed eyes, but his body language is still relaxed, easy. Manu can read people well — and he's known Oriol longer than just about anybody — but Oriol was trained from childhood to be whoever he needed to be.

And right now, even though he hates himself for it, Manu is wondering just who that is.

"Why now?" Manu says. "Why this moment to finally get in touch with me?"

"What the fuck, Manu."

"If this was a trap, I just want to know whether I was away from Jaantzen by coincidence or design."

"This is what you're asking me. If *I* betrayed your man."

"That's not what I'm asking," Manu says, though of course it sounds like it. "Somebody else could've pushed your timing."

"I came to you the only way I could think that didn't get me killed. I may not share your loyalty to the man, but I'm loyal to you," Oriol says quietly. "I hope you know that."

Manu nods, not trusting himself to speak.

"And if something's really going on, we don't have time for this shit."

Oriol puts the lift back in operation, and it begins to rise.

———

Toshiyo and Ximena are in the dark conference room, both bent over workstations on the far end of the conference table. Manu is relieved to see that the case is closed tight. He flips on the light; it must have gotten dark while the two women were working, and no one's bothered.

Oriol frowns at the half-assembled surveillance satellite that's now illuminated on the conference table. It takes up most of the room. "Is that . . . Why?"

"Oriol!"

Toshiyo is across the room and in Oriol's arms in seconds, face buried in his shoulder. "You smell terrible," she says.

"Perks of the road," he says. He kisses the top of her head. "You smell great." He lets her go, turns his attention on Ximena.

"Oriol Sina, meet Major Ximena Nayar."

"I don't think I have a rank anymore," Ximena says. She holds out her hand, and after a moment's hesitation, Oriol takes it.

"You're . . ."

"I'm Thala Coeur's sister," Ximena says, a hint of resignation in her voice.

Manu catches Oriol's side-eye. "We all have equally long stories to tell," he says. "Tosh, I need you to get me into Julieta's security system."

"Yeah, no problem."

She drops back into her chair and swipes away whatever she's been looking at.

"And tell me you two weren't messing around with whatever is in that case."

Toshiyo's lips purse as though she's about to answer, then she turns back to her workstation without a word. So, that's a yes. If whatever's inside does contain a plague that will wipe out all the scum of the world, Manu doesn't have time to worry whether or not Toshiyo has contracted it.

"How long have Jaantzen and Starla been gone?" Manu asks.

Toshiyo's frowning in concentration at streams of data;

it's Ximena who answers. "They left about forty-five minutes ago."

"So if they went straight there, they've been with her for about fifteen minutes."

"What's going on?" Ximena asks.

Manu watches her a moment, considering. He's viewed her as the enemy from the moment she arrived on their doorstep, but he doesn't believe she's working *for* Coeur — she's working to help her. And so long as he can convince her that working with them puts her sister's best interests first, she might be a valuable asset.

"We think Julieta Yang may be working with the Dawn. If this is a trap, we both know who they're after, and I can use every person I can get." Ximena nods slowly as understanding dawns, apparently already agreeing to whatever he's about to ask. "You've got a choice. Head back to your quarters and stay there under guard until this has all blown over, or follow my every word."

"I'm with you," she says.

"Okay. Tosh, you in?"

"Almost."

She's got a grainy feed of Julieta's property, which she swipes into a space on the conference table in front of Manu. "I'm going to be glad when I don't have to rely on hacking government satellites," she says. "Look at that resolution. Ridiculous."

Manu zooms in. Julieta's walled compound is unmistakable, the glass roof of the greenhouse reflecting sunset colors, the private water tower doubling as a lookout just to its north, her sprawling home facing it across the ring driveway. The black Dulciana JX is parked in front of the greenhouse, and Julieta's family's vehicles must be parked in the garage to the north of the driveway.

But there are also a spinner and a truck parked behind the greenhouse, near the loading dock.

That doesn't seem right.

"Tosh — "

"Shh." She taps one last sequence and then lets out a hiss of triumph. "Got it."

An array of video feeds projects into the air above the conference table. Toshiyo drifts her fingers through them, looking for the one she wants.

Manu's comm buzzes in his pocket: it's Lo.

"Call for you," she says; there's a catch in her voice that gives him pause. "Something about a hostage exchange. Manu, what's — "

"Send it through, Lo. Where are the Anahoys?"

"On their way."

With a sharp inhale and a click she's gone. Lo isn't core crew, but she's whip-smart and reliable — and he's long suspected she guesses at the darker side of the work he does for Willem Jaantzen. They're going to need to have a conversation, and soon.

Oriol has gone still. "Hostage exchange," he murmurs. "I lead the Dawn straight to you. If I put them in danger, Manu, I swear — "

Manu shakes his head. "It may not be you they want. And even if it is, these assholes aren't getting anybody from us."

Manu keys into the conference table. Accepts the call, and a man's face flickers to life over the table. He's pale, with a jagged scar on his cheek and cold blue eyes. Across the table, Oriol's eyes widen in recognition.

"Mr. Juric," Bennion Zacharia says. "I trust you know who I am."

"Yeah, I've seen your rap sheet," Manu says. "It's a pleasure, I'm sure."

"I have your employer here with me, and his daughter," Zacharia says. He looks away from the feed a moment, icy gaze fixing someone else a moment before returning his attention to Manu. "You have something — and someone — I would like to exchange."

Footsteps: the Anahoy siblings are at the door to the conference room. With the hand that's outside the camera's range, Manu beckons them in.

"You might need to be a little more specific," he says to Zacharia. "Not to brag, but we have a lot of things and people."

"I want you — and you alone — to bring the case and Thala Coeur to Julieta Yang's estate within thirty minutes. Otherwise Willem Jaantzen and his daughter die. Is that more clear?"

"Crystal. But it'll take us thirty just to drive there," Manu says. "And she's plugged into every IV we own — your people left her in pretty bad shape. You have to give us more time."

The connection goes out.

Manu's mind is racing. A simple hostage exchange is what it sounds like, and this should be one of the best kinds, too: give up the person you don't want in your home, get back the people you do. Plus, Coeur's already hooked up to any number of IVs — just press the sedative button and you don't even have to talk her into it.

Trouble is, Zacharia also wants a case full of prophecy plague or whatever it is. Add to that the fact that Thala Coeur may be their only chance at winning a fight against both Acheta's crew and the Dawn, and things get a lot more complicated.

Oriol is staring at him, wide-eyed. "Blackheart's alive?" he asks. "And here?"

"Unfortunately, yes on both counts." Manu brushes away the look Oriol's giving him. They can talk about how he feels about that when they're not in a room full of people. He puts a call through to the lead guard currently watching over Coeur's medical bay. "Get her ready for transport and bring her to the lobby on the fourth floor. I need her here in five. And bring me a vest."

When he looks up, Oriol's still watching him, with a look of fierce concern.

Manu ignores it, pushing back from the table. There's no time for a trip down terrible-memory lane. "Have you met Simca?" he asks Oriol. "El's sister? Good. We believe Jaantzen and Starla are being held at Julieta Yang's green-house," he says to the Anahoys. "Yang may be complicit, you heard their demands. Tosh, what do you see?"

Toshiyo has plucked a few key feeds from the array of Julieta's security system and blown them up over the table. "There aren't any cameras inside the greenhouse, just watching the doors," she says. "But on the front door feed you can see Julieta entering hours ago, Starla and Jaantzen coming in with Aster about twenty minutes ago. And the back door feed . . ."

She lets it play. Bennion Zacharia, T.J. Meijer, and a half-dozen soldiers.

Oriol reaches to stop the feed on Meijer. "I know her. She was with Zacharia on the *Dorothy Queen*."

"She led the crew that attacked Starla and us last night," says El. "Starla put her in the ditch, but she doesn't even look like she's limping now."

Oriol's pale finger scatters light as he touches the

woman's face. "I gave her that cut a couple of days back. It almost looks healed."

"Think she's one of those zombies, like the one El shot last night?" Simca asks.

Oriol looks up, surprised. "Those what?"

"We can speculate later," Manu says. And to Oriol, "Be advised that not all of Zacharia's crew die when you shoot them in the heart."

Fingers brush over his, and he looks down, startled. Toshiyo. He catches her hand and squeezes.

"Do you think he'll keep his word?" she asks.

Zacharia? Keep his word? Manu doesn't think so, not at all.

"It doesn't matter," he says. "We're not planning on keeping ours." He takes a deep breath, thinking. "They want me to take Coeur, and we have to assume Zacharia doesn't intend to let any of us go. El, you're in charge of getting us out of there. Use these two — you know what Oriol can do, and Major Nayar is a strong fighter and highly motivated." He meets Ximena's gaze, holds it for a beat. "We can't let them have this case, and" — god, he can't believe he's even about to say it — "we need Coeur alive."

"And Julieta?" Toshiyo asks.

"She may or may not be our enemy. Err on the side of caution." He touches the water tower on the north side of the greenhouse. "Julieta always has a lookout here. We have to assume her people are our enemies — or that Zacharia's people have taken the usual positions."

Manu's comm buzzes — it's Coeur's guard, they're on their way. He straightens, checks the time. "I need to go. Keep me updated on the plan." He nods solemnly to Oriol, who gives him a sharp "I'll see you soon" salute.

Manu picks up the case with the Coatlicue goddess

etched on the lid, then squeezes Toshiyo's shoulder. She grabs his hand fiercely without turning to look at him.

"There's a little green box on the table to the right of my office door, looks like a deck of cards?" she says. "You should take it. And *don't* drop it — at least, not until you need something destroyed."

"Thanks, Tosh."

"Tell me one of you knows how to skydive," Oriol says to the Anahoys as Manu walks out of the conference room.

"Oh hell yeah!" Simca bounces up on her toes.

"Major Nayar?" Oriol asks.

Ximena grimaces. "Not since basic."

"Perfect. We're going to need a plane, Manu," Oriol calls after him.

"I got a guy," Manu calls back. He steps out into the hall, thumbing through the contacts. *I, J, K* . . . Kulikutan. He initiates the call.

"Twin Star Salvage."

"Yeah, Beto, it's Manu Juric from RKE," Manu says. "I'm going to need you at the airfield as soon as possible."

A second of stunned silence on the other end of the line. Manu can hear chopsticks clacking.

"I'm sorry?" the other man says.

"I need a pilot, right now. You my man?"

"Ah. Yeah?"

A woman's voice in the background, calling Beto's name.

"Great. I'll be passing you off to my colleague, he'll explain what he needs," Manu says. "I'll owe you for this."

The sound of a chair scraping back from the table.

"Thanks?" Beto says.

And Manu patches his call through to Oriol.

No one's in the fourth-floor lobby when he arrives, and

Manu breathes a sigh of relief, allowing his shoulders just a moment of relaxation. He finds Toshiyo's little green box, slips it into the pocket of his suit. Inserts his earpiece and patches it into the network. There's a faint *pop*, and the connection takes.

"Oh, hello again," Toshiyo says in his ear.

"Hey, kid. You hear me all right?"

"I gotcha."

Across the lobby, a chime sounds. The lift doors open. A sliver of ice pierces Manu's gut.

The lift is crowded: a pair of guards, the medic, and Thala Coeur sagging in a wheelchair like a malevolent ghost.

Coeur sees him and breaks into a smile, those black eyes glittering as she drinks him in. It's like being under a magnifying glass, the pure speculative malice she can focus at will, like she's peeling back layers of his skin with her eyes, trying to imagine how his naked heart will look still beating beneath splayed ribs.

Manu ignores her, lifts his chin to the two guards. "You two, report to El Anahoy in the conference room down the hall," he says. "We have a situation."

The taller of the two guards furrows his brow. "Sir?" The man glances down at their prisoner.

"Go."

The medic, Elian, takes the slightest step back at being left alone with Thala Coeur.

"Is she ready to travel?" Manu asks without looking at Coeur.

"I'm not going anywhere," Coeur says.

"She shouldn't really be moved, she's not in a stable condition," Elian says. "But I've got her prepped as good as you're going to get."

"I don't care if it kills her, to be honest. But she's leaving now."

Coeur laughs. "You selling me back to the Dawn, Manu?"

Manu scans the lobby, going through one last sweep of his mental checklist. What is he forgetting?

"Manu Juric."

His name, in her lazy drawl. He glances down unwittingly and she fixes him with a haughty look that cuts like jagged shrapnel.

"Manu Juric," she repeats. "Tell me Jaantzen's selling me to the Dawn."

"No." He tries to force himself to relax his posture, fails. "They've got Jaantzen and Starla, and we're negotiating a hostage exchange."

She sighs with a smile. "Zacharia's finally gonna get his precious case," she says. "I suppose I'm just the cherry on top."

"I don't care why he wants you. He's not getting the case, or you."

"That's awfully gallant of you."

"I'm following orders," he says. "Let's go."

The interior of the lift is so much smaller than he wants it to be; he can feel the closeness of her arm to his like electric energy, singeing his skin through his suit jacket.

Coeur tilts her head, examining him; he forces himself to meet her gaze. She's wearing a loose floral blouse and linen trousers that someone must have scrounged from a guest bedroom, the thin fabric outlining knobbed shoulders, bladed hips. Her fine cheekbones are a mass of bruises. Her bandaged hands lie in her lap like clubs.

"Why should I trust you," she says finally.

"Because you have no choice," Manu snaps. "I would

love to see you dead, but that's not my call. Jaantzen thinks you're better off alive, and your sister's working with my team. Let that reassure you, or I'll have Elian sedate you and we can do this whole thing with you on a stretcher. It doesn't matter to me. What is it?"

Toshiyo's voice is insistent in his ear; he shifts away from Coeur.

"I just spotted two more squadrons approaching Julieta's from the canyon to the north."

"We're going to need a distraction," he says.

The corner of Coeur's mouth tugs up, ever so slightly. "I still got good crew who'll fight if they know I'm alive," she says. "Crew that's always ready to roll."

"Crew that's willing to follow orders from Jaantzen's man?"

"If I tell them to."

"Tell me."

"Castor Nikahr." She rattles off a fifteen-digit call number.

"Nikahr's not in your crew. He works for you?"

"Has done. Tell him he owes me for the Ruby Basin thing. He'll understand."

Manu messages the information to El; the lift doors open in the garage. "You got everyone's call numbers memorized?" he asks as Elian wheels her out.

"Everyone I might need," she says. She fixes him with a look. "I got a mind like that for those that cross me, too."

"I'm sure you do." Manu holds the spinner door open for her, checks the time again. They're cutting it so, so close. "Let's go."

19

JAANTZEN

The misters have come and gone again, and Jaantzen's gratified to see that Bennion Zacharia's crew seems to be just as unnerved by the cloying humidity and dripping foliage of Julieta's greenhouse as he is.

Zacharia himself, however, seems unperturbed. His calm mask hasn't cracked once while Jaantzen's been watching, not when he was speaking to Manu, not when giving orders to his team, not even at the success of his little mission. He's pulled up a short wooden stool and is watching Starla with interest. She's glaring daggers.

"What didn't you get from Coeur the first time around?" Jaantzen asks. The bindings dig into his forearms, though he's only trapped in one of Julieta's antique bamboo chairs. He could break the chair if he needed to — though he doubts he'd make it more than a few seconds before slugs and pulses from a half-dozen weapons would tear him to bits. But he'll try it if Zacharia touches his daughter.

Zacharia turns his cool gaze back to Jaantzen. "The satisfaction of breaking her," he says. "Unless you've done so already."

"Thala Coeur's health is unfortunately improving under my roof," Jaantzen says.

Jaantzen's imagining Zacharia interrogating Coeur, wearing that impassive mask while he prods for weaknesses Jaantzen's sure she doesn't have. He'd bet anything that Coeur made Zacharia's calm fray — the woman can destroy anyone's zen. Watching that demon rain down like hellfire on a common enemy would be a pleasant sight.

"No one who's met her wants Blackheart back," Jaantzen says. "What do you really want?"

Zacharia gives him a long look, evaluating. "I want the gift of the Fallen."

The case full of serum, of course. Coeur believed the Dawn wanted it so they, too, could take advantage of the riches that would come with terraforming and agricultural production. But Julieta had told him that Zacharia had offered Acheta some sort of drug that would make his soldiers invincible — like the man Jaantzen and his crew fought last night. Was the same serum that transformed the land also transforming Zacharia's soldiers?

Jaantzen spares a glance at the soldiers ringing them now. Which of these are also unkillable?

"Coeur thought you were in it for the money," Jaantzen says. "She forgot she was dealing with a religious zealot. Whatever this serum is, is it all part of this end-times delusion Aster was raving on about?"

A twitch of Zacharia's cheek. Jaantzen has learned from watching Coeur that it's all about finding the soft spots, then sinking in needle after needle until your prey is driven mad. She's also taught him that some prey are easier than others.

"Aster," Jaantzen says, fixing the girl with a look. Something that's been bothering him finally clicks into place. "I never saw you as a killer."

Her face blanches. "What — "

"Not getting your own hands dirty, of course. But luring me here? Sending Ximena to your mother's warehouse, the same time you knew Zacharia's crew was going to show up looking for the case? I didn't think you were this impressionable."

"What the prophet says, it's all true," says Aster. "It's — "

Zacharia turns his gaze on her and her mouth snaps shut. Color blotches her cheeks.

"I have no need to debate my religion with a nonbeliever," Zacharia says. "Though I would welcome an opportunity to show you what the serum does to those who aren't strong enough to walk through its flames." Zacharia leans forward, elbows on knees, fingers steepled in front of his lips. "I've developed a sense for who will and will not pass. And you, Willem Jaantzen, are black at the core."

There's venom in the way he says it, the first emotion Jaantzen's seen from him.

Good. He can use venom.

"I'm not interested in your afterlife," says Jaantzen. "But you're welcome to leave a pamphlet."

Zacharia's nostrils flare at that, just a touch. He tilts his head, turning his attention to Starla, who's watching him with the speculative look of a caged wolf who's become bored of captivity and is already reliving your death in its memory. And enjoying it.

It reminds him in no small part of Coeur. His chest tightens.

"The Dusai girl, on the other hand? She comes from good blood. When she walks through the fire, her soul will burn pure. I look forward to putting her through the test." A slow smile spreads across his face. "But don't worry, you can watch and see just what you could have become before going to meet your own fate."

"Tell me more about your nice delusion," Jaantzen says. He wants this man's attention as far away as possible from his daughter. "You've got a captive audience."

"I'm sure it's humiliating to be on this side of things," Zacharia says. "But you're handling it well."

"I didn't get where I am through pride," Jaantzen says.

"Pride is chief among weakness, deepest among traps," says Zacharia. Around him, his soldiers murmur assent; Aster does, too, her hands flying to press piously together in front of her as if in prayer.

"One of your prophet's little gems?"

"Universal truth. If we're to make way for a new era, we need to purge all weaknesses in ourselves — and in those around us."

"So you're a preacher."

Zacharia just smiles. "I am the prophet's tool."

"Purifying your own soul for heaven?"

That mask breaks, just for a moment, and a dark shadow flickers behind Zacharia's eyes. "There is no place in an ascendent world for my soul," he says. "The prophet will lead the worthy, but only because I and my people have taken on the sins of the world. We stain ourselves with blood so the prophet and the ascendent don't have to."

"What does that world look like?"

"A world at peace, united. Humans had it on the *Ark Matsya*, that togetherness of purpose and connection, but we destroyed our purpose by landing here, dividing up the land, crawling all over these rocks like vermin and snapping at each other for territory. We need to wipe the slate clean once again."

"Wipe the slate clean of humanity?"

"Just the weak."

"By poisoning them with shard."

Zacharia simply shrugs. "The good word needs funding," he says. "And it's better to destroy the weak now. Why let them hold us back during the final battle?"

"Since you're hell-bent on getting Coeur, the first thing you should know about her is that she doesn't care much for other people's plans. Not even your prophet's."

"She'll learn respect for his plans."

Jaantzen lets himself laugh at that. "If you figure out how to teach Blackheart to respect, you'll be the talk of the town."

Zacharia lifts his chin. "I assume we will be, soon."

"Isn't that pride?"

A twitch of his cheek, nostrils flaring wide this time. Zacharia smooths his palms down his thighs.

"Turn on some lights," he snaps at Aster. The sun has set while they've been talking, and Julieta's ambient lighting system has slowly spun up: running lights glowing softly along the paths between tables, witch lights suspended in the foliage. Aster disappears down one of the aisles, trailed by one of Zacharia's soldiers with a hand on his gun. Jaantzen notes that with interest. It seems Zacharia doesn't trust the girl any more than he does.

"Where are they?" Zacharia asks one of his soldiers, a woman about Jaantzen's age, with a thick braid of silver hair on one side. T.J. Meijer, Jaantzen remembers from the profile Toshiyo showed him.

"On their way," she says. "They should be here any minute."

"Good. Then we can — " Zacharia's full attention focuses suddenly on Starla. Jaantzen turns to see her watching Julieta, the older woman trying to indicate something with her gaze.

"What's happening here?" Zacharia asks, an icy purr in his voice. "If you have something to say, feel free to share." He smiles at that, knowing full well that he's silenced them both already, Starla with her bonds and Julieta with her gag. He strolls over to Julieta's work table, picks up a pair of pruning shears. Runs the sharp edge across his thumb.

"These look like they can do some damage to a plant — or a finger," he says. He smiles at Julieta. "One can tell a master's dedication to her art by how she keeps her tools."

"The deal was for Coeur for our lives," says Jaantzen sharply. "And she's on her way."

"Coeur for your lives," says Zacharia. "You think that snipping a few fingers off an old lady will give her a heart attack?"

Aster has returned and is watching, her face ashen. "Ben."

"'Ben,'" he repeats quietly. "I didn't realize you thought you were going home after this was all through. I thought you said the Dawn were your family now."

"Of course, but — "

"Then this old woman is a stranger to you."

He gives her a long, evaluating look. "You were so promising." And there's a sadness, a finality in the way he says it that sends a shiver down Jaantzen's spine. "But a young rich girl like you, you never truly believed you'd have to renounce it all."

"I did what you asked," Aster protests.

"And it cost you more than you expected. I pushed you too hard, too fast. I take responsibility."

Aster's eyes widen, lips parting in protest.

Zacharia lifts his chin to Meijer. The woman lashes out with the butt of her plasma carbine against the back of Aster's skull, so fast Jaantzen barely sees her move; Aster crumples to the ground, Julieta is screaming into her gag.

Zacharia steps over Aster's body. He's still holding the pruning shears, but his attention has shifted from Julieta to Starla.

Jaantzen strains sharply against his bonds, heart racing. "If you harm her — "

Zacharia lifts a fist and all weapons snap into place, aimed at Jaantzen.

"I don't want to hear from you again," Zacharia says. He turns his dead-eyed smile back at Starla. "But I am curious. Just how good a stock does this one come from?" He reaches for one of Starla's hands and she balls her fists, bares her teeth.

"What's that supposed to mean?" Jaantzen asks, desperate to regain Zacharia's attention.

The man spares him a glance. "Kill him if he says another word," he says. "It's been thirty minutes, hasn't it? It's time to begin a test. Let's show Mr. Jaantzen just how glorious the coming world will be."

Zacharia grasps Starla's left fist, slowly, inexorably prying out her index finger.

"You wouldn't fight me if you knew what was coming," he says to her patiently, like he's teaching catechism to a child. "Pain now gives you strength to withstand future trials. Starla Dusai, I am saving you."

He raises the pruning shears.

And he screams.

Starla drives the heel edge of her boot into the flesh of his calf, whatever blade she's got hidden there cutting deep enough that blood arcs across the greenhouse floor. Zacharia strikes back in fury, sending her crashing to the side in a tangled mess of splintered bamboo. He pulls his pistol, aims, and —

"Bennion."

The woman, Meijer, steps forward. Zacharia keeps his weapon leveled at Starla's head.

"He brought her," she says. "They're outside."

For a long moment, no one moves. Then Zacharia shoves his pistol back into its holster.

"Take her and the old woman," he says. He takes a limping step back from Starla, then gingerly touches the gash on his calf. "We'll finish this after we have Coeur and the case secured."

Manu's passed two spinners parked on the road just outside Julieta Yang's estate, where there should be none. Inside, men are armed to the teeth and not bothering to hide it.

"We've got sentries in these spinners I just passed," Manu says to Toshiyo. "One blue, one silver. You see them?"

"Copy that. I marked them," she says in his ear. "Nobody else has moved."

"Give me a knife," Coeur says from the passenger seat. She's leaned back in the seat, head lolling and eyes closed like she's gathering energy. Or about to keel over and finally die.

"No," Manu says.

"Wrap it up in my hands, they won't check there."

With anyone else, Manu might consider the idea a decent one. But with Thala Coeur? "I'm not giving you a knife and letting you loose. Especially not near my crew."

"You have issues with delegation and trust."

"Doesn't mean I'm not right." Manu glances over at her.

Her eyes are still closed. Her lips are thin with pain. "You know, if you hadn't double-crossed the Dawn, none of us would be here. Not double-crossing people is actually pretty easy."

She rolls her head to the side, opens her eyes. "It was a lot of money to leave on the table. Plus, they brought me back here, didn't they? If I'm gonna die anyway, it's gonna be in my city."

"You . . ." Manu frowns at her. "You thought if you double-crossed them, they'd capture you and bring you back here."

"Plan worked."

"They just about killed you."

"Nobody gets a free ride, Juric."

Manu doesn't have an answer to that.

"One knife," Coeur says. "That's it."

"I'm supposed to bring you back out of here alive," Manu says. "Giving you a knife seems like it'd put you in harm's way."

"Then what do you call sending me in unarmed? Fucking like this?" She lifts her bandaged hands.

"How will you even use it?"

And the scornful look she sends his way could be a weapon in its own right. "Bitch, who do you think you're talking to?"

The gate to Julieta's complex is wide-open, and though he doesn't see a guard here, their presence down the road has made a statement. No one's coming in or out without Bennion Zacharia's permission.

Manu slows the spinner to a crawl before making the turn into Julieta's long driveway. He reaches down, pulls the knife from his dress boot. It's slim but sturdy, a last

resort for fighting, and it won't add much bulk. She's right —
no one's likely to search her bandaged hands.

Coeur grins and begins undoing the bandages around
her left hand with her teeth. As the fabric unravels he
catches a glimpse of her skin: purpled and yellowed beneath
the earthy red, flaking scabs. He looks away.

Manu guides the spinner down the driveway, scanning
the dense desert foliage around them for signs of trouble; he
sees nothing. He parks in the center of the driveway.
Jaantzen's Dulciana JX is in front of the greenhouse, which
is where he and Starla must be. The greenhouse is the only
building with its lights on.

The greenhouse is to the left, the main house straight
ahead and wrapping around to the right. A beautifully land-
scaped dry fountain graces the center of the driveway,
generations of smugglers' wealth shaping this estate into
something with understated elegance.

It's eerie in the deep twilight gloom, with no one else
visible around them.

"They must be in the greenhouse," he says. "Let's go."

Coeur takes in a sharp breath. She doesn't move.

"Don't tell me you're scared."

Her eyes burn. "Of course not. But I can't — " She bites
down on the words, and Manu has the sudden realization
that Thala Coeur is trying to ask him for help. "I don't think I
can walk," she says finally, spitting the words out like bullets.

"That's fine," he says, holding her gaze. "I've been
there."

A muscle clenches in her jaw.

Manu exits, crosses to the passenger side, and helps
Coeur to her feet. She hisses with pain as he drapes her arm
over his shoulder.

"We're going in," he murmurs to Toshiyo.

"Two minutes," she replies.

Two full minutes. That could be an eternity, or not enough time — he has no way of knowing.

Manu pulls his pistol from its holster and aims it at Coeur's head.

"Grab the case. Let's go."

"Ah. Smart," she says.

"Shut up." He half carries, half drags her halfway between his spinner and the greenhouse. "I brought you Blackheart," he shouts, and, standing in the middle of an empty driveway with wind rustling the trees and the first glimmering stars fighting through the deepening night above, he feels ridiculous.

"Ninety seconds," Toshiyo says.

"C'mon," Manu whispers. From the hills behind Julieta's house comes the thin howl of a desert wolf. He feels each second ticking by in the slow, steady heartbeat of Thala Coeur's broken body against his own.

Finally, the door to the greenhouse opens and a single figure appears in the doorway: the woman with the silver braid. She holds a plasma carbine in chiseled arms which show that despite her age she's hardly past her prime. She waits until they've crossed the distance of the driveway — Coeur favoring her left foot badly — then motions to someone behind her.

Starla and Julieta appear in the doorway next, Starla helping the older woman walk. Neither looks injured, and Manu breathes a sigh of relief. He catches Starla's eye, nods towards the spinner. Traitor or not — he's still not sure which Yang Oriol's list refers to — they can deal with the old woman later.

"Where's Jaantzen?" he asks once he hears the spinner

doors close safely behind him. "I need to see him before she goes anywhere."

Meijer shakes her head. "Give me Coeur and the case, and you'll get your boss back."

Manu digs the pistol into Coeur's jaw. She takes a satisfyingly sharp, rasping breath. "I'd be very happy to kill her. Just give me a reason."

Oriol's voice sounds in his ear. "Keep her talking," he murmurs. "Almost there."

Manu needs Jaantzen out, or he needs to be in that building to protect him once everything starts going sideways. Manu takes a step forward, dragging Coeur at his side.

"You're not going anywhere, Juric," Meijer orders.

"We had a deal," Manu says. "Bring me Jaantzen, you can do whatever the hell you want with Coeur."

The woman finally turns to bark an order at someone behind her.

"Incoming," murmurs Oriol.

Shit, too soon, *too soon.*

A shot cracks in the night and the guard in the water tower falls, screaming.

Another, and Manu's lower back explodes with pain; he drops to his knees, Coeur's slight weight taking him down like an anchor. He manages to get a shot off at Meijer, but it goes wide and she only jerks back as his bullet catches her shoulder. It's not good enough. But it earns him just enough time to pull the green box Toshiyo gave him out of his pocket and fling it at the greenhouse's doorway.

Glass shatters. The blast rocks Meijer . . . not as much as it should. She snaps her plasma carbine back up.

The bolt hits Manu full in the chest.

The world goes black.

21

JAANTZEN

The overhead lights go out in a blast of energy from the front of the greenhouse. A rush of wind and heat, then drifting soot, choking smoke. Around them, the misters switch back on, aggressively watering plant and workbench, captor and captive.

Jaantzen's heart stops beating. Calculations rush through his mind: how long would it have taken for Starla and Julieta to get out, where were they when the blast went off? Through the muffled ringing in his ears he can make out shouts at the entryway, gunfire. Someone is out there fighting back.

One of Zacharia's soldiers slashes through his bonds.

"Move," the man barks, prodding him to his feet with his rifle. There's just the two soldiers, now, along with Zacharia. The other three went with Meijer to exchange Julieta and Starla for Coeur.

"Out the back," Zacharia says. "You're with us."

Whether they never intended to let him go or he's being used as insurance to help them escape, Jaantzen isn't certain. But if Zacharia wanted him dead, he would've had a bullet in him the moment things started to go south. Jaantzen doesn't move.

"Let's go!" Zacharia shouts.

"I'm not going anywhere with you," Jaantzen says.

Lightning tears through his chest, electricity shredding his organs. He collapses back into the bamboo chair, arching against the pain.

It stops abruptly.

He's doubled over, panting, muscles like water.

Zacharia's soldier clips the fist-sized electric barb back onto his belt.

"Next time it's a bullet," Zacharia says. "Now let's go."

Through the rush of blood in his ears, he hears the clobber of combat boots. The woman, Meijer, arrives with their prizes: Thala Coeur locked in one arm, the silver case tucked under the other. Jaantzen is almost surprised to see it — he'd wondered if that was what had blown up in the entrance.

Meijer's hauling Coeur like she's weightless or Meijer's invincible, and what with the way she's ignoring the blood streaming down her shoulder, it may be the latter. Zacharia motions for her to lead the way to the back of the green-house, and his two remaining soldiers wrestle Jaantzen to his feet, push him stumbling after with legs that have momentarily lost connection with the rest of his nervous system.

Jaantzen's threading his way through the narrow, leafy passages when the ceiling explodes, showering them all with broken glass. He covers his head with his arms, then looks up to see a figure in black combat gear land in a crouch in the center of the pathway, blocking their exit.

Oriol?

Meijer doesn't hesitate — she drops Coeur in the aisle

and sets the case on a table, then leaps after Oriol. He parries her blows, a kick from his prosthetic leg sending her staggering back with a grunt — but only for a second before she charges again, ducking the slash of his blade and aiming her own blow that sends him crashing through the foliage. She leaps after him.

"Take her," Zacharia shouts to Jaantzen. One of his soldiers has already grabbed the case and is on his way towards the back. Coeur is watching it go with a snarl of frustration.

Jaantzen pulls her to her feet. He can feel individual ribs through the thin blouse; they feel like they could snap under his broad palm. She smells both sharp and warm, a combination of astringent medical odors and beeswax. Her breath catches in pain as he hoists her arm over his shoulders; air moves on his cheek.

"Get me close to that asshole," she whispers.

She's impossibly light.

He stumbles with her out of the greenhouse.

22

STARLA

The concussion of the exploding warehouse rocks the Dulciana, and Starla pushes Julieta down to the floor and hopefully out of harm's way. At first she can't make sense of who's fighting whom — there's gunfire coming from the greenhouse and return fire coming from the other side of Julieta's fountain. A mass of parachute fabric billows just beyond it, cords tangling in the thornbrush and aloe that edge the driveway.

Someone's grabbed Coeur from where Starla saw her fall by the greenhouse door, but Manu's still lying motionless. She can't get to him, not with the crossfire. Not without a weapon.

She can't tell if he's breathing.

The Dulciana shudders as a spray of bullets from the greenhouse strafes the door. Starla covers Julieta's body with her own, peeks back through the window when the shaking stops.

One of the figures from the other side of the fountain has bridged the gap to the Dulciana. Simca. Her hands are too full of rifle to sign properly, but she pats the stock, points to Starla through the window: I've got one for you, too.

Excellent.

"Stay here," Starla signs to Julieta. "Lock the doors." She mimes door locking for good measure, and Julieta nods.

Starla waits for the all-clear from Simca, then slips out the spinner's door, keeping the Dulciana between herself and the greenhouse. She takes the rifle Simca offers and slips the strap over her shoulder to keep her hands free a moment longer.

"Jaantzen is still inside," she signs.

Simca nods. "Oriol went straight in," she signs. "We've got crew coming around the back."

Oriol? Starla doesn't have time to wonder or be grateful.

"Cover us, then get to Manu," Starla orders. "Follow us when he's safe." She's not entertaining the possibility that he doesn't need to be made safe.

Ximena is watching for direction from her position crouched behind the fountain. Starla gives her a thumbs-up, and in simplified military signs: "You're with me."

Ximena gives her a thumbs-up in return.

At her back, the Dulciana shudders again with gunfire; a blast from a pulse carbine sears past, charring the spines of a silver-needle fern cacti into a smoldering hand. Beside her, Simca leaps up from her crouch, aiming at the greenhouse.

Starla charges around the Dulciana as Simca lays down covering fire, leaping the rubble that used to be the greenhouse's door and taking out the Dawn soldier who ducked behind a twisted metal table. A bullet sparks off the table, coming from behind, and Starla whirls to face her new attacker.

But he's already slumped beside a toppled stone saint in a tangle of vines. Ximena nods to her.

They head into the greenhouse.

Three minutes ago, Starla had been tied to a chair in a brightly lit jungle; now, the greenhouse is in shambles. The overhead lights have gone out, leaving only the running lights and witch lights casting the foliage in flat, dimensionless color. Moonlight sparks off shattered glass and water pools on the floor as the misters drench the building.

The trio of chairs that held her, Jaantzen, and Julieta are empty; hers is splintered and twisted. At first glance, the greenhouse seems deserted. Then a lemon tree topples to the ground in the path before Starla, and two figures locked in battle crash through.

She recognizes Meijer, her silver braid whipping through the air as she spins, lands a kick behind her opponent's knee. Oriol staggers forward, then pivots and drives his fist forward and up into the woman's gut.

They're grappling in leaves slick with blood, and it's becoming abundantly clear who's winning. Despite the wounds Meijer has taken, she's still fighting precise, strong. Oriol's fit, but he's only human. And he's flagging.

Starla waves Ximena on and catches a clean shot at Meijer, just as the woman rears back to plunge her blade into Oriol's heart. Starla's bullet takes her through the chest, but Meijer doesn't fall. The pause gives Oriol enough time and momentum to throw her off.

Meijer rolls to a crouch.

She springs towards Starla.

Starla squeezes off another shot from her rifle before Meijer crashes into her. She deflects the flashing blade; Meijer buries it in the overturned wooden potting table behind Starla, pulls it out, stabs again.

Starla finds enough strength to shove the woman back; she's made of bands of steel, heavy as stone.

And Meijer's head snaps back, Oriol behind her with a handful of braid in one hand, a short yet wicked curved blade in his fist. He buries it in the base of her neck.

Meijer slumps to the ground.

Oriol reaches a blood-slicked hand to help Starla to her feet.

"They've got Jaantzen," he signs, and before he can say anything more she's running towards the back of the greenhouse.

23

JAANTZEN

The rear entrance of the greenhouse is a battlefield, too.

Julieta's greenhouse's loading dock opens onto a gravel lot leading to a gate that's always barred, but tonight that gate's flung wide-open and being defended against an attack from the outside. An armored truck and a four-doored spinner are docked and running.

Zacharia prods Jaantzen and Coeur towards the spinner with the muzzle of his gun; it jabs sharp against Jaantzen's spine. "Your people won't shoot if they know you're in here with me," he says.

"Leave us and I'll be sure they don't," Jaantzen says. Behind them, Jaantzen can still hear crashing, shouting as Oriol and Meijer battle it out. Someone is yelling orders in the distance beyond the wall.

Is it his people? Is Starla with them? He has no way of knowing.

The only thing he knows for sure is that the expiration date of his usefulness is rapidly approaching.

Cold metal presses against the base of his skull.

"Of course, they'll assume you're alive," Zacharia says.

"Willem."

He barely hears Coeur's whisper.

"Get me close to him," she'd said.

He can't do anything to help his crew with a bullet in his skull.

Slowly, Jaantzen bends to put Coeur into the spinner. The back is more for transport than comfort, with two bench seats facing each other across a cramped aisle. He sets Coeur in the far corner then sits opposite. In such a small space, she can't help but be close to Zacharia.

A shot rings out, meters away, and the soldier closest to Zacharia falls.

"Thala!"

Ximena Nayar is in the doorway to the greenhouse. She takes aim, clips Zacharia's remaining soldier. The impact of the bullet spiderwebs the back window of the spinner.

Coeur's halfway out of the spinner, but Zacharia's shot hits Ximena in the hip and she falls, then staggers to her feet and after them, raising her weapon once more.

Coeur screams her sister's name.

Zacharia shoots her in the head.

Ximena slumps to the ground, a mantle of black spreading beneath her shoulders, eyes wide-open to the night sky and already glazed. Beside him, Coeur is screaming.

Zacharia's soldier shoves Coeur back into the spinner and Zacharia slides in after, pulling the door closed. "Drive!" he yells.

They're skidding through the gate in seconds, the momentum knocking Jaantzen hard against the door. Coeur sobs out in pain. Through tinted windows in the dark night he can't tell who's fighting whom, but despite an initial spark of bullets against the spinner's sides, no one attacks them. Jaantzen's people must know he's in here, which means they'll follow him.

Which means they have a chance.

But — Ximena dead. Oriol paired with one of Zacharia's unkillable soldiers. Starla and Manu nowhere to be seen. He has no idea if anyone else has made it out.

"That was your sister, wasn't it?" Zacharia says. He checks the ammo in his gun, lays it across his lap so the barrel is pointing straight at Jaantzen. Across from Jaantzen, his soldier mirrors Zacharia's target. The case is cramping the meager leg room between them all.

Coeur's gone silent, slumped across from Zacharia. She's glassy-eyed and expressionless as she sways with the shifting of the spinner, the jostling of potholes on rough desert road. She looks destroyed, but she's watching Zacharia. Murder floats calmly in her gaze.

It chills Jaantzen to the bone. Before, he at least trusted that she wanted to get out of this alive. Now, she's smoldering with a fire meant to burn the whole world down with her.

Keep it together, he wills her. Wills them both.

Jaantzen's expecting them to head east, back to the Dry Creek neighborhood, but instead they turn north, heading farther out of the city and into the desert hills. He cranes his neck to follow their path, but he can't guess at their destination.

"Yes?"

Jaantzen turns back to Zacharia, but he's just answering a call. He lifts his weapon pointedly to Jaantzen as if to reassure him that he's paying attention.

Coeur's watching now, too, lids hooded and head bobbing loosely with the motions of the rough road. Despite her slumped posture, her eyes are clear and bright with fury. Jaantzen meets her gaze, calculating just how much strength she has left. And whether she'll use it to get them both out of this mess, or to destroy them all.

She raises an eyebrow, the flare of a question in her expression.

Jaantzen cuts his gaze to the soldier beside her, then back. Raises his own eyebrows.

That bitter quirk of her mouth: Who do you think you're asking?

Jaantzen gives her the faintest of nods.

Coeur breaks into a hacking cough, doubling over in her seat with hands hanging limply over her knees. The knobs of her rounded spine stand like knuckles through the thin fabric of her blouse. The soldier beside her looks over in alarm as she continues to cough; Zacharia pauses in his conversation, studying her.

"And just like that, Willem," she says when she's caught her breath. She wipes blood from her lips onto the back of her bandaged hand and he frowns at that; is she truly still coughing up blood? Did she bite her tongue for effect? Either is a possibility. "A little gun to your head is all it takes for you to give me up," Coeur says. "I thought we were friends."

"Quiet, please," Zacharia says, finger touching his ear. He's still trying to follow the conversation on the call.

"I'm not sure where you got that impression," Jaantzen says.

"You think you can sell me like this and take my crew? Like you could try — you're not half the man you'd need to be for that." Coeur laughs, showing that line of gleaming teeth with a gap where the Dawn knocked out an eyetooth. "You'll be bored without me."

"Quiet," says Zacharia.

"I have plenty of other enemies."

"Religious fanatics?" Coeur rolls her eyes. "Brainwashed idiots who got themselves an arsenal."

"We seem to have bested you," Zacharia says irritably. "Now please be quiet."

"Strong man's snatched an invalid," laughs Coeur. "Very impressive, I'm swooning."

Zacharia sighs sharply and gestures to the soldier beside Coeur. "Shut her up."

The soldier reaches for her with his electric barb but she deflects with her right arm, stabbing her bandaged left hand at his throat with a ferocious howl that's part rage, part agony. The barb's blast hits Coeur's headrest and leaves a smoking scorch; the state she's in, that shock probably would have killed her, not simply shut her up.

Jaantzen reacts the second she begins to move, well before Zacharia, grabbing the soldier's pistol and jamming the barrel into Zacharia's temple. Jaantzen is faintly aware of the flash of a silver razor in Coeur's bandaged hand, the acrid smoke from the scorched headrest, the sound of the soldier choking in his own blood.

Zacharia slowly raises his hands, but doesn't move to set down his pistol.

"Ben?" yells the driver.

"Keep driving!" Zacharia calls, and the spinner lurches as the driver punches the gas. Zacharia's gaze doesn't waver. Neither does Jaantzen's aim.

"I am not your enemy here," Zacharia says calmly.

"You're the one holding me hostage."

"Ignorance is the enemy. Kill me, and you won't do anything to stop the inevitable. Join me, and at least you'll go to your fate with your eyes open. Maybe your sacrifice will even help save some of your crew, your daughter."

Coeur laughs. "'Ignorance is the enemy.'"

"Tell me what's coming," Jaantzen says.

"Now he wants answers," Zacharia says with a faint smile. "I'll tell you. After we get Coeur and the case delivered safely."

"You're not listening to this," Coeur says.

"You and me, we have no chance to save ourselves," Zacharia says. "But if the work I do saves others, I consider my life well lived. And your daughter? She still has a chance. So long as you don't throw it away."

Jaantzen cuts his gaze to Coeur, who reaches for Zacharia's gun. She can't use it with her hands bandaged like that, but she tucks it out of reach; she's already got the soldier's electric barb held in one bandaged hand, thumb on the button.

"Tell me what you know."

The spinner's wheel drops into a pothole and Zacharia lunges for Jaantzen, using the momentum of the vehicle to knock his weapon out of the way. A bullet slams into the body of the spinner beside Jaantzen's head — the driver firing back over his shoulder — and they're grappling, punches thrown.

"Hold on," yells Coeur, and Jaantzen instinctively grabs for the safety harness, feels the crackle of energy as she barbs the driver, the wrench of the wheel, and the spinner tumbling off the road.

Everything goes impossibly bright, then viciously black; Jaantzen comes to in a familiar nightmare of choking smoke and burning plastic, charred metal, the rush of scalding fire licking at his skin, rippling heat blasting him in waves as a spinner burns around him.

He's had this nightmare before, night after night, and whereas in his dreams he's peaceful, ready to succumb and finally join the family that went before him, now his body reacts violently with a will to live.

He gasps for breath, eyes flying open.

"About fucking time," someone yells beside him.

In his recurring dreams, Thala Coeur is not beside him, shaking him awake, her legs crushed beneath the dead weight of the soldier.

Jaantzen wrenches free of his safety harness. Zacharia is nowhere to be seen. He tries to move the soldier off Coeur, but he's wedged.

"Go," Coeur yells. She's grinning, and there's not a hint of fear in her expression. Whatever part of Jaantzen's animal being that's screaming for him to save himself is missing from behind her eyes. "Right way for me to end, yeah?" she says, and he sees it's not just that she's trapped. Whether the smoke or a concussion or her previous injuries, she's starting to lose consciousness. "Always figured I'd deserve this."

And her eyes close.

The flames are getting hotter, the roar around him drowning out all else.

Jaantzen yanks his suit sleeve down over his hand and pulls up on the spinner's handle; it opens easily but the door jams against an outside obstacle. He slams his shoulder against it, once, twice, and the third time it breaks free. A rush of fresh air from outside fans the flames into an inferno.

Jaantzen turns away from the fresh air, grabs Coeur beneath the arms, and pulls with all his might. It seems like hours, but they're out and free in a moment, crawling away from the charred remains of the spinner as her eyes flutter back open.

A flash of silver catches Jaantzen's attention: Bennion Zacharia has the case and is scrambling away through the underbrush. Jaantzen picks up an abandoned rifle and aims. Fires.

The bullet tears through the case, and whatever Coeur did to booby-trap it works amazingly well. A chemical fireball consumes the road, a complicated, multipetaled bloom of retina-burning oranges and bloody reds. A wave of heat washes over Jaantzen. The scent of burnt hair and scorched underbrush. Flakes of grit drifting gently down to coat his face and fill his eyes.

Coeur is lying beside him, face a mask of shock.

"You missed," she hisses.

"I didn't," he replies.

"You're supposed to be resting."

Manu looks up from the tablet in his lap to find Oriol struggling through the door with an armload of bags.

"So are you," Manu answers.

"I was starving. You don't have anything to eat here."

"I've been busy."

These last two days of recovery were actually the most time he's spent in his own apartment in months. Lately he's even missed nights, sleeping instead on the cot he keeps in his office, and when he does come home he only showers, sleeps, dresses, goes out again. With such a schedule — and with Oriol gone — the main living area has been so devoid of signs of life, it looked like a hotel room.

Now Oriol's boots are kicked under one green linen armchair, his jacket rumpled over the back of the other, his satchel slumped in the middle of the entry next to the crutches he uses at home. One corner of the accent rug at the door to the balcony is folded over, and a painting — a Lu Shan — in the hallway is off-kilter. The dining table has been shoved against the wall to make space for Oriol's exercise routine. Wrappers from yesterday's dinner are still piled on the coffee table beside this morning's mugs, and Manu doesn't even care.

He's dragged his aching body from the bed out to the couch for a change of scenery, and is doing his best to coax his way past the security settings on the data chip that was embedded in the ring Oriol stole from the Dawn. The task is so absorbing he hadn't even realized how hungry he is.

He's expecting takeout, but instead Oriol begins to unload groceries.

"Wait," says Manu. "You're going to cook?"

"I learned how to make a thing on this last trip," Oriol says over his shoulder.

"One thing?"

"Gotta start somewhere. Don't make that face, I've gotten some rave reviews."

"From other crewmembers who are so sick of rations they'll eat anything?"

"I'll take any advantage I can get." Oriol opens a cabinet, frowns at what he sees — or doesn't see — inside. "You're not going to just hand that thing over to Tosh?"

Manu twirls the ring in his fingers; light glitters on its gaudy facets. "You don't think I can get into it on my own?"

"I think Tosh can get into it in thirty seconds flat."

"I'm hurt."

"You're better at shooting people than her. And you're prettier." Oriol winks, then lifts the lid off a wicker basket beside the sink, shakes papery fragments onto the counter. "You don't have any garlic?"

"You're the one who was just at the store."

"I assumed you had garlic. You always have garlic."

"It sprouted, I threw it out a month ago. And don't

worry, Tosh is right here advising me." He holds up the tablet so Oriol can see the chat screen.

"Hmm." Oriol leans over the kitchen counter, taps at something. Seconds later, a message appears on Manu's screen, addressed to both him and Toshiyo.

HE'S SUPPOSED TO BE RESTING.

Toshiyo responds with a smiley face.

"Where's your salt?" Oriol asks.

Manu scratches an ear pensively. "I'm out. I think."

"How are you out of salt, babe." Oriol opens another cupboard. "Out of plates too, yeah?"

"In the sanitizer, I think they're clean?" Manu hits play on the revised program Toshiyo has just sent him. "Work, goddammit," he mutters.

Oriol opens the sanitizer, sighs, and hits the button to start it. He collapses onto a stool at the kitchen counter with a wince of pain and taps at it again to pull up a screen.

"You never said what you were cooking," Manu says.

"I'm cooking fried chicken from Jade's," Oriol says. "Extra black bean sauce?"

"Yes, please."

The program's throwing itself against the chip's defenses, a maddeningly slow progress bar pulsing across the top of the tablet.

"Yucca chips and chutney?"

"Def."

Oriol finishes the order, then leans back against the back of the stool. "It'll be here in thirty," he says.

Cleaned up and shaved, his face is less haunted than when he rocketed back into Manu's life a few days ago, but he still looks like he's been through hell. Not that Manu looks any better, between the rainbow of bruises and stray plasma spatters over his torso and the cuts all over his face and hands from exploding glass.

None of them got out of Julieta's unscathed.

The tablet in Manu's lap chimes softly to let him know it's finished running the program, and he grins at the results. "I got in," he says, then waves a hand. "Toshiyo got in, whatever."

Oriol straightens. "Tell me I almost died for something juicy," he says. "State secrets, blackmail, that sort of thing."

Manu scans through the file names. "If you call 'Inventory of nitrogen, phosphorus, and potassium in Jupari Desert region three soil' juicy, then yeah. Ooh, look. Spreadsheets."

Oriol groans. "It's really just about farming? Throw it back to the Demosgas and kill me now."

"There's a lot of files on here. Could still be there's something scandalous about the governor's sex life."

"Some good dirt, you mean?" Oriol flashes him a grin; Manu rolls his eyes.

"I gotta let Jaantzen know."

"Manu."

Oriol slips out of the stool and limps over to the couch, then gently removes the tablet from Manu's hands, setting it and the ring on the coffee table. "Your man's supposed to be sleeping, too," he says.

"He'll want to know."

"And he will, but it ain't life or death for him to know right this second."

Oriol pulls up the ottoman from the far end of the couch, sinks onto it with a sigh. He tugs aside the throw pillow Manu's been using to prop up the tablet in his lap, and his hand lights on Manu's knee, the tendons in his forearm rippling beneath his gold-white skin as his fingers gently circle there. "But since you're already not resting," he says, leaning forward, his warm hand slowly sliding up, "we got a few minutes to work up an appetite before dinner."

He tastes like the desert air after rain.

———

Jaantzen can hear her downstairs, the scrape of a chair leg, the clink of glassware in the sink. Starla's been here every time he's woken these last two days — working from his conference table, maybe. He lies listening to her for a few moments until the scent of coffee rouses him. The clock tells him it's too late for coffee, but his circadian rhythm has been demolished anyway by the days of bed rest, and he doesn't care.

He hoists his legs over the side of his bed and pulls on a robe, then levers himself with muscles screaming to stand. He could call her to help him, but he's done with that.

Walking to the top of the stairs isn't bad, but his right knee complains at the thought of going down even a single step. Gia's been telling him it's due for surgery, and he's been putting her off for years. It's never a good time to be laid up healing; after this last escapade, he supposes he should give it another consideration.

Later.

When things have calmed down. Now, he still has the possibility of reprisals from the Dawn and Dry Creek to deal with, Acheta to placate or remove, and a complex web of shifting alliances and requests for meetings from Justice Leone's dinner crowd to navigate. Not to mention figuring out what to do with the demon woman in his medical bay, who's in even worse shape than when he dragged her home the first time.

If he can manage to keep this city from collapsing into another civil war, he doesn't give a damn what happens to his knee.

Starla's in the kitchen, making herself a coffee that's mostly milk. He can't see it, but Jaantzen knows a bead of milk has run down the edge of the container to pool on the countertop. He can't count the number of times he's wiped up that particular combination of stains after a visit from his daughter: a glossy milk ring, a muddy puddle where the spoon sat.

If things had gone differently at Julieta's, that number would have been finite.

The thought runs like water through his spine; his fingers tighten on the bannister.

He still has his daughter, and Julieta still has hers — and though the betrayal must pierce her to the core, Julieta's not told him a thing beyond having called her older daughter and son home to deal with Aster. In whatever form that takes.

There's danger over the horizon, and every fiber of his being screams that Starla's his weakness. When he closes his eyes, he dreams, and he doesn't dream of the crash or the exploding greenhouse or even Ximena's glassy gaze. He sees only Bennion Zacharia, standing over Starla with malice in his eyes.

Every impulse tells Jaantzen to send her away, to keep her from what's coming. But he's stronger with her by his side.

He needs her.

And maybe asking her to stay despite the danger is selfish — or maybe forcing her to the sidelines when she clearly wants to help is the selfish choice. He's not sure. He only knows that he loves her. And he'll kill to keep her safe.

Starla turns, then, and sees him standing on the landing above her just as she takes her first sip of coffee. Her eyes widen and she nearly spits in surprise. She sets the mug on the counter with a clatter; a trickle of coffee spills down the side to form yet another ring.

"You should be in bed," she signs, looking exasperated.

"I smelled coffee," he signs back.

She shoos at him. "I'll bring it up. Go."

Smiling, he goes.

Starla closes the door to Jaantzen's room as softly as she can — he's been having headaches, he said, and she's trying to avoid making potentially loud noises. It's getting late, but the coffee's still warm, and she still has work to do. Triple work, in fact. Besides playing catch-up on her work with Admant, she's also spent the past two days fielding hideously boring correspondence with both Jaantzen's and Manu's secretaries, as well as a woman named Cedra who apparently works for RKE and can't figure out how message priorities work.

Starla is debating calling it a night anyway when a vibration in her gauntlet tells her she has yet another message. She sighs — she wouldn't mind a nap, too, dammit — but it's Toshiyo, asking if she has a minute to check something out.

Starla's hoping it's something about the satellite they've been working on, some interesting mechanical problem she can use to distract herself and make it feel like everything's back to normal. Like Julieta's daughter hadn't led them into a trap. Like they hadn't just lost Ximena, someone she'd started to think of as crew.

An escape to the fourth floor could be exactly what she needs.

She flickers the lights as she enters Toshiyo's workshop, easily picks her way through machinery and half-finished projects. Toshiyo's at her desk, shoes kicked off and legs crossed beneath her on her chair. For the first time since Starla can remember, she's not working on something. She's just sitting. Staring into space.

Starla knocks on the side of a malfunctioning food rehydrator.

Toshiyo's gaze refocuses.

"What is it?" Starla signs.

"How are you?" Toshiyo asks.

Starla shrugs. "Fine."

She's not. She's been having visions, daydreams, she doesn't know what to call the sharp flashes of nightmare terror and imagery that have been interrupting her daily routine ever since they came across Jaantzen and Coeur beside a smoking pile of wrecked spinner. She's been taking them out in the training room, sparring until even Simca has tried to convince her to call it quits.

But physically, she's fine. "What is it?"

Toshiyo pushes gently at her desk; her chair spins in a slow circle.

"What's wrong?"

Toshiyo opens her mouth, closes it. Does so again. Starla's lens isn't transcribing anything, so she must not be speaking, but she's definitely got something to say.

Starla waits.

"You know that bean from the serum?" Toshiyo finally says, half signing, half rapid-fire fingerspelling. "I took it out to look at it and meant to put it back, but got distracted by . . . remember?"

Starla remembers talking about it, hadn't realized Toshiyo'd gone ahead and done it. In fact, Starla remembers telling Toshiyo specifically not to take it out. She had assumed — they've all assumed — that the little magic bean was destroyed along with the serum in the case Manu gave Zacharia.

But she shrugs. "Sure. What is it?"

Toshiyo brow furrows. "Come see."

She slips off her chair and into her shoes, then waves Starla past to her workbench, where she's got a magnifying glass set up. The bean is in a shallow, sealed dish in the tray below. It seems twice as big as it was a few days back, Starla's not sure if that's a trick of her memory. A lot has happened since she last looked at the thing.

But it *is* glowing a faint neon orange. She definitely doesn't remember that.

"Did you put something in there to make it glow?" she asks.

Toshiyo shakes her head. "It started this morning," she signs.

Starla bends her head to look. The bean fills the lens and she steps back, startled. She looks over at Toshiyo, confused.

Toshiyo's gnawing on her lip.

Starla looks again.

It's still colored like a black-eyed pea: pale but for the splash of black on the belly. But close up it doesn't look like a bean so much as an egg, with a pearly, translucent shell. And contained within that shell, she can make out the faint outline of miniature limbs, a zipper-tooth spine. It pulses rhythmically, like a heartbeat.

Starla straightens, an uneasiness growing in her belly.

Toshiyo cracks her ring fingers. "I think it's alive," she signs. "And it's not a plant."

"Is there one like it in the other case?"

"I haven't opened that one."

"Do it."

The case found stowed in the RKE shipment is farther down the workbench. Toshiyo works her thumbs under the goddess's snake heads just like Ximena had — Starla lets a wave of sorrow wash through her — then lifts the faceplate off. She enters the code Ximena used, then gives Starla a thumbs-up. Together, they work the case apart.

Toshiyo nearly drops the lid as it comes free, her eyes going wide. Starla catches it and places it carefully aside — she saw the crater that remained after Jaantzen shot the other case, and she has no intention of blasting a similar hole in Cobalt Tower.

She turns back.

Stifles a scream.

Inside is a glass ball same as in Ximena's case, and inside the ball is a creature that could be a human fetus — if humans had fish tails and leathery wings tipped with razor-sharp claws. It floats in a liquid that glows a faintly pulsing pink, seemingly its own light source.

Dead, Starla thinks, but when she leans in to take a closer look, it opens its eyes and stares right at her.

She jerks back, startled.

Toshiyo leans over it, the pink light playing off her pupils and giving her pale skin a rosy glow. The thing's head seems to be following her movements. Its eyes lock on hers, in curiosity, maybe. Or malice; it's impossible to tell.

Either way, Starla needs an escape from its gaze.

She slides the case's cover back into place; the creature thrashes angrily against the glass of its tank as though trying to keep her from sending it into darkness again. She feels the positive click as the case shuts, but Starla isn't any more comforted to have the thing out of sight.

She and Toshiyo stare at each other a moment, neither sure what to say.

"Didn't get out before, huh?" Toshiyo finally says with a falsely cheerful grin. "Do we bother the boss now, or?"

He's supposed to be resting, but . . . Starla nods. Stares back at the little bean under the magnifying glass. It already seems bigger, and *that* is definitely a trick of her imagination. Right?

Toshiyo hits a button on her desk. "Boss?" she says after a moment. "I'm sorry to bother you right now. But you really need to see this."

AUTHOR'S NOTE

Sometimes I think I'm writing a single, standalone book. And sometimes my characters think otherwise. I plot out my books ahead of time, but I also listen when my instincts tell me I'm uncovering a much larger story.

Double Edged became one of *those books*.

From its initial inception years ago, *Double Edged* sprawled from a standalone novel into a full-on series (*The Bulari Saga*) and a set of novellas centered around individual characters.

I even found myself with too much story to tell in the timeline of this particular book! So if you're dying for more and want to know exactly what Oriol got up to in between shooting up the *Dorothy Queen* casino and hooking back up with Manu, download the free short story at:

WWW.JESSIEKWAK.COM/TROUBLE.

The Bulari Saga is just getting started — and, as you may have gathered, things are about to get . . . interesting. If you're the sort who enjoys bonus excerpts, read on to find a sneak peek at the second book in the series, *Crossfire*.

If you just want to dive in and figure out what the hell Starla and Toshiyo found in the case, buy *Crossfire* now at:

WWW.JESSIEKWAK.COM/BOOK/CROSSFIRE

Thank you for reading!

If you enjoyed *Double Edged*, I'd love to hear your feedback. Leave a review on your favorite retailer to let me know what you thought.

See you in the next book,

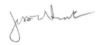

ACKNOWLEDGMENTS

I couldn't have done this without all of my early cheerleaders, from good friends to complete strangers who joined my mailing list and/or sent me notes that made my day. Knowing that you all loved Starla, Jaantzen, Manu, and the rest kept me going through the long slog that is writing a series.

You know who you are. Hugs!

Thank you to my writing community and to the various brain trusts who have helped me strategize about both business and plots over the past years: my powerful Trifecta ladies, my Tiara Club guys, the Indie Finishers group, the Stone Table's distracting Slack channel, the Oregon Writer's Network, my #VanSushi lunch friends, the Monday Night Write-In, the Writer's Social crowd, and my freelance accountability ladies.

A huge thanks to Kate Pickford, my story coach with Lisa Cron and Jennie Nash's *Story Genius* program, who helped me take this book from a chaotic idea to a living, breathing thing. Whenever I'm tempted to take the easy route, I hear your voice telling me to keep digging, to go deeper.

Thanks to Elly Blue and Joe Biel of Microcosm Publishing, who encouraged me to write this book, then graciously supported my decision to let the story take me far away from "bikes in space" into "gangsters in space."

And on that note, thanks to Kathy Kwak, Andrea Rangel, and Robert Kittilson for reading so many damned versions of this novel. Your support and feedback made the Durga System what it is.

Finally, thanks to Fiona Jayde (fionajaydemedia.com) for the brilliant cover design, to Kyra Freestar (Bridge Creek Editing) for the phenomenal editing, and to Jenna Beacom for consulting with me as a sensitivity editor for Starla. You folks all rock.

BONUS EXCERPT

CROSSFIRE: BOOK 2 OF THE BULARI SAGA

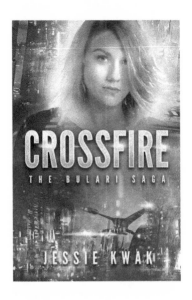

CROSSFIRE
THE BULARI SAGA
JESSIE KWAK

Trouble is dead. Long live trouble.

Killing the leader of a violent cult was supposed to make the city a safer place, but instead it created a power imbalance that's left a deadly war raging in the streets of Bulari.

When Willem Jaantzen is approached for help by local casino magnate Phaera D, he has the sinking feeling the only way to end this war is to betray the people he loves the most. And he's starting to suspect that Phaera wants more from him than just his help.

Whatever decision he makes feels like the wrong one. And as his goddaughter chips away at the mystery surrounding their latest discovery, bringing peace back to the Bulari underground is quickly becoming the least of his worries.

Turn the page to read the first chapter.

CROSSFIRE

He'd been told this place was a temple.

Levi Acheta hasn't been in any temples or churches or whatevers before, but he watched plenty of religious promo vids in exchange for free meals back in rougher times. He knows what they look like: ornamental and opaque in a way meant to comfort believers and disorient outsiders.

This place? It looks like a fortress.

It's cavernous, an abandoned factory on the outskirts of Dry Creek, the northernmost of Bulari's Finger slums. If he takes this place, he'll push the farthest reaches that Blackheart's territory — Acheta's territory, he reminds himself — has ever stretched. Getting here before the Dry Creek crew did had been a gamble.

But Acheta's spent the past few days mopping up the remnants of the Dawn cult, taking the opening left after their leader, Bennion Zacharia, disappeared. And he isn't about to stop before he takes their prize.

This temple, or whatever it is, is definitely going to pay off in weaponry, and — if Acheta's very, very lucky — in some fancy relics and whatnot he can sell off. His crew's stuck with him this long, but the winds are going to shift if he puts off paying them any longer.

Only one problem.

There are plenty of signs of habitation here: sleeping cots in unorganized clusters, salvaged food rehydrators buried in reeking mounds of discarded containers, the shitters out back.

But no people. And no bodies, except for the ones he and his crew left in the street outside.

Maybe the cultists packed up and left after Zacharia's death, and to avoid the fighting between Acheta and the Dry Creek crew in the week that followed. Maybe the rumors are right and the Dawn actually was just a bunch of brainwashed rich kids who ran back to their mansions once things got tough.

Or maybe it's a trap.

The only nod to their weird-ass cult is a small shrine on the northern wall: a black-ink drawing of something that looks like a desert mountaintop, a rickety bookshelf full of what looks like their prophet's holy ravings, and somebody's desiccated hand holding an unfilled shard tab. The tab's razor-sharp waffled edges glitter in the dark.

It's fucking disturbing.

"We hit the jackpot, man."

Acheta turns away from the shrine to find Aden Damyati behind him, his silver hair glinting blood red in the abandoned factory's emergency lighting. Acheta lifts his chin and Damyati continues.

"Some of the weapons lockers were emptied out, but they left behind some real good stuff," Damyati says. "Plasma carbines, shotguns. And check this out." He spins a grenade charge in the palm of his broad brown hand like an egg, flips it in his fingers to show the stamp on the back.

Acheta winces inwardly at the oldtimer's lack of caution, then swears sharply under his breath at what Damyati's showing him.

The back of the grenade is stamped with the seal of the Indiran Alliance.

"Where'd the cult get Alliance shit?" Acheta says, and Damyati shrugs. "Pack it all up," he orders, and for a moment Damyati looks like he's got something else to say, but the oldtimer doesn't challenge him.

Not yet, at least.

Acheta'll need to get rid of him before too long, but Damyati hasn't done anything outwardly disloyal — and Acheta's not going to fool himself. He doesn't have a strong enough command to start killing people who've served this crew since Blackheart days. Not on a gut feeling.

Plus, the man's a magician with a gun. Acheta can't afford to be down by even one more good soldier while he's in a full-on fight with Dry Creek.

Damyati strolls back to the other side of the cavernous factory, shouting orders to fill duffel bags full of weaponry. Acheta should be feeling elated at the haul, but instead he feels uneasy. With this much firepower just sitting around, how did he and his crew manage to bring the Dawn to their knees?

Those aren't words he'll say aloud. But he also won't waltz into the next battle without some serious searching into what the hell.

"Almost clear here, boss," Sjel calls from the entrance to the factory's offices, just to the right of the altar. Acheta promoted Sjel to his lieutenant the moment he killed Naali Hinoja and took over the crew, and he hasn't regretted the decision. There's a man who knows the meaning of loyalty.

"You meet anyone?" Acheta asks.

"Just checking the back rooms for stragglers. All sugar, now," Sjel says; he's grinning, a good sign. "And we found a stash of shard, gotta be a hundred thousand marks here."

A hundred thousand marks.

Acheta doesn't allow the relief to show on his face, but it flushes through his body just the same. They sell that shard and he can pay his crew. It's his lifeline until he gets the shard production facilities already captured from the Dawn up and running.

"Pack it up and ship it to the street dealers. Tonight."

"On it, boss."

"Keep sharp," snaps Acheta. "I don't like how easy this was."

Sjel ducks his head in agreement, then turns to bark orders down the chain, leaving Acheta staring at the abandoned shrine again as though it'll give him a clue.

Clue is, the Dawn lost.

The cultists got greedy, is what it was. They thought they could spin alliances with his crew and the Dry Creek crew, both. And Acheta ground them into sand.

Dry Creek is still fighting strong, but Acheta feels it in his bones that they're on the run. If he can just keep up the onslaught — and this new source of revenue will help — he'll wipe them off the map.

Then, all those who whisper that Levi Acheta isn't half the leader Blackheart was — that he isn't half the leader her lieutenant Naali Hinoja was — will either be dead or proven wrong.

Naali would never have seen the potential of joining with the Dawn to cement their hold on the drug trade. She wouldn't have had the strength or foresight to turn on them the minute Zacharia was killed and it looked like the deal would go bad. She didn't want anything to do with the shard — she'd said it again and again.

But without the shard they don't have the cash to operate.

Naali was the reason Blackheart's crew had been buckling under pressure from Dry Creek and the other crews on the edges of their territory. And Acheta is the reason Blackheart's crew — fuck that, *his* crew — is going to be feared in this city once more.

He's broken the Dawn, he'll break the Dry Creek crew, and he'll cement his control over the most lucrative business in the city. Everything in Dry Creek? That'll be his by the end of the week. All the shard manufacturing facilities, all the workers — so blitzed that none of them will even notice a change in masters so long as the masters keep feeding them what they're making.

It's all within his reach, provided he can keep his crew happy. Pay those that are grumbling for their hard-earned cash and shut down those — like Damyati — who are putting him on shaky ground.

He's jostled from his thoughts by a disturbance at the door. Voices raised, menacing. The faint whine of pistols and carbines warming to their owners.

"Boss!" yells Bull.

Acheta jogs across the expanse of the old factory, shoulders loose and ready; he'd expected far more of a fight tonight, and he's floating high on unspent battle adrenaline.

Bull is arguing with someone outside the door. The two soldiers around him have weapons drawn, but Bull doesn't. He doesn't need to; his fists could pound rocks, his bulk fills the door.

"What is it?" Acheta calls.

Bull steps back to reveal a woman standing just outside the door to the factory. She's dressed outlandishly, like she's in some rom vid about a bounty hunter who falls for the scum she's supposed to kill: tight purple leggings and a practical yet formfitting biosilk baselayer top under a cropped black jacket that would provide a year's meals for some street kid if it was made out of real leather. Her black hair is pulled back in a short, shaggy ponytail; stray strands spear across copper cheeks.

"Says she's part of Blackheart's crew," Bull says. "But I ain't ever seen her before."

The woman examines Acheta, dark eyes glinting in the beams of tactical flashlights and red emergency lighting.

"You never ran with Blackheart," Acheta says. What kind of suicidal person thinks she can pull that line here? He rests his palm on his pistol. Everyone in the room tenses at the whine as it warms to his hand. "I been with Blackheart since before she ever left New Sarjun. Who the fuck are you?"

"I am Norah é Vega," the woman says, simply, like he should know the name. He doesn't, but at the Arquellian accent he knows one thing at least: that jacket probably *is* real leather. His first thought is that it will be a pity if it gets shot up.

His second thought is shame that the money stress of the past week has turned him back into the desperate kid he'd been before he started running with Blackheart, sizing up a woman's jacket for what it might be worth.

"And who's that?" Acheta asks. "I never heard of you."

"I was Blackheart's right hand on Indira."

And at that, the name does ring a bell, just vaguely. Maybe he read it in a memo. Maybe he heard Naali talking about her.

He doesn't let recognition show.

"And you're what," Acheta says. "Here to help?"

Here to challenge him is more likely. Adrenaline courses through him: Let her come. Let him have yet another chance to prove his strength to the unbelievers on his crew. Out of the corner of his eye he can see them — Damyati, Sui, Talla, all the others watching to see how he leads.

"I'm here to take revenge for Coeur's death," é Vega says.

Acheta lifts his chin at that, and é Vega seems to see the sea of weapons around her for the first time. "Revenge on the Dawn," she adds.

Beside him, Bull tilts his thick head. Pistols lower as people process what she said.

"Revenge?" Acheta asks.

"My way of showing respect," she says, like she doesn't get the question. "It's mine to avenge her death before taking her mantle back on Indira."

"Very nice," says Acheta. "Except seems you should've stayed on Indira, since that's where she got done."

She frowns at him. "I see you don't have that tradition here."

"We have our own ways of showing respect," says Acheta. "I'm showing mine by taking Dry Creek out at the knees and expanding her territory."

Or whatever. Let her think his actions had anything to do with avenging Blackheart, Acheta thinks. He'd been low and desperate in the crew back when the old bitch ran things. Cranky old Blackheart with her antiquated ways of doing things and her delusions that she could have it all. Then she'd hamstrung her own people for years by trying to run things from off-planet with Naali as her puppet. Refusing to go quietly into exile to Indira and let her people here run things on New Sarjun without her interference, that was what had driven this organization into the ground.

Good riddance. He's happy she's dead.

His crew will thrive now that there's a real leader at the helm.

Only.

Blackheart was killed on Indira in some random break-in, right? A weak way to go, he'd thought at the time. Fitting for a failed, exiled queen.

É Vega is watching him like he's missing a piece of the puzzle.

Fuck it, he'll bite.

"Let her in," he snaps at Bull, who pivots like a door to let the Arquellian woman pass. Acheta turns to Damyati and his team at the weapons lockers. "You done there or just gawking?" he yells. Damyati waves his team back to work.

The only place away from prying eyes and pricked ears is by the disturbing shrine. A shadow in the doorway to the back rooms; Sjel has slunk out, watching his boss's back like a good lieutenant should. É Vega ignores Sjel, walking past Acheta to study the shrine. She tilts her chin as she takes in the desiccated hand with the unfilled shard tab in the palm.

"Blackheart died on Indira," Acheta says, voice low. "So why are you really on New Sarjun."

É Vega turns back to him; she doesn't look scared. She has that same haughty look Naali Hinoja always had, like there wasn't a damned thing in the world worth losing her cool over. Blackheart had a type when it came to the tough bitches she picked for lieutenants, that's for sure.

"Thala didn't die on Indira," é Vega says. "She died ten blocks from here in a prison run by Dry Creek and financed by the Dawn. Do you want to know why?"

Until this moment, Acheta hadn't cared who offed

Blackheart. He figured he owed them a nice bottle of gin, but he hadn't thought much more about it. "Why don't you tell me your theory?"

"It's no theory," é Vega says, the barest flick of her attention to Sjel. "The Dawn kidnapped Thala and paid Dry Creek to secure her in their territory. She was guarded and tortured by Dry Creek soldiers. They broke her hands. And they killed her."

"Well, it looks like I took care of your revenge for you, then," he says. "Sorry you made the trip."

"You don't need help?" É Vega raises her gaze to take in the whole abandoned factory, sweeping over the cots, the weapons lockers, the shrine.

"The Dawn are done," Acheta says. "This was their last stronghold."

"You're sure?"

No, no he's not. This shrine in front of them with its holy books and desiccated hand, that arsenal abandoned, nothing here feels like vanquishing an enemy should feel. Unease radiates out like an itch between his shoulder blades.

But he'll never show that. Acheta spreads his arms and turns a slow circle to show off the place, this last stronghold. He's not sure what's worse: turning his back on é Vega or on the strange shrine with its wilting books and eerie images.

"What do you think, yeah? They look dead to me."

He grins at her. She's not smiling. "And Dry Creek?"

"Why the fuck does the Dawn kidnap Blackheart?" he asks. Just so they could come straight to him with the shard connection? Blackheart would've been fine with it; it was leaving Naali Hinoja in charge that messed up their chances there.

É Vega's smiling like she knows something that'll blow

his mind. She turns back to the shrine, picking up the desiccated human hand with reverence.

"Have you heard of the Gift of the Fallen?" she asks.

Someone screams behind them and Acheta whirls from é Vega with his pistol drawn. A pair of his people — Masso and a new recruit named Liari — are dragging a struggling man between them.

"We found him hiding in one of these rooms," Masso says. "One of their priests, looks like. Do you want us to — "

But in that moment, the priest breaks a hand free, grabs something from his pocket, and slips it into his mouth.

The priest screams again, this time in rage, and throws Acheta's two crew back from him. Masso crashes against the wall, head cracking back and legs buckling as he slides to the floor. Liari isn't thrown quite as far. She stumbles, rolls, grabs her gun. With another screech, the priest flings himself after Liari, wrestles the gun from her hand. But not before the new recruit gets off a pair of shots, both burying themselves in the priest's chest.

Acheta relaxes, but it's only a fraction of a second before the priest staggers back to his feet and lunges, grabbing Liari's head and snapping her neck with a sickening crunch.

The priest spins with an animal look in his eyes, blood washing down his torso from the bullet holes in his chest.

How is he still standing?

Acheta fires; the bullet tears through the man's shoulder but doesn't drop him. It only draws his attention.

"Aim for the head!" é Vega yells, and at her voice, the priest seems to find his focus once more, swiveling his head to notice Acheta and é Vega and the knot of crew running to surround them. He tenses as if to run, and Sjel wings him with a burst from his plasma carbine. The scents of ozone and scorched flesh fill the room.

The priest sprints towards Acheta and Sjel, howling. Acheta fires, the priest manages to dodge the bullets — how is he moving this fast? — and launches himself into the air towards Sjel.

Acheta lunges himself, tearing the priest off his lieutenant's back before he can do much damage. Acheta's tough, he knows, but this wiry priest? He's unimaginably strong. And none of his injuries seem to have slowed him down one bit. He writhes in Acheta's grasp, breaking free and wrapping his hands around Acheta's throat.

Acheta hears é Vega's shout and she slashes at the priest's neck with a knife in her hand; the priest shifts and she misses, burying the blade in his shoulder.

It doesn't slow down him any more than the bullet wounds in his chest did, but it does divide his attention. Acheta kicks him off and rolls to a crouch with his gun in his hand just as the priest pivots and launches himself at é Vega. Acheta fires; the man's face disappears in a fine red mist.

Panting, Acheta rolls the man over to make sure he's really gone.

Alive, the priest had had the weight and strength of three men. Dead, he weighs as little as his scrawny frame looks like it should.

In the last weeks of fighting, the closest Acheta's come to dying is at the hands of this old man. The thought blooms bright and fiery and blinding, and he fights down adrenaline-fueled rage before he slips and turns it on his people. He didn't know what this man was — how could he expect it of any of them?

Except.

He turns to é Vega; she's radiating post-fight adrenaline. "You said to aim for the head. Why."

"I suspected once I saw what he was."

"And what was he?" Acheta asks coldly. "What did he take?"

"The Gift of the Fallen," she says, her Arquellian drawl sharpening with insistence. "I've never seen it in real life, I've only read about it in the Dawn's holy books."

Acheta suddenly realizes he's still crouched over the priest's body like a predator; he pushes himself to his feet. "Holy books." He glances at the shrine, though he doesn't turn his back on the priest. Not until he's sure the headshot is enough to keep him down.

"It's a drug. Zacharia and the Dawn were using it to make their people fast and strong. Invincible. It's what they killed Blackheart over."

Acheta frowns down at the priest's body, crumpled in a pool of blood on the factory floor. "He doesn't look very invincible to me."

"He wasn't a fighter. He was naturally weak." É Vega picks up the dried hand once more, touches a finger to the empty shard tab in its palm. "Still, you saw what he could do, how strong he was. Imagine giving that gift to a soldier."

Acheta is definitely imagining.

Imagining a world where finally defeating the Dry Creek crew is a given. Where he doesn't have to worry about someone coming after his position the way he came after Naali's. Because he may have gotten rid of her most vocal followers, but there are plenty in the crowd around him who are only waiting to see what kind of leader he'll be. To see if he'll be a strong, invincible commander, or if he'll simply be the next target.

No way is Levi Acheta a target.

"You said they killed Blackheart over this," he says. "Why."

"She was supposed to steal two cases of it from the Alliance on Indira and ship it to the Dawn here on New Sarjun," é Vega says. "But she double-crossed them, shipped it somewhere else instead. Somewhere only she could get it. One case was destroyed, but as far as I can tell the other is still intact."

"Where?" growls Acheta.

É Vega's watching him, he gets the sense that she sees his need, but he doesn't care. He's proven himself this far, and he'll continue to make good on his leadership. Especially once he has this gift.

"Where is it?" he asks, quieter.

"Do you know a man named Willem Jaantzen?"

Like what you read?

Get *Crossfire* at www.jessiekwak.com/book/crossfire

ABOUT THE AUTHOR

Jessie Kwak is a freelance writer and novelist living in Portland, Oregon. When she's not working with B2B marketers, you can find her scribbling away on her latest novel, riding her bike to the brewpub, or sewing something fun.

Connect with me:
www.jessiekwak.com
jessie@jessiekwak.com

THE DURGA SYSTEM SERIES

STANDALONE NOVELLAS

Starla Dusai is fifteen, deaf — and being held as an enemy combatant by the Indiran Alliance.

Willem Jaantzen is about to end a fearsome vendetta — and most probably his life.

When he learns his goddaughter has been captured by the Alliance, will he be able to save her? And her, him?

Manu Juric's quick wit and knack for creating unexpected explosions has taken him a long way in the hitman business.

At least, until he signs on to a job that might just be out of his league: taking out one of Bulari's most notorious underworld figures, Willem Jaantzen.

When Starla receives a tip that her beloved cousin Mona is alive and well on an astroid station out in Durga's Belt, she drops everything to find her.

But saving her might just mean giving up the new family she's come to love. If it doesn't get them both killed first.

Find bonus Durga System stories and more:
www.jessiekwak.com/durga-system

CPSIA information can be obtained
at www.ICGtesting.com
Printed in the USA
FFHW021801120919
54911577-60621FF